Long Overdue at the Lakeside Library

Also available by Holly Danvers

Lakeside Library Mysteries

Murder at the Lakeside Library

(Writing as Holly Quinn)

Handcrafted Mysteries

A Crafter Quilts a Crime
A Crafter Hooks a Killer
A Crafter Knits a Clue

Long Overdue at the Lakeside Library

A LAKESIDE LIBRARY MYSTERY

Holly Danvers

CROOKED LANE

NEW YORK

Published in the United States by Crooked Lane Books, an imprint of The Quick Brown Fox & Company LLC.

Crooked Lane Books and its logo are trademarks of The Quick Brown Fox & Company LLC.

Library of Congress Catalog-in-Publication data available upon request.

ISBN (hardcover): 978-1-64385-890-6
ISBN (ebook): 978-1-64385-891-3

Cover illustration by Jesse Reisch

Printed in the United States.

www.crookedlanebooks.com

Crooked Lane Books
34 West 27th St., 10th Floor
New York, NY 10001

First Edition: February 2022

10 9 8 7 6 5 4 3 2 1

To my nephew, Conor Powers—
brilliant in both mind and spirit

Disclaimer

Lofty Pines is not a real place; it's a place the author dreamed up. The characters and events are completely fictional, and any similarity is completely coincidental.

Chapter One

Change. So much had happened in the last nine months, Rain Wilmot almost didn't recognize her own life. Everything about her world had shifted, as if another life force had been busy scripting an entirely new novel in her own personal story.

There was one thing Rain had made final, and that was her decision to make Lofty Pines a permanent year-round residence. As the leaves changed color and the wind shifted cold, she hadn't been ready to part with her family's generationally owned log cabin compound, perched on Pine Lake, in the Northwoods of Wisconsin. She'd grown accustomed to the acreage. And the neighbors whom she'd reconnected with had been the icing on the cake, rounding out her world and settling her into a new place of belonging.

The grounds included a log cabin library, attached via a catwalk, which was typically open only for the summer months, to accommodate the swell of lakeside vacationers. After a long heart-to-heart with her parents, who lived a few hours south, they all were in favor of her decision to come back full-time.

Especially since it was her mother whose name was technically deeded on the property, Rain felt she needed permission to remain in the Northwoods. They had all agreed it was in her best interest to stay on at least another year, until her thirty-third birthday, and then take time to reevaluate her life once again. And so she did.

After making the decision to reside in the Northwoods year-round, Rain was determined to keep the library open throughout the winter too. She couldn't bear to leave the library closed to patrons and boarded up for the winter, especially when she discovered that the population had suddenly swelled. More and more Wisconsinites were making the choice to transplant permanently, after a downhill ski hill, suitably named Eagle Peak due to its many feathery denizens, had been built forty-five minutes from Lofty Pines. Families now enjoyed the pleasure of downhill skiing and snowboarding there, which led to other winter sports popping up on nearby trails as well, such as cross-country skiing, snowmobiling, and snowshoeing. It was clear the winter tourism was thriving even closer to home too. Rain had noticed this during her frequent trips to the grocery store. From the longer lines on the weekends, to the numerous Illinois plates she had seen darting through the snow-covered parking lot at the market, Lofty Pines was officially becoming a winter hot spot.

The sound of ice pellets hitting the window drew Rain from her reverie and prompted her to investigate. She pulled back the muslin curtain, noting the snow droplets streaking slowly down the window like worms tunneling through the earth. She shivered and then wrapped her lean arms around herself in a meager attempt to warm up. Despite the small library's electric heat source, the loose chinking of the log cabin walls sometimes allowed cold air to seep in. Rain had finally convinced her mother to add a wood stove, to make the library a viable year-round option. It was a bit of a compromise since she'd hoped to refurbish the outer walls as well. But her mother had initially balked at the idea of renovations, for fear the structure would lose its character and, along with it, the memory of her great-grandfather, whose hands had originally built it. Despite Willow's hesitation, an installation appointment was made, finalizing the decision.

Rain reached for a nearby belted cardigan that she'd brought over from the main cabin, wrapped it around herself, and then tied the strap in a knot around her narrow waist. She could hardly wait for the contractor to arrive and install the new Franklin stove.

Winter in northern Wisconsin was not for the faint of heart. Only the locals could withstand the biting windchills yet willingly partake in the outdoor festivities. Rain pondered this, as she noted the swell of ice shanties popping up on Pine Lake for the upcoming ice-fishing tournament. She'd heard through the grapevine that there were a record number of entrants eager to participate this year, including her neighbor Nick. She hoped, for her own sake, he'd win. The winner would be awarded a thousand dollars and the latest and greatest UTV—a coveted Polaris utility task vehicle, outfitted with all the latest bells and whistles. If Nick won, she was sure his wife, Julia, who was the closest thing Rain had to a sister, would take her for a joyride. Ever since they were kids, Julia had always been game for just about anything.

Those who owned lake property adjacent to Pine Lake—the people commonly referred to as Lakers, were expected to attend the ice-fishing tournament. Those from surrounding areas were also welcome, as a chili dump would also take place. Rain wondered if that was a way to get the non–ice-fishing population involved in the tournament by encouraging them to feed the hungry participants and partake in the camaraderie too. Maybe she'd get a chance to connect with neighbors she hadn't met yet, and reconnect with those she hadn't seen in years, who lived farther down the lake.

The tinkling of a bell, followed by the sound of stomping boots, thwarted her musings and alerted Rain that someone had entered the library. She turned to greet the newcomer with a welcoming smile.

"Well, hello there! I see someone fought the elements to make it out this morning?" Rain retreated from the window, tucked her long raven hair behind one ear, and then rushed to hold the door as the man filled the doorframe while he continuously attempted to remove snow from his boots.

"I'm so sorry—it's a bit of a mess out there." His eyes reached hers and his face turned from a smile mirroring hers, to a cringing look as he mouthed the words, *Please forgive me.*

"Oh, don't worry about it," Rain said with a wave of dismissal, regarding the puddle beneath his feet. "'Tis the season. And we have months of wet slop ahead of us—this is only the beginning." She grinned.

The man removed his winter cap, leaned against the door, and shook the snow from his hat before officially stepping over the threshold. "Are you sure you don't want me to slip off my boots? It would be no bother." He looked down, showing the balding of his head, before his eyes returned to hers as he waited for permission to enter.

"Nah, but thanks for asking. I see the snow has changed to ice pellets." Rain clucked her tongue after looking beyond his shoulder at the mess outside. "Honestly, it's my fault—I probably need to buy a larger doormat. This is the first winter season we're open to the public, so I guess I have a few minor adjustments to make. I'll run to the hardware store later and see if they have a larger mat that might work a bit better," she said, tapping her finger to her lips and speaking more to herself than addressing the newcomer. "Anything I can help you find? Or are you just here to browse and find an escape from this miserable weather?" She shivered from the wind that blew in from the open door and rushed to close it behind him.

A sheepish grin washed over his face. "Have any cookbooks? I'm hoping to add something to the chili dump for the tourney. But . . ." The man hesitated after throwing his hands up in defeat. "I don't want to be the one that adds the chili that ruins the entire batch. Who knows? Maybe I have a chance of winning the chili contest if I find the right recipe." He smirked.

"Oh? That's a contest too? I just thought it was a chili dump."

"Yes, they're having a chili taste test before they dump them all together into the cauldron. I'm afraid I might need a cooking lesson; I've never made chili before—or much else for that matter. My wife used to do the cooking in our house but . . ." He let the comment linger, and based on the sad look in his eyes, Rain didn't dig for more. She knew that look. She'd felt it once too—the loss of a spouse, either from death or a roving eye. Her own loss had been due to both. Her heart silently ached for the man. It was like ripping off a Band-Aid on her own heart and revealing a gaping wound.

She deflected their grief by pointing to a shelf located behind him. "Plenty of cookbooks. I think there's even a few, authored by the local church groups, those are always loaded with amazing recipes. I'm sure you'll find what you're looking for." Rain briefly touched him on the arm to encourage his efforts, and then dropped her hand to her side, as the man seemed to flinch, like a dog cowering from the slightest pat on the head. "You don't fish?"

His thin eyebrows rose in amusement, and his face suddenly lit in pure animation. Rain had struck the right chord. "Oh, dear girl, I'm fishing too. In fact, my shanty is parked right out in front of your place." He lowered his tone to a whisper as if he was sharing a big secret. "I hauled it out there just as soon as the ice was able to hold its weight." He flung a finger in the direction of the window. "Primo spot! Largest walleye can be found right out yonder. I snatched it up before anyone had a chance to take it. It's usually one of the first spots taken, but this year I beat the other guys to it." He brought a finger to his lips. "I'm sure I ruffled some feathers over it, but ah well, all's fair in fishing. The early bird gets the worm, isn't that right?" His eyes rose to glance at the tongue-and-groove ceiling. "Or maybe it's the largemouth bass that gets the worm?" He chuckled to himself as he unzipped his long parka but kept the coat on. He then shoved one reddened hand into his pocket, then the other was used to tuck his cap beneath his arm.

"I've heard that," Rain said with a nod. "I mean, that it's a great fishing location. Good for you for landing the spot, and I wish you the best of luck at the tournament."

"Thanks." He grinned, revealing teeth that had splintered with age. "You in?"

"You mean, the tournament?" Rain questioned, and the man nodded in eager anticipation of her answer. "I'll probably add to the chili dump, but no, I'm not fishing this year. Though I am looking forward to the community coming out. It'll definitely be fun to see everyone before I officially go into hibernation mode and hide in this library for the rest of the winter." She folded her arms across her chest, as if hugging herself, and smiled. Truth be told, it wasn't easy for her to participate in community events. Being a single woman after so many years of marriage to Max left her feeling awkward and alone sometimes in social settings, but she was trying her best. She had pushed herself on more than one occasion and found herself growing braver with each attempt. But if she spent too much time weighing the pros and cons about whether she'd take part in the event, she could easily weasel out.

"Well, you just remember to listen for my name being called, 'cause I'll be the one on top of the leader board." He poked a thumb at his chest. "I'm walking away with the big prize this year—I promise you that." His lips turned up in a knowing smile, and he replaced the wet knit cap on his head and adjusted it in place. Then he shoved both hands back into his pockets.

"I sure do admire your enthusiasm. What's your name? I want to be sure I know it when I hear it being called over the intercom," Rain said teasingly.

"Oh, forgive my manners." He thrust out a hand. Rain accepted his calloused hand in hers and gave it a firm shake. "The name's Wallace. Wallace Benson. Number-one walleye angler." He held up a long finger and nodded curtly with solid conviction.

"Nice to meet you, Wallace. I'm Rain."

"Rain?"

"Yep."

"What a cool name."

Rain smiled. "Thanks. I wish I could take the credit, but alas, it was my mother's choosing. She's a bit of an earth child, as you can imagine."

"Miss Rain, you just remember this face, as this is the face of a winner!" He grinned as he circled the outline of his face with his finger.

"Well, I certainly admire your confidence, Mr. Benson. I hear it's quite the competition. I believe the winner has their picture taken for the local newspaper, and I also heard that an enlargement is posted in the bait shop for an entire year for all to see. Isn't that right?"

"Yep, bragging rights for an entire year. Quite a competition. That it is!" His eyes danced in merriment. "Yep, I can't wait. I got a good feeling; this just might be my year."

"Well, I'll tell you what: we'll both try our hand at something new. You try making a chili recipe from one of those cookbooks, and I'll try my hand at making a fish fry. I've always gone out to a restaurant for Friday night fish fry but never tried making it at home myself. How about we both try a new skill?" Rain grinned.

The bell on the door sounded again, drawing Rain's attention. She noticed her next-door neighbor, Julia, stepping inside, with a bag of what she anticipated was doughnut holes in her hand. Rain's stomach leapt in anticipation. "Can you excuse me, Wallace?"

"You bet—thanks for pointing me in the right direction," he said, wandering away from her.

"I'll help you check out the books whenever you're ready; just meet me over at the circulation desk," Rain continued with a wave of her hand at a small desk that held a laptop by the door. It was a meager attempt at keeping records, but it was the best she could do until she decided on the proper library software. Her spreadsheet seemed to work during the summer months, so she'd decided to continue with it since the library was small and most folks were fairly good about returning materials. Besides, she wasn't sure how busy the library would be during the long Wisconsin winter that was sure to roll on endlessly. Only time would tell if she'd need to come up with a better system.

Rain smiled inwardly when she noted that Wallace had turned his interest toward the bookshelf and begun flipping through a variety of cookbooks. Hopefully, he'd give a recipe a whirl. Meanwhile, she returned her own attention to Julia, who was in the process of removing her winter hat. As Julia did so, Rain brought her hands to her cheeks. "You colored your hair!"

"I sure did. Do you like it?" Julia tossed her platinum head from side to side for inspection. "I kept a sliver of pink, but that's the extent of it. I couldn't let the pink completely go. To be honest, it sort of grew on me, I guess." She shrugged.

"I don't like it—I love it!" Rain exclaimed. "You look be-a-utiful!"

"What? The hair? Or the doughnuts?" Julia asked with a raised brow and a knowing smile, as she held up a bag from their favorite coffee shop. "I picked up these babies when I left the salon."

Rain laughed. "Well, Brewin' Time doughnut holes might have your hair beat, just a tad," she teased as she squeezed her thumb and index finger together to demonstrate. "How'd you know I was starving?" She laid her hands on her lean tummy, which seemed to roll eagerly.

Wallace brought two books over to the circulation desk, and Rain headed over to assist him. "Don't start without me," Rain said over her shoulder to Julia, her dark eyes lasered in on the bag of treats.

"Oh, I wouldn't dare." Julia's light brows danced in amusement. "Now would I?"

"You found what you need, did ya?" Rain asked, stepping behind the desk.

Wallace nodded appreciatively.

After printing out a receipt for Wallace, Rain handed it to him and said, "These cookbooks are due back in a month. Hang on to them; maybe you'll find a few other recipes you'd like to try. And good luck at the ice-fishing tournament tomorrow. I wish you the very best."

"Just remember, it's like I said: luck doesn't have anything to do with it. It's all skill. And don't you worry about that—I have plenty of it. Cooking, on the other hand? Well, I guess that's to be determined," Wallace said with a chuckle as he gathered the books in his arms and then turned on his heel, heading out the door into the icy rain that had now morphed back into quarter-sized shavings of snow.

Rain rushed to close the door tightly behind him as the flakes blew in from the outdoors like unwanted guests. "It's nasty out there today," she muttered to herself as she retreated into the room, seeking Julia. She found her hiding behind a bookshelf, powdered sugar dotting her lips.

"I thought you were waiting for me?" Rain grinned.

Julia attempted to answer, but her mouth was full, causing Rain to laugh aloud.

"I think we might need coffee too?" Rain chewed at her lip and waited. "Shall I head back to the main cabin and brew some for us?"

Julia swallowed, wiped her mouth with the back of her hand, and then held up a finger for Rain to hang on a second. "Actually, I have an idea," she said finally after she fully swallowed.

"An idea?"

Julia led Rain by the arm to where the comfy chairs and a side table were located at the end of a bookcase.

"Picture this." Julia placed the bag of donut holes on the chair and then lifted her hands as if she was holding up a picture frame. "How about we set up a coffee bar over here? You know, so patrons can enjoy a cup while they peruse? Wouldn't that be cozy?" Julia's eyes danced at the thought. "I can bring over some paper cups and those individual non-dairy creamer pods, to make it easy on us, if you'd like."

"I love it! We could add cocoa and tea options too," Rain answered enthusiastically. "Why on earth didn't I think of that before?" She clasped her hands to her heart. "I'm already picturing those fancy marshmallows—and cinnamon sticks. Oh, I could go wild with this."

"Hey, that's what I'm here for. Besides, in the summer we were roasting to death. No wonder you didn't think about it then, but now that the library is open all winter long, can you imagine how nice it would it be, to sit back with a book and hot drink . . .?" Julia let the comment linger as she leaned back on her heels and patted her own back dramatically, as if approving her own fantastic idea. Rain nodded her assent.

"You know, we could talk to the owner of Brewin' Time to see if they want to supply us with donuts to share too."

"Now that's an idea I can get behind," Julia said with a laugh.

"On second thought, the crumbs would probably end up all over the books." Rain frowned, as she looked adoringly at the volumes that surrounded them. "I think I'm getting ahead of myself."

"Oh shoot, just when I thought I had you on the hook for pastry too." Julia grinned after a shoulder bump. "Although it probably wouldn't be wise with my growing waistline." She grimaced.

"You know, I can't tell you how happy I am that you and Nick decided to make Lofty Pines a year-round residence too.

Honestly, nothing could be better than having my favorite pair close by." Rain beamed. "And I really do appreciate you working at the library on your days off," she continued. "Did you get a permanent teaching position yet? Or is that still on hold?"

Julia's smile grew wider at each additional comment. "No, I'm still subbing, but it's okay. If Malory doesn't come back from maternity leave, I'm a shoo-in for her position. She hasn't quite decided yet. This is her first baby, so . . . in her words, if she can balance both, she'll continue to teach."

"Ah, I see."

"She's due to deliver this week, then she's taking six weeks off. After that, she'll be forced to decide. I guess I'll just take it one day at a time." Julia lifted the bag of doughnut holes from the chair and reached in for another.

"Good attitude. If things surprise us and we stay busy over the winter, maybe you can work here full-time instead of just on your days off. Maybe you wouldn't even have to go back to teaching if you didn't want to," Rain hinted. "What do you think of that idea?"

"Don't tease me like that," Julia said, taking a bite. "That would be ideal. Honestly, having to commute just next door would be an absolute dream! Especially in weather like this. Ugh. I'll tell ya, if Nick wasn't doing residential plowing this winter, I don't know what I'd do. I'd probably become a hermit," she said, chuckling. "Lofty Pines is great, but they don't seem to be in a rush to plow the roads around here. It's like they're still on Laker time, even in the winter!"

"Believe me, I hear you, and I'm a very thankful customer too. If it wasn't for your husband, I doubt I'd go anywhere in the snow." Rain then tapped the small pub table located between the two chairs. "All righty then, now: about that coffee machine. I have an extra one that I brought up from my Milwaukee move still in storage. I think I stuffed it somewhere in the back of the pantry. How about I set it up over here? I think this'll be great." She lifted a finger to her lips as she thought it through. "If I go get it from the main cabin, are you going to eat all the doughnuts you brought? Or are you gonna save me a few?" Rain eyed the bag again with longing.

Julia shrugged. "Hey, I can't guarantee anything," she confessed, licking her lips, apparently seeking any remnants of powdered sugar. "I'm just kidding. Go!" She set the bag of donuts down and took a step backward and then brushed the powdered sugar from her hands, as if proving the point.

Rain chuckled. "I'll hurry back then, just in case." She winked and then turned toward the door, but didn't reach for a coat. Instead, she opted to rush across the catwalk to the main cabin. Flakes stung her eyes when she opened the door, and she blinked several times before catching her bearings. She was surprised to find Wallace was only a few feet away, eyes to the sky, watching the snow fall, as if in some sort of a trance.

After wrapping the belt on her cardigan tighter, Rain cupped her hands beside her mouth and hollered to him, "Hey, Mr. Benson, everything okay?"

Wallace turned and smiled. "Yeah, I'm fine. I just stopped to admire the beauty of it. It's quite magical if you take the time to watch. Almost angelic, isn't it? The way it sparkles. I wonder if heaven is this way . . . all iridescent and clean," he answered pensively before turning his back to her and walking slowly in the direction of his car.

Later, in retrospect, Rain wished she'd stopped and watched the beauty of the falling snow with the man and had appeased his divine request. Because that was the last time she'd see Wallace Benson alive.

Chapter Two

The day of the ice-fishing jamboree arrived, and as Rain zipped the navy parka up to her chin and lifted the hood, she grew flustered. The down coat fell to her knees, which was saying something, because she was every bit as tall as the average American man. The artificial fur from the hood tickled her cheeks, and she pushed it away with her hand. Maybe she'd overdone the number of layers, and she should just start over or—better yet—stay home. Her willingness to abandon the idea of attending the contest completely and remain in the safety of the log cabin was not due simply to the bone-chilling cold, or even an overstuffed coat that made her feel like a sausage crammed into its casing. No. She was self-aware enough to know the issue ran a little deeper than that.

Rain knew in her heart she was just making excuses. She just wasn't ready to go and face the community alone. But she also knew that once she got to talking to people, she'd carry on just fine. Especially if Julia and Nick were already out on the lake—she could easily slip in and out of conversation and tag along with them. Rain had gotten to know a few other friendly faces from the community, folks who had perused the library shelves too. Heck, even just yesterday, she'd met Wallace, and he had mentioned his ice shanty parked a few feet from where her own pier had stood during the summer months. *Before* the water had morphed into an ice-skating rink. She frowned.

Again, Rain chastised herself for being ridiculous, as she knew she was being totally irrational. It was an ice-fishing tournament, for Pete's sake, not a visit with the queen. Why was she getting so worked up about it? She needed to just get over herself.

It was strange how quickly life plunged her into these new realities. She was reminded again of how she'd allowed her confidence to slip away, along with her husband, without even being aware of it. When she and Max had gone places, she had never thought twice about carrying on conversations with strangers because Max had been so personable with everyone who'd crossed their path. He'd been a stellar salesman for Harley Davidson, and his salesmanship had oozed into their social life. There was never an awkward pause in a conversation. He'd crack a joke, break the ice, and conversation would flow like a rambling river. Times like these, she almost ached for her wingman.

Now alone and officially stuck in the singles category, thoughts of insecurity and every potential way to back out of social situations easily took over Rain's mind. Rain didn't suffer from FOMO, or the fear of missing out. Instead, she suffered from FOGO, the fear of *going* out (her own personal acronym.) *Alone.* Such a dreadful word. It bothered her that even though she had lost Max well over a year ago, she still struggled at times to gain her sea legs in society.

Rain unzipped her coat. She removed the bulky sweatshirt, cast it on a nearby chair, and left a thin layer of Cuddl Duds for a second skin, then slipped her arms back into the soft down. That felt better. Now it was as if she were wearing a comforter, and the switch did the trick—a fresh wave of comfort. She smiled inwardly.

The aroma of cumin and chili powder reminded Rain to sample her chili batch one last time before unplugging the crockpot. It was perfect. She thought back to Wallace again and wondered if the library patron had found a decent recipe in one of the cookbooks he'd borrowed. She'd have to seek him out to see if his first attempt at cooking had paid off. She carefully ladled the hot mixture into an oversized thermos and capped it tightly for the journey down to the lake. Instead of cleaning up the excess, she decided to let the rest of the chili cool inside the crockpot. It gave her one more excuse to return to the cabin, if need be. She inwardly scolded herself once again for already concocting a quick exit plan before she'd even left the house, then squared her shoulders in resolve.

Growing up in Wisconsin, this wouldn't be the first chili dump Rain had attended—not by a long shot. She loved the idea of everyone blending their own recipes into one big cauldron to share out on the lake while the fishing competition took place. It reminded her of blending people: some sweet, some spicy, and some full of hot air, but together the perfect mixture. She let out a nervous giggle. Before she gave her mind a chance to thwart her again, she plucked her thermos from the countertop and headed down to the event.

The previous night, the weather forecast had called for below-freezing temps, which would cause an added sheet of ice to form atop Pine Lake. Rain was relieved by this, as the lake would then be able to handle all the added trucks, snow-mobiles, and ATVs without anyone cracking the ice and slipping under. Over the years, thin ice had claimed the lives of a few reckless wanderers on other lakes peppered throughout the state. Pine Lake, however, had already been measured at well over a foot of formed ice, so yesterday's icy rain wouldn't hamper the event. And for this Rain was relieved, that this type of tragedy might be avoided.

The gale off the frozen lake was biting, and Rain shivered despite the warmth of her parka. Her face felt as if it'd been slapped a hundred times by an angry fishtail, and she could almost bet her cheeks were as red as a ripe strawberry. Despite the plethora of shanties scattered all around her, there was no escaping the conniving wind. From the sting of it, Rain calculated the windchill was well below zero, and the overcast sky was bound to keep it that way. Every cell in her body screamed for her to go back inside, but she refused to succumb.

Rain looked up and noticed an oversized outdoor party tent was located not too far from her log cabin. The tent was close enough that, if she squinted, she could read the blue-lettered sign attached to it, which read "Pine Lake Ice-Fishing Jamboree." She assumed that was where the registration, chili dump, and raffles would take place, and decided to head immediately in that direction.

Rain's feet glided across the ice as if her boots were ice skates, and she kept her feet carefully planted so as not to slip.

She wondered if she should turn around and strap ice grips onto her boots to make the journey easier, but then decided that if she turned back now, she'd probably throw a log inside the stacked stone fireplace and curl up in the chair along with a good book. Instead, she pushed on and continued to maneuver her way across the frozen lake, catching the smell of smoke from the ice shanty roofs, billowing a campfire scent. This made her wish she was tucked inside of one of them, to warm her gloved hands. Even with leather gloves, her hands felt naked.

When she arrived a few feet away from her destination, Julia stepped halfway out from the tent and shared a friendly wave.

"Oh, hey, you're here! I'm so glad you made it. I thought you might be helping someone at the library." Her smile grew wide as she carefully took the thermos out of Rain's hands and laid it gently on the table just inside the tent before returning to her friend's side.

"Nah, I actually hung a "Closed" sign on the door today. I wrote a note that says something like: *Instead of reading about adventure today, how about joining us down at the lake for the ice-fishing tourney? For your convenience, materials can be returned in the outdoor box.* I figured it would be better to coax others out into the community today instead of encouraging them to hide away in a book." Rain didn't add that reading was exactly what she wished she was doing. Instead, she said, "After all, this only happens once a year, and soon we'll be tucked away by our fireplaces for the remainder of the winter, eh? At least I will." She teasingly bumped Julia lightly with her shoulder. "The time for socializing is now." She grinned, and when she did, it felt as if her face might crack wide open. No doubt the day would provide one heck of a windburn.

"I'm so glad, Rain. You could use a day off, and I'm sure Nick will be thrilled that you're making use of the outdoor return box that he built for the library. He worked so hard on that."

"Yeah, that reminds me: I need to thank him again. I absolutely *love* that box. It's the perfect size, and best of all, it keeps the books dry from our crazy weather when the library is closed. I haven't had one patron leave a book out next to the door like they used to. Nick is so incredibly handy, I wish I could be half as talented. Where is he, anyway? Is he already registered and headed off to his fishing hole?" Although people scurried all around them, she hadn't yet caught sight of Nick from her vantage point. Neither inside nor outside the tent.

"I dunno where he disappeared to." Julia shrugged. "He's here somewhere."

Rain again peeked over Julia's head, but her friend's husband was still missing from view.

"Actually, I think the last place I saw him was over by that shanty there—the one a few yards from his own." Julia pointed to the ice house that was located directly in front of Rain's property. "He was a bit perturbed that someone actually had the nerve to park there and steal the spot he'd coveted the last few years, and decided to give him or her a piece of his mind." Julia grimaced.

"Oh boy. I'd heard that fishermen can get a bit territorial over it. How do they get their spots? Do they keep them for the entire season?"

"Yeah, it's ridiculously competitive." Julia rolled her eyes. "These people build elaborate shelters before the snow flies. It's almost comical how decked out they are inside. To be honest, I think a lot of guys create a place to escape from their wives all winter long." She grinned.

"Surprising as this might sound, I don't think I've ever been up here during ice-fishing season. I've only been up north in the summer, so I guess I figured they just built the shanties directly on the ice."

"Oh no. They pull the shanties on with four-wheelers or UTV's as soon as the ice can hold 'em, when the ice hits about six inches thick. And they set them up for the entire winter, until the first week in March, when they're told to take them off before the big melt. Of course, if they're using trucks to drag 'em out, they need at least ten inches of ice. Otherwise, bye-bye truck," she said, chuckling.

"I suppose it could get pretty upsetting then if someone stole your spot, eh? I notice some are kinda on top of each other, I'd be frustrated if someone parked that close to me too, especially if I parked there year after year."

"They're *supposed* to be at least ten feet apart. I can see, because of this big prize, people are getting a little out of hand."

"Ah, I can see how that could tick Nick off then."

"Yeah. Nick's not one to get angry about stuff—he's usually a pretty placid, even-keel type of guy, but steal a man's fishing hole, and watch my husband turn from a turtle to an angry bear. Just because he set up his shanty there for the last few years doesn't make it his. I mean, hey, the first one to take the spot gets it, right? Nick can be so territorial over something that doesn't technically belong to him." She winked and then a grin washed over her face.

Rain hadn't passed Nick on her trek over, so she wondered if Julia could be mistaken. "Wait. You mean Wallace's shanty?" she asked, looking back to verify.

"Hang on a second." Julia held up a palm. "You know the guy that parked there? A few yards from Nick? Did this person ask you if he could drop his shanty in front of your cabin? Did you happen to hold a special spot for the guy? Ooh, do spill it—is he cute?" Julia's eyebrows danced up and down teasingly. "Am I sensing a love connection?" She closed her eyes and put her gloved fingers together as if she were calling on the spirits for an answer.

Rain laughed aloud and then slapped her hands to her side. "You have a wild imagination, my friend. In fact, you've met him." When Julia didn't seem overly convinced, she continued, "He was at the library yesterday. Remember? The gentleman that checked out the cookbooks. When you brought in the doughnuts . . ."

"Oh. *Him?*" Julia's face fell. The look of sheer letdown did not go unnoticed.

"Why do you sound so disappointed?"

"No, it's not that. I was just hoping maybe you might meet someone. You know, a potential suitor?" Julia said out the side of her mouth while she nudged Rain playfully with her elbow.

"Suitor? You've been reading historical romance again, haven't you?"

Julia frowned. "How'd you guess?"

"Because every time you start reading historical romance novels, you encourage 'set-ups.'" Rain lifted her gloved fingers in air quotes. "And use words like *suitor*," she added with an eye roll. "Don't worry about me. I'm just fine and can find my own *suitor*." She emphasized the word to drive the point home. "That is, if I were even looking. Which clearly, I'm not. I'm perfectly happy going solo," Rain said with a smile, even though inwardly she felt a twinge of regret, as if she'd just spat out a bold-faced lie to her best friend.

"Oh, I see. Maybe your heart's leading you in another direction." Julia tapped her fingers together conspiratorially. "Like maybe my brother is on your radar? Hey, I'm not blind—I've seen you around Jace." Julia then cupped her hand over her mouth, as if she could rewind her outburst.

"I'm going to pretend I didn't hear that," Rain said flatly. But she secretly wondered exactly what Julia's brother thought of her, if he even thought of her at all. Did he think of her like a younger tagalong from their youth? Or had the last investigation they'd helped him with in their little sleepy town of Lofty Pines given the police officer a chance to see her as a mature woman? Had Jace mentioned something to Julia in passing? If she were to admit it, Rain had thought about it on more than one occasion. But she wouldn't dare share this with Julia, as she knew her girlfriend would absolutely run wild with it, so she closed her lips tight. Tighter than a locked cedar chest.

"Oh, here's my better half! The man of the hour. My darling, my sweetheart!" Julia gushed, and the two eased farther away from the tent to greet Nick.

"Please help, Rain. Stop lending Julia that romance crap, will you? You need to cut her off at the library." Nick made a cutthroat gesture across his neck. "My wife keeps calling me *darling* and *sweetheart*. It's weirding me out!" He elbowed Rain teasingly and sent her a conspiratorial wink.

"Oh, I hear you, and believe me, I sympathize loud and clear." Rain laughed.

Julia pouted at them both and then regarded her husband. "I actually think *darling* and *sweetheart* are quite endearing terms, but apparently you don't? Would you rather me call you something else?" Julia asked as she reached up and adjusted the Green Bay Packer hat atop Nick's head so that the big *G* was facing forward.

"Like what?" Nick said, waving her away with his hand, and then tucking his mop of dark hair beneath his hat and readjusting it tightly over his ears.

"How 'bout *fish head*," Julia huffed, squinting her eyes at him.

"Well, I'll take *fish head* over *darling*. It's just too sugary for a mean ole chap like me." Nick threw out a few fake punches playfully.

"Chap?" Rain asked. "I get the feeling you've been sneaking a peek at her romance novels after she dozes off." She raised a brow. "You two deserve each other."

Nick laughed heartily. "Hey, now don't be givin' away my secrets." He shrugged. "I guess I'll play the part if it can gain me points with the Mrs. I'll be whatever she wants me to be." He winked playfully and then sent an alluring glance over to his wife. His brows danced as he glanced over at her.

"Hubba-hubba!" he added as he removed his gloves and then swatted his wife on the backside, and Julia brushed him away with her hand, clearly growing annoyed.

Nick then gave his wife the puppy-dog eyes and melted her gruff exterior.

Suddenly Rain noticed the large gash on the side of Nick's hand. "Oh heavens, what happened to your hand?"

"Oh, I tore it with a loose hook or something. I snagged it when I was diggin' through my gear. Total rookie move," Nick answered, as he popped the fresh wound into his mouth.

"You probably ought to head back to the house and apply some antibiotic ointment before you get back to your fishing hole," Julia said, leaning in to take a closer look at her husband's injury.

Nick waved her off, as if Julia was mothering him.

"So, tell me. How does this competition work anyhow? Julia and I want you to win so you can take us for a spin on that brand-new, shiny toy." Rain grinned.

"It's based on species and length. For example, if you and I both caught a walleye or a Northern, and they were the same length, then they take the one that weighs the most as the winner. It's got to be a game fish, though. There're smaller prizes for the panfish winners—I'm talking perch, crappie. Anyhow, everyone brings their catch in to the registration tent at the end of the competition. You should stick around for that. It's great fun to see what everyone caught."

"I bet. I'm getting the impression there're rivalries too, which adds to the hype. Am I right?"

"On target," Nick started, before a rude interruption.

A woman Rain didn't recognize rushed toward the three of them so quickly Rain didn't know how the woman had managed to maneuver across the ice with such speed, or where on earth she'd come from. The stranger's eyes were blazing, and her hair was askew—as if she'd just removed a winter hat or she hadn't showered in a day or two. Because of her wild and dramatic entrance, folks around them began to surround and watch like a school of hungry fish.

With an outstretched shaky finger, the woman pointed accusingly in Nick's direction, and seethed through gritted teeth, "Murderer!"

Julia's eyes darted from her husband to Rain and then back to this woman who looked like a caged animal just released from captivity. Julia and Nick then shared a baffled glance, too stunned to speak.

"Whoa! Hold on, ma'am. What are you talking about?" Rain placed her hand on the woman's arm to calm her, but the woman flailed away from her touch, as if she'd been poked with a hot iron.

The growing crowd grew more and more silent, not wanting to miss a syllable of the conversation. The only sound that could be heard was that of the ice expanding and contracting. As if a loud booming thunderclap sang out from beneath their feet.

"Someone call the police! This man was the last person to walk out of my husband's shanty. And now my husband's dead! *Dead!* The man I spent over two decades with is *gone!* And you—" The woman brought her pointed finger closer to Nick's nose. "You killed him!"

Chapter Three

Julia looked to Rain for confirmation and let out a nervous giggle. "She's joking. Clearly the woman's joking! Right?" Julia's eyes darted around the crowd that now surrounded them, as if this were all a big joke that they weren't yet privy to, and at any moment now they'd all have a good laugh. But the crowd remained somber.

"I'm not getting that vibe," Nick said out of the side of his mouth, causing Rain to crack a weak smile.

"Yeah, me neither," Rain said.

"She seems pretty serious," Nick added.

They watched as the woman slowly shook her head and circled Nick, her eyes penetrating back at Julia, as if ready to pounce at a moment's notice.

"Now just wait a minute! This is really getting outta hand." Julia glared back at the accuser, and Nick had to hold his wife back from lunging at the woman. Rain feared if Nick let his wife go, Julia might attempt to punch the woman right in the nose. In all the years Rain had known Julia, she'd never seen her friend so upset.

"What the hockey puck are you sayin'?" Julia continued. "This really isn't funny. Why don't you go and bother someone else?"

Rain's heart thumped so hard in her chest, it felt as if she suddenly couldn't breathe. As if some force was constricting her rib cage in an unwanted hug. An attempt at a big gulp of oxygen didn't help either, as the cold air simply squeezed her lungs, making it worse. It was imperative she get herself together and steady herself on her own two feet, though, as both Nick and Julia's faces were growing as white as the snow that was beginning to fall from the sky.

Clearly, neither Julia nor Nick had taken the accusation lightly. The aftermath of the spewing attack was still written all over their anxious faces. And Rain couldn't half blame them. To date, it was the oddest thing she had ever personally witnessed.

Before Rain had another moment to think, Julia's brother pushed his way through the crowd and rushed toward them. Jace wasn't dressed in his police uniform. Instead, he was wearing a buffalo plaid hunter's cap that covered both his blond head and his ears with flaps. A Carhartt sandstone jacket finished off the ensemble. Judging by his attire, Rain assumed Jace was at the jamboree to fish, not to work, but suddenly the job had been thrust on him as escalating chaos ensued.

"What's going on here?" he asked.

After he'd licked his cracked lips and flung a hand in the direction of the woman with the blazing eyes, Nick finally spoke up. "This deranged woman is accusing me of murdering her husband. Heck if I know what's going on!" His hands landed in a defensive stance at his sides. "Why don't you ask *her*?" he added in a bitter tone.

"Ma'am, I'm off-duty but I can help. What seems to be the problem?" Jace asked.

Apparently overcome by emotion, the woman began to shake uncontrollably. She then dropped to her knees and began to weep. As she sobbed, she rocked back and forth on her knees, hugging her torso tight and making a moaning sound.

Jace scanned the crowd before yelling, "Anybody here with medical training? Can I get a medic over here!"

A young woman wearing a pink camo hunting jacket picked her way through the crowd, knelt by the woman, and said to her in a soothing voice, "Ma'am, I'm a nurse . . . let me take a look at you." After checking the woman over, the nurse yelled, "Her eyes are dilated—she's going into shock. Someone call an ambulance!"

Jace ripped his cellphone from his jacket pocket and called one in. He too then knelt by the woman. "Where is your husband?"

The woman hung her head and wept harder before stretching her arm out and pointing her finger. The crowd parted like the Red Sea, leaving a path in the direction of Rain's log cabin.

Rain reached for Jace's arm to gain his attention. "I think she might be talking about Wallace's shanty." Rain then directed her question to the weeping woman: "Is that right?"

The woman looked up and stared vacantly, as if she were looking at a ghost.

Jace turned to the nurse and asked, "Can you stay with her until the ambulance comes?"

The nurse nodded and rested a hand of comfort on the woman's shoulder.

Without any further prompting, Jace, Nick, Julia, and Rain rushed as quickly as they could in the direction of Wallace's ice house. Smoke, coming from a woodstove, was billowing from the roof of the russet-painted shanty, as if nothing was amiss. On the way over, Rain replayed over and over in her mind her earlier conversation with Wallace. She'd assumed the man was divorced or that his wife had passed away. Had she mirrored her own life story onto his and misinterpreted his body language? She had no way of telling if the accuser was suffering from psychosis. Or had she actually seen something that had made her react like a deranged lunatic? Rain didn't know what to think.

The sky opened, and the snow fell thicker now as quarter-sized flakes blinded their journey. Rain was trying to hurry, but she had fallen a bit behind. She was aware that one narrow misstep would have her landing on her backside or twisting an ankle. The last thing she wanted was to be laid up all winter. The newly fallen snow atop the sheet of ice was making it even more treacherous—she hadn't even thought that was possible. She heard a gasp from Julia after Jace flung open the door to Wallace's shanty. Rain scurried forward to get a view with her own two eyes.

"Oh nooo! What happened?" Rain asked as she peered over Julia's shoulder. It was then that she saw for the first time the body of Wallace Benson lying on the cold, hard floor. Blood was dripping from his neck into the carved hole in the ice. The erect flag on the tip-up signified that a fish was on. Rain's mind flew back to the last conversation she'd had with the library patron. He had wanted to win the tournament. He had so desperately wanted to win. And here a fish was obviously on his hook, and Wallace would never get the chance to see it. Rain could feel the tears welling in her eyes.

They all squeezed into the small space, careful not to get too close to the compact wood stove, the hole in the ice, or the victim.

The reality of what Rain was witnessing suddenly hit harder, and she held her breath for a moment and buried her face in her hands before uttering, "I can't believe this! This is awful." Then a silence fell heavily over them all. Rain shook her head in disbelief, wiped the tear that had fallen to her cheek, and covered her mouth with her gloved hands. A lump in her throat was forming, and she swallowed in an attempt to clear it.

"Nick, did you talk to this guy today?" Jace asked, planting his hands firmly on his hips.

Rain's eyes darted to Nick who stood stoically looking at the lifeless body. He removed his Green Bay Packer hat and rubbed his hands through his mop of thick hair leaving it to flop to one side.

"Yeah," he answered through a puff of frustration, and then scratched his head before returning his hat to his head and pulling it down tight, as if for protection.

"When?" Jace pushed.

Nick held out his hands in defense. "I don't know, man! A little bit ago."

"Were you in here? Alone with him? Please tell me you weren't in here alone with him inside this shanty." Jace gestured to the victim.

Nick hung his head and uttered quietly, "I don't believe this."

"Now wait a minute," Julia pipped up. "What are you getting at?" Her eyes flashed to her brother. And then she shot a glance to Rain, which Rain interpreted as complete panic.

"I'm getting at the fact that Nick might have been one of the last people to see this poor man alive before he hit the floor," Jace said evenly, as if he was trying to pacify his sister. But the implication only egged her on.

"So, what is that supposed to mean? Are you accusing my husband? You actually *believe* that crazy woman?"

All eyes flew to Jace, waiting for an answer, but he remained stoic.

"It sounds to me like you're saying my husband had something to do with this. You're acting like he's a *suspect*!" Julia's voice rose an octave with each additional question. "Are you out of your fish flippin' mind?" Julia's hands landed at her sides in balled fists as she waited for an answer from her brother.

"I'm just collecting the facts, Julia, ease up." Jace put his hands up as if he were now the suspect under interrogation. "Don't get your toes in a tangle."

Rain knew Julia always came up with unique idioms when she felt cornered or upset. Julia had confided in her on multiple occasions that she had done that to prevent herself from swearing accidently in front of her teenage students during her teaching tenure. She'd never heard Jace talk that way before though. Rain wanted to say something to soothe the growing tension in the tight space, but for the life of her she couldn't find the right words, so she remained closed lipped. Between the heat bellowing from the wood stove and the escalating uneasiness that could be cut with a knife, her down coat started to feel less like a comforter and more like a straitjacket.

Jace kneeled close to Wallace's body to seemingly get a better look, and find the cause, or get a closer view of the laceration.

Rain noticed one of Wallace's hands was curled and colored an odd shade of blue and purple. The other hand, however, was covered with a heavy work glove. A wet stain was evident around the collar of his shirt, and she couldn't determine if was soggy from perspiration, or if someone had splashed him with clear liquid.

"Was he shot? Why didn't anyone hear it?" Julia asked. "Someone must've heard something!" she added shrilly.

"No. Looks like a stab wound. Though I don't see any-thing that could've caused this type of injury. Unless the perp dumped it down the fishing hole or took it with him." Jace's eyes scanned the area beneath their feet and down the hole, but the look on his face remained baffled. "I'll have to wait for the coroner to make that call. In the meantime, you all better step outside. This is officially a crime scene. Don't go far, Nick, I still need to ask you a few more questions."

Julia looked as if she was going to spit more words at her brother, and Nick somberly shook his head at his wife as a warning, then dragged Julia outside by the arm.

Rain held back a minute before following them. "Please tell me you don't think Nick had anything to do with this," Rain whispered.

"Doesn't matter what I think. If he was the last person in here, and Wallace's wife is calling Nick a murderer . . . Rain, what am I supposed to do?" Jace lowered his voice to barely a whisper. "Right now, my brother-in-law looks like the number one suspect, and I need to figure out how to fix that."

Chapter Four

"This is absurd! I can't *believe* this is happening." Julia's eyes flashed hot anger as she flung a hand in the direction of where Jace and her husband stood talking privately in hushed tones. "Why is my brother even interrogating him? This is ridiculous!"

Rain was at a loss for words. She wasn't exactly sure what to say to help ease her friend's mind. Since they had been kids, she had never seen Julia this angry, although she could completely understand where her friend's fury was coming from. Some stranger accused her husband of murder? In front of a large crowd of people? Not exactly an ordinary occurrence. Only Julia's behavior wasn't exactly fixing the problem. The animated superlatives that were spewing out of her mouth were causing onlookers to gape open-mouthed. Rain knew she needed to say something to calm the situation.

"They're just talking at this point, Julia. Try not to assume that your brother already has Nick tried and convicted—he's totally on your husband's side. Jace is only trying to get information at this point. You know that—it's his job."

"I do know that. But did you see my brother's expression, Rain? He looked like a deer in the headlights. Like he was scared out of his freakin' mind! Problem is, Jace doesn't scare easily." Julia frowned after blowing out a breath of hot air that sent a cloud of steam to rise in front of her face. "I know my brother better than I know myself. He was never any good at hiding anything from me." She shook her head and dropped her gaze. "Right now, I really wish I didn't know him so well."

"It's going to be okay. Everything is going to work out. You'll see," Rain soothed. Though in her own mind, she wasn't sure how anything would ever be okay.

"Anyone who knows Nick knows he's not capable of murder! This is ludicrous!" Julia continued. "The fear in Jace's eyes is freaking me out and not helping—at all. I can't even look at them right now." She turned her head and folded her arms across her chest.

Rain reached for her friend, gathered her into her arms, cocooning and enveloping Julia into the safety of her puffy coat. When she released her, she held her friend at arm's length. "I know you're upset; I hear you. No one would ever believe Nick capable of such a heinous act. The only thing that woman can be basing her accusations on is maybe seeing Wallace and Nick together. Or Nick leaving the shanty. Is she even his wife? When I talked to Wallace at the library yesterday, I didn't think he was even married. He gave me the impression that his wife was either deceased or he was divorced. I don't get it."

"I have no idea who she is. I'm surprised, in our small town, that I've never seen the woman. Maybe they don't even live in Lofty Pines. They're not Lakers, I can tell you that!"

"No, they actually do live in the area. They don't live around Pine Lake, but they're not too far from the library actually. I confirmed Wallace's address when I checked out the cookbooks yesterday and he flashed his library card. If I remember correctly, I think it was Acorn Lane? I'd have to double-check, but if my memory serves me right . . ." Rain put a finger to her lips.

"Acorn Lane is on the border of Lofty Pines, way out in the sticks. No wonder I don't know her. And I'm glad I don't. If I got flippin' close to her right now, I'd wring her scrawny little neck like a dishrag, because of these allegations," Julia spat.

"Hey, don't worry—I promise you, we're gonna fix this! What else does she have for proof? There's no murder weapon. The only thing pointing toward Nick was her own little finger. I'm sure this will all blow over. Jace is just doing his due diligence by asking a few questions. That's his job, Julia," she reminded her friend again. "You, of all people, know it's standard practice to speak to those who were last seen with a victim. Clearly, someone slipped into the shanty after Nick left."

A lull fell between them.

"Besides," Rain continued, as she wagged a finger between them, "we've read enough mysteries back on that library shelf to understand small-town police procedures. Please try and cut your brother some slack. He's totally convinced of Nick's innocence—I'm sure of it."

The sound of sirens filled the air, and soon ambulance personnel were traipsing through the snow by way of Rain's property. Jace moved to greet them. He pointed out the woman waiting by the registration tent, and then the medical personnel rushed quickly in that direction. One attempted to enter Wallace's shanty, but Jace answered with a sad shake of his head. No emergency personnel could bring back the man that was lying inside. Rain secretly wondered if the EMTs had a sedative she could slip to Julia, as her worry for her friend was escalating by the minute. She looked to the ground and noticed all the additional footprints that had muddied the ground around Wallace's shanty, and quickly realized that the crime scene was indeed contaminated. Jace and others on his police crew would have their work cut out for them. You couldn't even follow a footprint to see who had stepped inside, or outside, the ice house at this point.

Julia must've read her mind as she too scanned the fallen snow beneath their feet and then said, "look, we can't even track a print in the snow to see who actually entered Wallace's shanty. We all rushed in there, not thinking. I bet Jace is rethinking the fact that he allowed that to happen right about now."

Rain noticed that Jace had returned to Nick's side, and the two were back to speaking in hushed tones.

"It's not entirely Jace's fault. We ran in there on pure adrenalin. He probably wouldn't have been able to stop us even if he'd tried."

"That's true." Julia puffed out her cheeks. "The problem is, footprints might've been the proof we needed to show that Nick wasn't the only one that went in there. And now look: what a cluster mess." Her eyes finally rested on the door of Wallace's shanty, seemingly begging for answers to what had happened inside the four walls not long ago. "There's no blood on the ground outside—did you notice that?"

"Yeah, whatever happened clearly happened inside the shanty away from view, and the murder weapon was probably tossed down the hole, like Jace said." Rain chewed her lip and noticed her lips were starting to crack. She reached into her coat pocket in search of ChapStick. After she applied the cherry lip balm, she added, "let's go back to what we do know. We know someone besides Nick entered the shanty. What we don't know, is what time. Maybe your husband can share that, and we can nail down a time of death. That will give us a window of when this horrible incident occurred. As it is, it's a small window. I didn't see Nick on my way over to the tent, so he must've been with Wallace around that time. Unless he stopped to visit with another fisherman. Maybe we can ask around to see if anyone saw Nick chatting with anybody? Hopefully, someone can provide an alibi."

Rain let her musings linger between them like dangling icicles from the roofline before she noticed familiar people beelining in their direction. Kim, a former member of the water-ski team, whom they'd hung out with quite a bit in their youth, was gripping the arm of her husband, Seth, as the two quickly made their way toward them. Their faces were marked by obvious concern.

Upon her arrival, Kim reached out for Julia and immediately folded her into an embrace. Her red hair screamed out from beneath a light-colored hat.

"Are you okay?" Seth asked. He stretched a long arm out, to pat Julia on the shoulder after his wife had taken a step backward and moved to greet Rain with a half hug.

"Define *okay*." Julia's gaze dropped to the ground, and she slowly shook her head. Her shoulders slumped in defeat, and her arms hung limply by her sides.

"We took the four-wheelers back to the house to drop the twins off with Grandma, and it feels like we've just walked into a hornet's nest!" Kim's green eyes darted toward Jace and Nick, who were still huddled in quiet conversation. "How the heck did this happen?"

"Boy, wouldn't we like to know. So, how'd you hear the news then, if you were taking care of the twins?" Rain asked.

"How could you not? Everyone's talking about how Nick offed some guy!" Kim covered her mouth with her mitten when she noticed her comment was clearly a sucker punch to Julia. "Goodness, I'm so sorry! I didn't mean—"

"Are you kidding?" Julia's tone was incredulous. She looked toward Rain, and then her eyes searched Kim's for answers. Answers that neither woman could give.

"When you said you'd heard the news," Rain stuttered, "I thought you meant you'd heard that a man was murdered. You're not serious. People actually believe Nick was involved in this?"

Seth's face morphed from concern to chagrin. "Everyone knew Nick was ticked off that someone had stolen his fishing hole. It's not like it was something he'd kept to himself. We all knew it! And besides that, the victim's own wife is accusing him—" Seth stopped short when the searing eyes from the group of women focused in on him incredulously.

"And you really think . . ." Julia's voice lifted to an octave that was almost uncomfortable for the human ear. Her lip began to quiver.

"Nooo, of course not, honey," Kim interrupted in a soothing tone. "We don't think that at all, right, Seth?" The softness in her eyes turned to a glare when she prompted her husband to help console Julia and to choose his words carefully.

"Of course not," Seth said flatly.

"So, neither of you actually saw Nick or anyone else coming from Wallace's shanty? Or did you?" Rain pressed. "Anything that might help clear him of this?"

Seth swallowed, his large Adam's apple bobbed, and his eyes avoided her gaze. It was obvious to Rain he was holding something back and that whatever it was, would not be in Nick's favor.

"What?" Rain pressed.

"Nick was really mad, okay? You might think losing a fishing hole is no big thing, but when there's a big money prize and the latest Polaris on the table . . . decked out with all the bells and whistles . . ." He didn't finish his sentence as his wife shot him a dagger look that would silence anyone in an instant. Seth seemed relieved when Jace beckoned, with a wave of his hand, for Seth to join him and Nick.

"Excuse me, ladies, I'm being summoned," Seth said in a tone of relief before rushing away from them and heading toward his fishing buddies.

"I'm going with him. Maybe I can talk some sense into all these men. And find out what exactly is going on here." Kim gave Julia an encouraging smile. "Call me later?"

Julia answered with a bob of her head before Kim went to join her husband. Rain watched as Nick crumpled to his knees and put his head in his hands, as if he'd just received very bad news. Jace placed a steadying hand on his brother-in-law's shoulder. Julia noticed this too and reached to grip Rain's arm tight.

"Rain, you gotta help me. We need to prove Nick is innocent! Someone else must've been seen entering Wallace's ice shanty. Or there's another clue . . . somewhere. I just need to find it . . ." Julia's tone was growing more and more desperate, and her voice was strained. "We need to find something to clear his name." Her breath grew ragged, as if she were a heavy smoker.

"Deep breaths, Julia. Don't worry—we're gonna figure this out. I promise." Rain touched her friend's hand where Julia continued to hold Rain's arm in a death grip. The trembling of Julia's lips told Rain everything. She realized in that moment that her friend's anger had been a disguise for pure adrenalin and fear. Julia was scared out of her mind. And she had reason to be. Rain couldn't help but remember, Nick also had blood on his hands. That ominous cut that she had seen earlier, which Nick had brushed off as being nothing. Things were starting to add up . . . in the wrong direction.

Chapter Five

Rain watched in disbelief as Nick ducked his head before slipping into the backseat of a police cruiser. Jace was talking to the new officer in charge, and Rain was doing everything in her power to calm her friend. "It's gonna be okay, Julia."

"Why are they taking him *in*?" Julia's face sagged. Her voice was now coming out as a whisper, as if all her adrenaline had depleted and she had officially hit the wall.

Rain couldn't believe what was happening either, but she did her best to hide it. The last thing she wanted was to encourage her friend's insecurities. "Jace told you. It's just a formality at this point. He couldn't just let Nick go because he was the last person to see Wallace alive. And besides, if Jace had let Nick walk, it would've looked as if he was giving him preferential treatment. His conflict of interest has given him no other choice than to have another officer take over. Which, honestly, is best for everyone. This is all going to work out, I promise. I'm sure Nick'll be home within the hour." Rain hoped she wasn't making empty promises.

"I suppose you're right."

"Let's get you inside where it's warm, and we'll talk this through over a cup of herbal tea. Or maybe something a bit stronger. Whaddya say? We need to make a plan."

Julia nodded solemnly and reached for Rain's arm, to steady herself, before the two maneuvered through the newly fallen snow, back to the warmth of the main cabin.

The scent of chili still hung in the air, though Rain guessed her friend probably wouldn't have much of an appetite. She immediately shed her coat and hung it on a nearby hook and gathered Julia's coat to do the same as her friend numbly followed.

Rain headed to the kitchen and picked up the kettle. "Peppermint or chamomile?"

"Peppermint, with a hit of schnapps if you've got it. I think you're right; I might need something a bit stronger," Julia said quietly as she sank onto the stool at the kitchen island and rested her head in her hands.

"I'm assuming you don't have an appetite. I still have some chili in the Crock-Pot, which is probably cold at this point, but I could warm it back up if you'd like."

"No, thanks." Julia lifted her head and made eye contact with Rain. "What motive would my husband have to harm Wallace? I mean, the police can't get this to stick, right? There's no motive! Don't they need means, motive, and opportunity?" she said sarcastically. "Right now, they only have opportunity . . . and potentially means? But motive? No way!"

"I'm sure you don't want to hear this, especially coming from my lips, but you were the one that mentioned Nick was furious that Wallace had stolen his fishing spot. Remember? Seth alluded to it too. If you two were aware of that fact, I'm sure there were many others that knew how Nick felt about it." Rain reached for the tea bags and dropped two into oversized mugs. She slid the bottle of Peppermint schnapps over next to it. "Take what you need, hon."

Julia rolled her eyes and then hung her head. "Seriously, Nick's gonna kill someone over a stupid fishing hole? That's what the police think? Gimme a break," she huffed. "That's lame."

Rain shrugged. "Large money prize, a coveted UTV. Hey, people have killed for less."

"You're not helping."

Rain winced. "Sorry. You asked!"

"I did, didn't I?" Julia cracked open the schnapps and took a swig directly from the bottle before dousing her tea. She then hovered over the mug of tea, deflated. "I appreciate you being straight with me. Holding things back at this point isn't gonna solve this crime, is it? You don't need to mince words with me—you know that. Besides, we need to lay everything out on the table. Then we can dissect it and figure this out."

"Exactly. We'll hash all this out and have it wrapped up by nightfall," Rain said convincingly. More to convince herself than anything, if she was being honest, as she had no clue how they would figure any of this out.

"Boy, waking up this morning for the fishing tournament, this was the last thing I thought would happen. Life is chock full of surprises, isn't it?" Julia smoothed the static from her hair with her fingers after removing her winter hat and setting it down in her lap, and then dug her fingers into her forehead.

Rain added more hot water to the mug in front of her friend, then took a deep breath. "Do you know of anyone else that might have had an issue with Wallace? Do you know anything about him?"

Julia blew into her mug and shook her head before taking a slurpy sip.

"I think if we do a little digging about our victim, maybe we can understand why someone would want to kill him. We need to find out if he had any ongoing problems or issues with anyone. I just don't know where to begin digging into a stranger's past. Or how we find out any information about him. Where do we even start?" Rain rested her chin on her hand and searched her mind.

"Yeah, I agree, we need to get to know our victim." Julia nodded slowly. "Wait. How about library books? Maybe we should see what books he's borrowed in the past? It might give us a clue about his interests and such? Outside of fishing that is."

"Actually, Julia, that's a great idea." Rain stood upright. "Although, I'd never met him before yesterday, so it must have been a while since he last visited the library. But it's all we've got to go on right now. And it's something we have immediate access to. Hey, it's a start, right?"

Julia slipped off the stool and reached for her mug. "No time like the present. Let's go find out everything we can about the man."

Rain followed Julia to the back door and reached for the key before the two rushed across the slippery catwalk to the safety of the library. The cold followed them inside, and Rain rubbed her hands up and down her arms to get the blood pumping again after closing the door. The smell of books and the sight of the leather spines meticulously organized on the shelves always calmed Rain, and she could sense Julia felt the same as she watched her friend relax a little in the space. The library was their sanctuary, a place of safety and quiet that enveloped them with some semblance of normalcy and hope. And answers. Hopefully, a lot of answers.

Rain woke up the laptop and immediately ran a search. Her eyes scanned the information, and she read it aloud to Julia. "I put Benson into the library database, and three names popped up: Wallace, Tina, and Greg. When I input Tina, she and Wallace share the same address. I guess he is married, after all."

"You mean Tina's my husband's accuser? Oh, Tina-bobina, what am I gonna do with you?" Julia sighed.

Rain looked up and made eye contact with Julia before dropping her glance back to the screen. "They live on Acorn Lane, and the last books Wallace's wife borrowed from the library were a book about ceramics and one about plaster crafts."

"What about Wallace?"

"Unfortunately, it doesn't look like he's been here all that much. The last time he borrowed a book, before yesterday, was two years ago, and it was on birds of Wisconsin and bird watching." Rain shrugged. "I'm not sure that's much help."

"Well, no, you're right, that doesn't really help at all. What about the other Benson? Did you say Greg? Any relation?"

"I'm not sure, but let's take down his address and maybe pay him a visit? Whaddya say? It's something, right?"

"That's a good idea. We have to do something. I can't let this go, Rain. Not until my husband is home free will I be able to rest."

For the first time, Julia looked encouraged. As if having a plan might make this pill easier to swallow. One step in a direction, hopefully the right one, was bound to be reassuring.

After searching his name further, Rain realized that Greg had an overdue library book. "Looks like our friend Greg here didn't return a book the last time my mother was up here as library director. Apparently, she didn't follow up. In any event, he lives right here in town." Rain reached for a piece of scrap paper and a pen and scribbled down the address. "Should we go?"

"Yeah, maybe we should call Willow and see what she knows about any of these patrons?"

"Yeah, we can give her a call. Should we do it before we go?" Rain dug into her pocket, plucked out her cell, and held it up in one hand.

Julia nodded. "I can't just sit here and wait for the gavel to come down on my husband. And right now, we don't have much to go on. Let's find out everything we can about Wallace Benson. Someone besides my husband had to have means, motive, and opportunity. And I guess it's up to us to find out."

The door of the library opened then, startling them both. Rain lifted her hand to her heart and evened her breath. A man filled the doorframe, and before he had a chance to knock the snow from his boots and cross the threshold, Julia said, "I'm sorry, we're closed today because of the ice-fishing jamboree."

"Not here for books, ma'am. I'm here to install the chimney for the Franklin stove before the storm hits."

"Oh," Julia turned to Rain and waited expectantly.

Rain placed her phone on the desk and then tapped her friend encouragingly on the shoulder. "We'll still go. We still have plenty of daylight."

Julia didn't look convinced.

"I promise we'll get there today, okay?" Rain said gently.

"Okay, if you're gonna need some time to get this started, I'm gonna run home and change. I think I need to get outta these snow pants before I roast to death. Meet you back here?"

"Sure," Rain answered before turning her attention back to the man who had filled the room with a commanding presence.

He removed his coat, revealing a long-sleeved shirt that said: "Wright Installation: We Get it RIGHT the First Time!"

Rain couldn't help but notice the bulge to his biceps when he dropped his coat by the entrance and rolled up his sleeves. Even his forearms flexed, as if he'd just finished a workout. His feathered hair was peppered with the slightest hint of silver at the temples, almost unnoticeable, but the rest of his hair remained the color of coal.

"Where's Howard? I thought he was handling the install?"

"Forgive my manners. Ryan Wright, Wright Installation." He held out a hand for her to shake. "Howard's my dad."

"Nice to meet you, Mr. Wright. I mean not Mr. *Right*, I mean . . . Ryan." She could feel her face growing hot.

Ryan chuckled. "And you must be Rain? Although to me, your smile is every bit a sunny day," he said with a gleaming smile that could make any girl swoon. His attempt to help her relax worked, as it was impossible for her not to return his smile.

And charming too. A dangerous combination.

Though out of nowhere a sudden feeling of guilt washed over her as if she was betraying Max in some way. The thought surprised her as Max had been gone well over a year now. It had been a long time since a stranger could make her heart skip a beat. Jace had caused that to happen too, but she knew Jace, had grown up with him. Would Max approve? And why was Max occupying her mind and drawing comparisons to the way Ryan looked. He was much more rugged. Max barely had an unclean fingernail a day in his life.

"You still with me? I lost you?" Ryan's eyes narrowed in concern.

Rain cleared her throat and smiled. "Sorry—thanks for coming over."

"You bet," he said, tugging his sleeves up higher on his arms. "I'm only installing the chimney today. I'll be back with the stove as soon as we get it in stock. Should be any day now."

"Not taking part in the jamboree?"

"Nah, duty calls. I have a few of these stoves to get in before the big snow hits and piles up on the roofs. I couldn't take the chance."

"Ahh, I believe it. So, you didn't hear what happened out there today?" Rain sat on the corner of the desk, folded her arms across her chest, and waited.

"Uh-uh. I've had my hands full all mornin'. Why? What did I miss? Someone catch something big out there?" He grinned.

"Not exactly. You know a guy named Wallace Benson?"

"Can't say I do."

"Oh."

"Why do you ask?"

"He was murdered today." Rain watched Ryan's reaction closely, and his eyes, the color of copper pennies, doubled in size. She couldn't stop herself from thinking that everyone who crossed her path could be a potential suspect or might be withholding information. Her distrust of the human condition sometimes alarmed her. Max had really done a number on her by cheating before he died.

"You're joking."

"No, unfortunately, I'm not."

"They catch who did it?" He raked a hand through his hair and then landed his hands on his hips. Rain noticed how broad his shoulders were in comparison to his narrow waist when he did so.

"No . . . not yet." Rain hesitated to take the conversation further, as she could feel a lump forming in her throat when her thoughts turned to Nick. She moved away and adjusted a few items on the desk that didn't need adjusting, and then turned back to him. "Anything I can I do to help you get started?" She followed him to the spot where the stove would eventually be installed.

"How good are you at clearing snow off a roof?" he asked over his shoulder.

"Excuse me?"

"I'm just kiddin'. I've got this handled. I'm just bummed it started to snow already. I'll give 'er a quick sweep. You don't even have to be here if you have somewhere else you need to be."

"Actually, yeah, I was just going to run an errand with my friend before you arrived." Rain jutted a thumb toward the door.

"It's no problem. Really, go on ahead. No need for you to stick around."

Rain looked to the shelves of books, clearly with an expression of uncertainty because Ryan continued, "I'll tarp the bookshelves before I cut the hole in the ceiling. No worries—not my first rodeo. You won't even know I was here," he added confidently. "I won't leave a speck of dust." He winked.

"Oh, I'm sorry, I didn't mean to come off as if I didn't trust you with this . . . I'm a bit protective of my collection here. My grandfather Luis was an author, and my great-grandfather built this log cabin with his own two hands." Rain glanced at the walls and then back to him.

"You don't say?" He took in the room with fresh eyes and nodded approvingly. "Nice workmanship—it's a gorgeous cabin. It's actually a dream of mine to build one someday. You know, a bucket list–type of thing . . . when I ever get some free time." He chuckled. "Not sure when that'll ever be, but—"

"Yep, so please excuse my hesitation. It's not at all a reflection of you. I had to practically beg my mother to take on this project. She didn't want me to make any big changes to the library cabin. We have a long history here." Rain touched the bookshelf with reverence.

"Totally understand. But again"—he pointed to the logo on his shirt—"we get it right . . ."

"The first time," Rain finished with a smile.

Ryan grinned, showing an almost perfect set of teeth. His smile was contagious. "You got it," he added convincingly, and something told her the cabin was in good hands.

She was so glad Julia had been preoccupied upon Ryan's arrival and hadn't witnessed this conversation unfold. Because she just knew that her friend would have teased her about it for weeks.

Chapter Six

The only sound on the ride over to Greg Benson's house was the wipers squeaking in perfect rhythm across the windshield. Rain was glad that she'd recently topped off the windshield wiper fluid to prepare for the sloppy winter months ahead. Unfortunately, the *only* thing keeping up were the wipers. The roads were becoming treacherous because of the snow falling at a rate of almost an inch an hour, and Rain was relieved to know that, according to Google Maps, they didn't have much farther to go. Julia was unusually subdued, and Rain wondered what kind of chaos was raging inside her friend's noggin. She reached out a hand and tapped Julia on the leg.

"How you holdin' up?"

Julia stifled a yawn with the back of her hand. "Honestly, this whole thing has me beat. I think I may have worn myself out back there with all my freakin' out. If I wasn't so desperate for answers, I'd go crash on the couch in front of the TV or, better yet, go for a long winter's nap." She yawned again, this time with her mouth wide open. "I doubt I'd be able to rest, though, even if given the chance," she admitted with a frown.

"I believe it. We'll be quick, and hopefully Nick will be back home soon, and you both can do just that," Rain said as she gripped the steering wheel tighter. "The roads are getting slick." She adjusted the wipers to a faster speed to keep up with the sudden burst of flakes that made it look as if they were driving through the opening credits of *Star Wars*.

"Yeah, well, without Nick to do the plowing, I guess we won't be the only ones who'll be stuck at home after this. Right?" Julia looked out the passenger window to the sky. "It looks like we're in for a doozy of a storm. They'd better not keep him long."

Rain hadn't thought of that. So many people relied on Nick to dig them out. This could be bad on so many levels. "I doubt they'll keep him overnight. They just brought him in for questioning. Seriously, besides Tina's account, the police have nothing to hold him on, and I doubt hearsay is enough to make any charges stick."

"I really hope you're right." Julia sounded defeated.

Rain wondered if her friend had even a glimmer of hope left, from the tone of Julia's voice. She flipped on the radio for a quick weather update and then turned it off when she could only find music. She reached for her phone and handed it to Julia. "We forgot—let's call Mom and see what she knows."

When Willow answered the phone, both Rain and Julia instantly said hello in unison, causing them to chuckle.

"You're on speaker, Mom. We're in the car," Rain said finally when the laughter subsided.

"Where are you two headed off to? I heard the North-woods is in for a humdinger! Are you running to stock up on some essentials? I do hope you're both prepared. It can get pretty nasty, pretty quick up there," Willow said with a hint of concern.

After explaining about the murder and the conundrum Nick was in, Rain could tell from the sound of her mother's voice that she had made the turn from simple unease to grave concern, like the rest of them. "I wish I had more information on the Bensons, but you know how it can be in the summer up there. The library is like a revolving door. I really can't put my finger on anything that stands out about either of them. Do you need me to come up? If I leave now, I might be able to beat the storm."

"No. We've got everything handled, Willow, and the last thing you need is to head directly into a blizzard—it's too dangerous. Just pray," Julia said wearily.

"You've got it, honey," Willow answered. "I'm sure it'll all smooth over soon. Try not to worry."

But Willow's words were hollow, because Rain could tell they were all worried. "Here we are. Mom, sorry to cut you off, but we gotta go. Love you—say hi to Dad for me."

"Wait!"

"Don't worry, we'll be in touch, Willow," Julia added.

"If you change your mind, I can come up after the storm if you need me . . . Love you girls. Please be safe out there," Willow said hesitantly before Rain ended the call. It was obvious that her mother was now added on to the list of those who were deeply concerned.

Rain maneuvered the car along where she thought the sidewalk would be if the roads hadn't been covered in fresh snow. She checked the address on the mailbox for confirmation. "Yep, looks like this is it."

"Okay. we'd better hurry so we can get back home. I know you depend on your SUV to do the job, but sometimes these storms are too big for even your Ford Explorer to handle." Julia smirked.

Rain hoped for both their sakes that Julia wasn't right and this wouldn't turn into some type of psychic foreshadowing of how the remainder of the afternoon would go.

The two trekked through the deepening un-shoveled snow to the front door of Greg Benson's house. Rain pressed the doorbell with a gloved finger, and they waited with chattering teeth. A light flickered in the front room, reflecting through the privacy glass on the door, and Rain saw a figure appear. A man opened the door, wearing a perplexed look on his pasty face.

"Can I help you?" He looked past them for a quick moment and then regarded them with confused, narrowed eyes. "Jehovah's witnesses? In a snowstorm?"

"Greg Benson?" Rain asked.

"Yeah. Do I know you?" The lines on his forehead deepened. Then he wiped a hand wearily across his face as if he was attempting to wake from a nap.

"No, but you might remember my mother, Willow. My name's Rain, from the Lofty Pines Library, the one located on Pine Lake at the log cabin. And this is my coworker and friend, Julia." She gestured a hand to where Julia stood shivering next to her. "You're familiar with the library, yes? You have a library card with us."

Greg immediately shook his head as if dumfounded. "Is this about a book?"

Rain and Julia shared a glace before she continued. "Um . . ."

"Let me get this straight. You mean to tell me you came out in a winter storm, looking for an overdue book? This couldn't wait. What's the title?" His eyes widened and then his gaze dropped to the ground, as if he was seeking answers. "I don't even remember . . ." He rubbed his hand across the back of his neck. His brow remained furrowed.

Julia smiled genuinely for the first time since all the craziness had occurred. "Actually, Mr. Benson, it's not really about the book. Only partly," she admitted.

"What's this about then? If not chasing down overdue books?" His confusion morphed to a tone of frustration. "And why in the world would you choose to do this in the middle of a snowstorm?"

After seeing firsthand Greg's reaction and growing agitation, Rain hoped he wouldn't throw them both off his front step into a snowbank. "I think it was a Michael Connelly novel, or was it a Grisham book?" She shot a glance to Julia and then back to Greg. "Do either of those ring a bell?" For the life of her, Rain couldn't remember the name of the title, as it was currently the least of her concerns. But now she wished she could, because an awkward silence hung over them.

Rain elbowed Julia, who just stood there like a deer in the headlights.

Greg's eyes narrowed. "I don't know what to make of this. You could've called. I'll send a check to replace the cost of the book, if that's what you're after."

Rain bit her lip and then went for it. "Okay, the truth is, we're not here to fine you for a lost book. We're here because we were wondering if you were any relation to Wallace Benson. We wanted to pay our respects . . . we're so sorry for your loss . . ." Rain's voice trailed off as she looked at Julia expectantly, hoping she'd jump in at any time with a comment or to rescue her. She didn't.

"Loss? Wallace Benson? Did something happen to him?" His hand gripped the side of the door tighter, and he looked past them as if expecting the deceased man himself to be next to walk up the snow-covered path.

Rain chewed the inside of her cheek. This was a bad idea. If his relative had been murdered, and they had beaten the police to share the news with him, this could prove to be an unbelievably bad idea indeed. What were they thinking? They were making poor decisions based on pure emotion and fear. So much for digging for answers. Rain was going to have to rethink this whole idea of leading Julia on a wild goose chase before they got themselves into hot water for impeding an ongoing investigation. She looked to her friend for guidance.

Meanwhile, Julia shuffled her feet, leaving fresh paths on the snow-covered porch, and then started making what looked like rainbow patterns in the snow with her foot. "Yeah, we're so sorry . . ." she added with her glance downcast, as if mesmerized by her winter art.

"Although I appreciate your condolences, Wallace shares no relation to me. We just share the same last name." Greg held the door as if he wasn't sure whether he should let them inside his house or slam the door in their face. Rain thought at this point it could go either way. She could hardly blame the man.

"Oh." Julia stopped making patterns in the snow and looked up.

Greg let out a long, slow whistle. "Well, I hate to be the one to say it, but that's karma for you. I wonder how Danny's gonna take the news."

"Danny? Who's he? And what do you mean, *karma*?" Rain's interest was piqued. "I'm confused . . ."

Greg rubbed his fingers across his forehead and then answered, "Isn't that what they say when things boomerang in your direction after you do something horrific? It's karma, right? Fate steps in?"

Julia finally jumped into the conversation with something of value. "Yeah, but how do you know Wallace had something coming to him?"

Greg completely dodged the question and said, "You weren't the first to think I was related to the guy. A lot of people thought we were related, but Wallace seemed to drag negativity wherever he went." He frowned. "I'm not sure he had many coworkers that he could actually call friends. A bit of a loner."

"Negativity?" Julia leaned in expectantly. "You worked together?"

"Yeah, over at Smith Brothers Logging. Hey, I'm not trying to spit on his grave or anything like that. I just think Wallace ruffled a few feathers at work. Seemed he left a path of destruction in his wake before he finally quit. I probably would've quit too with all that hanging over my head."

Julia's ears seemed to perk up even more. "You don't say? What kind of destruction?"

"Wallace was considered reckless on the job. He didn't take the necessary OSHA precautions. Rumor was that Danny lost his arm because of that guy. Didn't you hear about the logging accident a few months ago? It was all over the news. If it wasn't for Wallace, Danny might still have two hands and not be outta work on disability. The accident destroyed him—and his family. He has two small kids to raise. On disability? Come to think of it, I think his wife was even pregnant with a third. How's Danny gonna make that work? With one arm? I feel bad for the guy."

Rain looked to Julia after that bit of information sank in. She could almost see the wheels in her friend's brain spinning rapidly. The loss of an arm and the inability to work and provide for his growing family could surely prove to be a motive. Revenge? The question was, could a one-armed man pull off the murder of a man as large as Wallace Benson?

Greg surprised Rain when he quickly changed the subject and said, "By the way, I have no idea where that book is. I'm going to need a few days to dig though my shelves to locate it. If I owe you a fine, so be it." His gaze moved away from them and toured the sky. "Anyway, by the looks of this weather, you two better be getting on your way. Unless you plan on spending the night in your car. It's getting dark."

"Yeah, no problem," Rain said. "Just drop it off as soon as you can, okay? We won't worry about a fine if you get it back to us by the end of next week. After the storm—no rush," she added with a light smile.

"You bet," he said before closing the door and abruptly ending the conversation.

"Well, that was awkward," Julia said out of the side of her mouth before taking a step backward, doing a military-fashion about-face and heading toward the car as if now wanting a quick getaway.

"No kidding." Rain rushed behind her, shuffling her feet through the snow so as not to slip, and then wiped the driver's-side window with the sleeve of her coat before sinking behind the wheel. As she let the engine warm up, she turned to Julia.

"What do you make of that?"

"I think we found a motive for murder. That's what I think."

Chapter Seven

The previous night, Rain had tossed and turned throughout a fitful sleep, worrying about her best friend and what they should do next to clear Nick's name once and for all. The police had allowed Nick to return home, but they were keeping the pressure on, like a tourniquet, adding that they might be in touch with more questions. Basically, any wrong move, or any additional evidence, and Nick would be going away in handcuffs. The dark cloud over his head was real, and Rain was desperate to bring back the sunshine.

Rain stifled a yawn as she tucked another returned book back onto the shelf where it belonged. She scanned the library and noticed she wasn't alone. A few patrons were scattered throughout the room, hushed, with heads deep into hardcovers. Thankfully, all were consumed in the books they were reading. Rain was glad for the silence, but her own mind was so noisy, she wondered how she would continue to focus, if at all.

Who could've done this to Wallace? Why was Tina so adamant this was Nick's doing? Did Danny hold a grudge? Was this a revenge killing?

Her train of thought was diverted when she noticed Ryan entering the library. He summoned her to the door as soon as he had her attention.

"Ryan, what a nice surprise. I wasn't expecting you today."

"We got a few stoves in stock, so I'm only here to drop and go. I can always do the install when the weather gets worse, but I can't deliver then. Is this a bad time?" He looked over her shoulder as if he was examining the space for room.

"No, it's okay. We can move outta the way if you're just bringing it in and placing it."

"Yeah, Dad's in the truck; he's on the phone with a customer. As soon as he's finished, we'll bring it in, if that's okay with you."

His eyes held her gaze momentarily, and Rain felt a hot rush to her cheeks. "Sounds perfect. I can't tell you how much I'm looking forward to warming this place up for my patrons."

He smiled. "I could see myself kickin' back over there where the stove's goin' with a bit of Thoreau." He pointed to where the phantom stove stood.

"Henry David Thoreau?" Rain's mouth dropped.

"Why do you look so surprised? Haven't you ever been told not to judge a book by its cover?" he said teasingly, throwing his arms out wide, as if he himself were on display.

Rain could see that Ryan would make a great model for one of Julia's historical romance novels. She could picture his rugged hands cupping the face of a beautiful woman. She shook her head to remove the thought. "No, it's not that. I just didn't expect . . ."

Ryan smiled, *"Rather than love, than money, than fame . . ."* he started.

"Give me truth," they finished in unison.

"I love that quote." Rain held a hand to her heart. Little did Ryan know just how important truth was to her. "You surprise me, Mr. Wright."

"Here you go again, calling me 'Mr. Right.' Hey, you never know," he teased with an uplifted brow. "May I call you Sunshine? Rain just doesn't fit you. Or am I being too presumptuous?" A slight flush washed over his cheeks, but he recovered with a broad smile.

"Call me whatever you like." Rain shrugged. "Doesn't bother me a bit. Just don't tell my mother—she named me."

"I won't tell a soul." He lifted a finger to his lips, where Rain's eyes couldn't resist lingering.

An older woman approached with a frown and an uplifted finger, interrupting their banter.

"Excuse me. Can you help me find something for my grand-daughter? She's coming to stay with me for a few days, and I haven't a clue what kind of book would be appropriate for her age group. Things have changed so much over the years." She put a hand aside her cheek and shook her head in dismay. "Kids today," she whispered. "They learn so much on the computer, there's little left to the imagination." She feigned a laugh.

Rain smiled. "I hear you. How old is she?"

"She's twelve."

"Can you excuse me, Ryan?"

"Sure, no problem. Dad and I will be outta your hair in no time," he said with a salute, and then turned on his heel away from them. "I'll be back in a few days to install it," he added over his shoulder.

"Looking forward to it," Rain answered before she led the woman to the Young Adult section of the library. When they arrived, she turned and asked, "Can you share some of her interests? Maybe I can help pick something specific to her liking."

"Cassie likes horses, but I don't know if that helps any. I just know the poor girl needs an escape. Hopefully, you can help me find a novel that she can't put down. Something that will take her mind off things and distract her for a bit." The woman lowered her voice again to a whisper. "Her neighbor died this week, and my daughter-in-law says Cassie's been absolutely distraught over it. My granddaughter can't sleep, can't eat—she thinks she's next."

"Oh, that's awful. Why would she think that? I know that death can really rattle a person. Especially if she's young—it's like they finally come to understand they're not invincible."

"Apparently awhile back, another house down the road was burglarized. Now Cassie has it in her head that her neighborhood is being targeted by some sort of serial killer. I say, my daughter-in-law lets her watch too many PG movies, and she gets these crazy ideas in her mind! The poor little thing. That's why she's coming to my house for the weekend. We're hoping to keep her away until things die down a bit. Oh, dear, I didn't mean 'die down,' I meant *settle* down." She put her head in her hands in shame and then toyed with her thinning hair before making eye contact with Rain again, albeit with her face still riddled with guilt.

Rain's heart hammered in her chest, and a throbbing vibration suddenly thrummed in her ears. She checked over each shoulder to be sure another patron wasn't in earshot before whispering, "Wait. Now I think I understand . . . She thinks she's next? Was her neighbor murdered by chance?"

"Why, yes! How did you know?" The woman's eyes doubled in size. "Has word gotten out already of this horrible tragedy? Oh, it's just awful. I can't believe my son's neighbor has . . . well . . ." Her voice trailed off, and she covered her mouth with her hand.

"I'm guessing their neighbor is Wallace Benson?"

"I do believe that was the neighbor's name." Her head bobbed vigorously in agreement. "It's absolutely a disgrace what happened to him, in our own town no less! Did you know him?"

"Yes, he was a patron here. Actually, he had paid us a visit the day before he passed. So incredibly sad." Rain swallowed the lump forming in her throat and then continued. "What do you know about him? Anything?"

"What do you mean?" The woman's thin brows, which were painted thick with pencil, came together in a frown.

"Was he married? Or divorced? Anything you can share about him? I'd like to send a card to his family." Rain's mouth went dry as the little white lie escaped from her mouth.

"Oh. Yes, his wife's name is Tina, but I heard some rumblings that maybe they were on the brink of a divorce. They may have even been separated—I'm not exactly sure. I have to admit I'd only met the neighbor a handful of times. Mostly, the kids come by my house for dinners and such. I don't like to be that kind of mother-in-law." She pursed her lips, and her expression pinched. "If you know what I mean."

Rain actually wasn't sure what she meant, and her face must've shown it because the woman continued.

"I try not to meddle. Once my son married his wife, I promised myself I'd wait for my daughter-in-law to extend the invites to visit. Well, let me tell you, the invitations are few and far between." She rolled her eyes. "If I want to see my family, I have to be the one to prepare a big meal and have everyone over for Sunday dinner. The kids all seem to land at my house. Then I'm not intruding on their home turf, you see," she added with a curt nod and a frown. "As if I'd be critical or something like that because my daughter-in-law can't keep a clean house."

"Ah, I see what you mean," Rain said, although she was sad for the woman who seemed to be missing the invitations she clearly desired, and was looking for a way to fit into her grown children's lives.

"Anyhow." The older woman fluttered a hand. "Despite the circumstances, I'm glad to have Cassie coming to stay with me for a few days." She smiled and then added under her breath, "Though, it took a murder for this to happen. But I'm not complaining. Cassie needs me right now," she said, lifting her chin.

Rain turned her attention back to the shelf and plucked a book she thought might be a good fit and handed it to the woman. "She might like this one, but if not, please be sure and bring your granddaughter over. I'd be happy to exchange it for something else. She might like to take a look at the Young

Adult section herself. Kids can be a bit finicky at times when it comes to reading."

The woman accepted the book and held it to her chest, beaming. "That's a wonderful idea! We might do just that! But I'll take this one along for now. What else might you have? Maybe I'll take two," she added, tucking the book under the crook of her arm.

Rain felt slightly guilty that she wanted the woman's granddaughter not to like the book, because she wanted the chance to question Cassie. But she decided she would make a point of it, even if she had to seek out the girl herself.

Chapter Eight

Rain scanned the items on the kitchen island one more time before beginning to assemble dinner. She had already decided that the enchilada lasagna recipe that she'd concocted just a few weeks prior, which Nick had absolutely raved about, was just what the doctor ordered. Comfort food on a blustery evening always had a way of making things better. At the moment, it was all Rain could think of to do that might help calm her friends' frayed nerves. She hoped filling their stomachs, and lending a listening ear, might ease some of their growing anxiety, if even for just a few moments.

Rain layered the enchilada sauce, the meat mixture packed with onions, tomatoes, corn, and green chilies, and then topped the final layer off with cheddar cheese. She slipped the baking pan into the oven and then wiped her hands on a dishrag. After looking around, she began to clean the ungodly mess she'd left in her wake. The sound of the plow scraping ground caught her attention, and she smiled inwardly. Nick was working to clear her driveway for the second time that afternoon, and for that she was forever grateful.

Rain reached for her cell phone to call Julia, put the phone on speaker, and continued to load the dishwasher while she waited for her friend to pick up. When Julia answered, she moved closer to the phone and said, "Hey, I know I can't fix all this, but one thing I can do is cook. You guys hungry? I'm cooking like a madwoman over here." She grinned.

"Whatcha have in mind?"

"Well, I had planned on bringing dinner over for you both, but now I'm rethinking it. Would you mind coming over here to eat, and I'll just send home the leftovers with you? I'm not sure traipsing across the yard in knee-deep snow with a hot lasagna pan would be a good idea." Rain chewed her lip. "Although Nick is out there plowing, I'm assuming the drifts outside my door need to be shoveled again. This time I'm waiting until tomorrow. I've had enough shoveling for one day. But there's probably enough of a path for you to get in, just not enough to navigate with an armful of food," she added with a chuckle.

"Did you say lasagna? Girl, you speak my language. Sounds yummy!"

Based on her tone, Rain could tell Julia was smiling, and she was glad her plan was working. "Actually, it's my enchilada lasagna, the one Nick really liked when I tested the recipe out on you guys last time."

"Aw, you're too kind, friend. He really did talk about that recipe for days. He even pestered me to make it—but I haven't gotten a chance yet. But Jace is over here right now, so I'm not sure we can break away," Julia answered with a deflated tone. "As enticing as it sounds."

"The more the merrier. Your brother is welcome to join us."

"Are you sure? Hold on." Rain heard a rustling and then a short pause on the line before Julia returned. "Jace said yes. Apparently, Nick must've told him about your recipe too, and now he wants to try the famous enchilada lasagna." Julia giggled.

"Come over whenever you're ready—it's already in the oven," Rain said before hitting the "End" button on her cell.

Rain bustled about the kitchen, tidying and then setting the long wooden table, before she heard a hard knock on the door and the sound of boots shuffling around on the inside mat. Rain and Julia had an open-door policy. Neither waited for the other before entering each other's house. Rain dropped the dishrag into the sink and brushed her damp hands against her jeans before going to greet them.

"Just hang your coats on the rack or pile them on the bench—your call," she said as she gestured to the wooden bench her grandfather had built back when she was a child and which stood proudly against the wall in memory of him.

"No, they're wet," Julia said, and gathered the coats from Nick and Jace and piled them on the already over-stacked rack. "I don't want to ruin the wood after all the work your grandad went through to build that beautiful piece with his own two hands. Bless his heart."

"They're wet? Please tell me it's not snowing again!" Rain placed her hands on her hips and blew out a frustrated breath.

Julia nodded. "Yep, it just started up again."

"Welcome to the Northwoods. It'll probably spit all winter long. Which for me is good for business, so bring it on!" Nick teased with a grin. "I can't wait for the next big storm!"

Rain slapped Nick with a high five and said, "Yeah, put it on my tab, will ya? I heard you out there earlier, and I can't thank you enough! You're a lifesaver."

Her guests all removed their boots before following Rain and the scent of smoky spices directly into the kitchen.

Jace rubbed his hands together vigorously and smiled. "It smells amazeballs in here!"

Julia jabbed her brother teasingly with her elbow. "Wait till you taste it. Rain made up the recipe all on her own, and I, for one, think she's brilliant for it," she added proudly. Julia then leaned into her friend and spoke in hushed tones so the men couldn't overhear. "You know the way to a man's heart is good food." Her eyebrows rose and fell like a clown's, as a deep smile formed on her lips.

Rain smirked when she realized Julia was referring to Jace.

"What did you say?" Nick asked.

"Nothin', honey." Julia swatted her husband on the backside and then returned her attention to Rain. "Anything I can do to help?"

"Nope. I think I have it all under control." Rain nodded as she looked around her kitchen that was now back into some semblance of order. She peeked into the oven and noticed the cheese bubbling on the top, removed the pan, and set the dish on the stovetop to cool just enough to serve.

"Oh, shoot. I forgot to bring over my bottle of wine." Julia slapped her hand to her forehead. "And after all that's gone on this week, I could really use it," she added with a sigh.

Rain winced. "Sorry, Julia, I don't have any wine. I have beer, though. You want one?"

"I'll go back and get it," Jace said.

"You will?" Julia pleaded with her eyes. "Have I told you lately how much I love you, my dear ole bro?"

Jace didn't respond to Julia's overt display of love. "Yea, I think you, of all people, could use a little loosening up, so I'll gladly go and get it. I'll be right back," Jace added, turning on his heel before Julia had a chance to react to his minor dig.

"What was that about?" Rain looked at Julia, who responded with a shrug.

"The last few days haven't been easy. I guess I've been a little hard to get along with," Julia admitted. "I've been pestering my brother for details on the case, to the point of being annoying."

"What? You?" Nick teased.

Rain was glad to see glimmers of Nick's old ribbing self despite the growing lines across his forehead and the gray shadow that had formed beneath his weary eyes. She noticed Nick toying with the injury on his hand, covered with a bandage, and asked, "How's the cut healing?"

Nick blushed. "Oh, it's nothing. You know Julia—she lathered me in antibiotic ointment like I was gonna get gangrene or somethin'. I was glad I didn't need stiches." He smiled weakly before brushing her off with a cool smile.

"As I said, I do have beer from the last time you were here, if either of you'd like one." Rain opened the refrigerator and Nick followed like an excited puppy and reached over her shoulder to grab a bottle.

"Don't mind if I do!" he said with a grin and immediately cracked open the amber bottle and tossed the cap expertly into the trashcan. "Score!" he chuckled. "I should've been a Milwaukee Buck; I definitely missed my calling in the NBA."

"Yeah, right." Rain chuckled. "I'm sure the basketball league sees bottle caps in a trashcan as a winning score! And what would you like, my dear?" Rain turned her attention to Julia.

"I'll wait for Jace to bring over my Chardonnay. I don't want to ruin my tastebuds on the likes of that," Julia said, pointing to the bottle held tightly in her spouse's hand.

"Suit yourself," Rain said, closing the refrigerator door and then leaning her weight up against it. "I hate to even ask, as I don't want to kill the mood, but have either of you heard anything at all? You mentioned pestering your brother. Did you get *anything* of value out of Jace? Has he shared anything new about the investigation? Or has he remained tight-lipped? Fill me in before he gets back and we have to keep our mouths shut on the subject."

Julia blew her face up like a blowfish. "He hasn't shared squat. They officially took Jace off the case completely. Conflict of interest," she grumbled.

"Oh." Rain folder her arms across her chest. "I guess that's for the best. We'd probably drive him crazy otherwise, eh?"

Nick wiped his mouth with the back of his hand after taking a swig of beer and said, "Yeah, but he's hoping his buddies at the station will keep him abreast of new details as they become available. I'm not out of the woods yet." He grimaced before taking a longer sip. "I was warned they might have more questions for me," he added in a sarcastic tone as he waggled a finger like a parent scolding a naughty child.

"They're just being thorough. Don't take it personally," Rain said.

"Yeah, seems the police weren't satisfied with any of my answers. I get the feeling they didn't believe me; they're solely basing their decisions on Wallace's wife and her ridiculous accusations. The woman is clearly out of her mind. What a nutcase!"

"Oh, I'm sure this will all blow over. You'll see." Rain's attempt to downplay the situation brought a disgruntled shrug from Nick.

"I'm not sure about that, but there's one thing I did learn in this whole situation, and it's been a hard lesson."

"What's that?" Julia asked.

"Never to open my mouth about another human being ever again! If I hadn't been running my mouth about that stupid fishing hole, I wouldn't be in this kind of trouble. I need to learn to shut my big fat pie hole!" Nick said as he circled his mouth with his finger and then stuck out his tongue.

Rain shared a conspiratorial smile with Julia before she answered. "Trust me, I'm sure we could all use that advice from time to time. We all know how to put our foot in our mouth. We're not immune either, right, Julia?"

Julia soothed Nick by wrapping an arm around her husband's waist and giving a quick squeeze before letting go. She then curled her hair between her fingers, and her eyes glazed over in a vacant stare.

Nick caught onto it too. "Hellooo, earth to Julia!"

"There was one thing Jace let slip before he was shoved off the case . . ." Julia bit at her fingernail as if she thought maybe she should hold back what she was about to share. "Although I don't think it'll come as any surprise to either one of you."

Nick shoulder-bumped his wife to nudge her to keep talking.

"I suppose it's worth mentioning." Julia frowned.

"What's that?" Rain unlaced her arms and dropped her hands to her sides before reaching for nearby potholders to move the enchilada lasagna to the trivet located at the center of the table. Nick and Julia followed suit and took a seat around the table. Nick eyes tracked the wafting dish, as if he didn't want the food to disappear from his line of sight.

"The coroner confirmed that Wallace died as a result of stab wounds. He thinks with a knife. Possibly a fish gutting knife, which makes sense since the man was killed at an ice-fishing event. He's also gonna run a toxicology screening for some reason—I'm really not sure why. Perhaps those details will come in later. I'm not even sure we'll be privy to them with Jace off the case, which totally sucks."

Rain took that information in and let it settle deep within her brain. "I see . . . well at least it's some sort of clue."

"Thank you for making this, Rain," Nick said, interrupting them with a tone of deep appreciation. He fluttered a hand in front of himself, as if to catch the aroma lifting from the steaming pan. "After all the plowing I did today, I didn't stop for lunch. I'm officially starving to death." He wiped a hand across his weary face. "It feels like I haven't eaten in weeks."

"I told you to bring an apple on your route," Julia scoffed.

"And I've told you before, honey, that apples only make my stomach growl harder. I swear they make me even more hungry. Must be the acid or something . . ." Nick frowned, and Julia rolled her eyes. "Do we have to wait for Jace to come back to dig in?" he pressed.

"Um, yeah, we're not going to be rude, *Nick*. Just hold your horses."

"All right, you two." Rain held up the napkin and fluttered it between them to stop the banter. "Looks like we're all getting a little hangry. And tired. We're all definitely a bit overtired."

The sound of the door opening and a shuffling of footsteps after boots were wiped brought a fresh wave of smiles around the table. They looked up to find Jace walking into the room with a grim expression. Unfortunately, he was not alone. And the man standing behind him made the collective smiles immediately drop from their faces.

Chapter Nine

Rain felt her mouth go instantly dry. The look on Jace's face was one of fear and apprehension. His shoulders sagged, his hazel eyes were double the usual size, and his dimples were hidden behind a bleak appearance. And the officer standing behind him did not give her a warm fuzzy feeling either. The seriousness of his stance, how he planted his feet firmly on the floor, and his rigid spine spoke volumes.

"Nick. Julia," Jace said, addressing them both individually, before clearing his throat. "The police department brought over a warrant to search your property. I let them inside already, as you really have no other choice at this point." His glance dropped to the floor. When his eyes rose to meet theirs again, he gestured a hand to the officer. "This is Officer Bentley, one of our newer officers in Lofty Pines."

Officer Bentley's penetrating stare seemed accusatory as he gave both Nick and Julia a once-over. He handed paperwork to Nick, which Rain assumed was the warrant.

Suddenly, Rain's stomach flopped, and she officially lost her appetite.

"What could they possibly be looking for?" Julia asked in a completely incredulous tone. "At *our* house?" She leaned over the table to eye the documents.

Officer Bentley snorted. "Isn't it obvious? Evidence in a murder investigation." The officer then hooked his thumbs inside his police belt and adjusted his stance as he continued looking at them through a haze of disapproval.

"Should we go over there? I'm not exactly comfortable with them digging through our things without us present." Nick slid the papers over to Julia, rose from the chair, and raked a hand through his thick, dark, hair. His eyes darted around the room like a ball in a pinball machine, racking up serious points.

"You can if you want to. Either way, they've got a job to do, and they'll do it without any approval from you," Jace acknowledged with a resigned nod. "Maybe that's best, though, if it makes you more comfortable."

Nick looked at the center of the table, where the enchilada lasagna waited for them, and then back at Rain. "I'm sorry, I can't just stay here. I gotta go over there. You understand . . ."

"Of course! Absolutely, no worries. Food will be here for you when the police are through. I'll just put tin foil over the top, and it'll be ready whenever you are." Rain sent him an encouraging smile but had to remind herself to take a breath. She couldn't fathom why the police had moved forward and issued a warrant. Something had prompted them; she just had no idea what it could be.

Nick moved quickly away from the table, beelining a direct path to the door, and Julia hollered, "Wait!"

Nick turned to address his wife and threw up his hands in frustration. "For what, Julia?"

Julia leapt from the chair. "For me, silly. I'm coming too." Her glance darted to Rain. "You comin'?"

The fear in Julia's tone made Rain's stomach flop for the second time. "I'm right behind you," she said evenly.

Jace held Rain back by the shoulder and let the others pass and get a head start to the neighboring property before lowering his voice to a murmur. "This is not good for Nick, Rain. Not good at all."

"It's not like they're gonna find anything. I don't even know why they're wasting their time. This is nuts!" Rain vigorously shook her head, and Jace surprised her by reaching for her, and turning her body to squarely face him. He lifted her chin so she faced him directly, and they stood but a mere foot apart. They were so close; she could feel the heat of his breath on her face.

Jace lowered his voice to a whisper. "The police wouldn't do this unless they had just cause. Are you hearing me?" His eyes narrowed. "I need you to be strong for Julia. Can I count on you?" The vein in his temple pulsated.

Rain shook her head in denial. This wasn't happening. She wanted to call them all back, seat them around the table and feed them, and tell them everything was going to be okay. But deep in her heart, there remained a flutter of fear.

Jace gave her a little shake as if to wake her. "Rain, will you do that for me?" The intensity in his eyes was palpable and she almost wanted to break away and run from the horror of it all.

"Yes. Of course. But . . . I . . ."

"Come on, let's go. I need to be there and watch this unfold." Jace turned on his heel and summoned her closer to the door, where Rain quickly slipped into her boots but completely abandoned the idea of a coat. Her heart now raced erratically in her chest as she quietly allowed her mind to mull over the implication of what Jace had said.

Just cause? What just cause had led the police to conduct this search? And why now? Had it taken them this long to issue the warrant? Was that the delay? What on earth was happening? Quickly her world, and everything in it, was spinning wildly out of control.

Snow stung her eyes and caused Rain to grab Jace's arm and grip it tightly, to keep up with his stride, as the two rushed across the plowed driveway. She didn't feel the chill in the air, despite having no coat. Or the wind whipping in their direction or the fluttering snow curling around their heads. No. All she could feel was the sudden heat in her cheeks, brought on by an erratic thumping heart. When they entered the house, they immediately joined Nick and Julia, who were huddled together on the sofa, with eyes wide and faces riddled with apprehension. The couple was holding hands and talking in muffled tones between themselves, but stopped when they noticed Rain approach.

"Hey," Rain said as she took a seat beside Julia. Her friend responded by resting her head against her shoulder for a moment, but never uttered a word. She watched as multiple officers opened drawers, flipped cushions, and emptied cabinets. It was horrifying to see Nick and Julia's life being turned upside down. It seemed over the top, like a cruel invasion of privacy.

One of the police officers stepped into the room and looked toward Nick. "In order to clear you, I'm gonna need to check everything you had in your ice shanty on the day of the murder. Where's your tackle box? Show me the gear that you brought to the ice-fishing jamboree. I want to see it. *All* of it." His accusatory tone caused Rain's mouth to go dry. It was almost as if this man had already tried and convicted Nick, and she couldn't believe it.

Nick rose from the couch and turned to his wife with a furrowed brow. "Is it still in the shanty? Or did I leave my gear in the garage? Where the heck did I put it?" He raked his hand through his hair and waited for his wife's assistance. "So much has happened, I can't think straight." He pounded his forehead with a closed fist. "Can ya help me out here?"

"Honey, it's okay," Julia soothed. "I think I put your stuff in the closet. After you injured your hand, I don't think it made it back out to the garage." Julia bit her lip. "I know it wasn't left in the shanty . . ." She gestured a hand to the nearby closet, and the officer went ahead and opened the door. After putting on a set of gloves, he stepped inside and returned with a large tackle box, which he displayed in front of them. When he flipped the top open, a gasp shot from Julia's lips.

The officer lifted a knife and dangled it from his gloved hand. The knife was smeared with dried red patches, and one could only conclude the blood had belonged to Wallace Benson. The officer slipped it into an evidence bag and closed it tight. A grim look passed across his face.

Rain immediately turned to Jace, whose jaw dropped, and his complexion instantly turned from ruddy pink to ashen in a matter of seconds.

Nick leapt from the sofa like an animal ready to pounce. He pointed to the weapon and shouted, "That knife is not *mine*! Man, come on!" He raked both hands through his hair. "That's not mine! I've never seen it before in my life! Julia! Tell 'em! That's not mine!" He threw up his hands in frustration and then landed them in balled fists by his side. "I never even looked inside my tackle! I just dug through it and stopped when I cut myself!"

A pulsating throb pounded in Rain's ears when she heard, "Nick Reynolds, you're under arrest for the murder of Wallace Benson. You have the right to remain silent . . ."

Nick adamantly shook his head. "Wait! This is all wrong! You guys got this all wrong!"

These were the last words Rain heard before she looked over to see Julia slumping to the floor in a faint.

Chapter Ten

The wind whistled around the log cabin library, and Rain was thankful for the protection of the hand-hewn walls. She could hardly wait for the installation of the wood stove. The windchill had dipped to a dangerous level, and as she looked around at the shelves of leather spines that surrounded her and the patrons that were tucked deep within them, she breathed deeply again. She had been involuntarily holding her breath for what seemed like hours now, and she needed to let the books around her soothe her as they once had. Anyone that would dare brave the cold for a chance to join her in this cozy library could only share a love of books as deep as her own.

They were her people.

Julia was huddled in the guest bedroom back at the main cabin, taking a well-needed nap, as she hadn't slept a wink the previous night. Rain knew this because she'd finally convinced her best friend to stay with her at the cabin. The last thing Rain wanted was for Julia to be alone, and besides, she'd promised Jace she'd care for her. Jace had insisted his sister go to the hospital and get checked out after she'd fainted, but Julia had adamantly refused. She hated hospitals and would do almost anything to avoid them. Rain also thought the change of scenery was needed; she didn't think pacing a hole in her living room floor would allow Julia to momentarily forget what had taken place just a few hours prior. After Nick's arrest, they had returned to the main cabin, put a few logs on the fire, and allowed the warmth of the licking flames to reflect off the pine log walls and comfort them throughout the night. Rain had watched like a mother hen and held Julia's hand as she cried most of the night, until her friend's sobs became like hiccups, and she'd finally succumbed to sleep in the wee hours of the morning. School had been canceled because of the dangerous wind chill factor, and both Rain and Julia were relieved by this. Rain didn't know how Julia would be able to function patiently in her substitute teacher role with everything in her life falling apart around her. It would be the only time Rain wished more cold weather on them—if only to keep the students from going to school and Julia from needing to go back to work.

Rain reshelved the work of nonfiction that she'd been holding in her hand and turned to find a woman scratching her head as she eyed the spines of books in front of her.

"Something I can help you find?"

"Oh." The woman put her hand to her heart, obviously startled as she backed a step away from the shelf and sighed. "I was just looking for books on bereavement, just scanning to see what you have available. At times like these, I just don't have the right words to say, and I really want to be a comfort to my friend. She's a bit of a sensitive type, you know. I'm never sure if what I say will set her off or be of help. I thought maybe I could find something that might give me the right words to explain this whole mess to my daughter. I don't even know where to begin to explain the horrors of the human condition."

"Your daughter?" Rain asked, her heart skipping a beat.

"Yes. I'm sorry, let me backtrack a bit here, and introduce myself. My name's Melissa." The woman, who looked as if she were in her mid-fifties because of her 1980s blue eyeshadow, stretched out a hand to Rain. She shook Rain's hand so limply, it felt like a mere brushstroke against her skin. "My mother-in-law was in recently and mentioned how you had helped her find something for my daughter to read. Thank you, by the way. Apparently, Cassie hasn't been able to put the book down the entire time she's been with her grandma. It's exactly what my daughter needed. I guess I thought the library might have something that could help me too," she added with a resigned sigh.

A new hit of adrenaline surged through Rain. "Oh, you're Cassie's mother." She clenched her sweater against her chest and pulled it closer. When she realized what she was doing, she let go. She smoothed the fabric with her hand, before dropping her sweaty palms to her sides and pasting on a smile.

"Yeah." Melissa mirrored her smile and brushed Rain's arm lightly. "I can't thank you enough. Cassie is really taking the death of our neighbor so hard. It's been such a shock! So, giving her mind a diversion has been such a blessing. A blessing indeed! My mother-in-law mentioned she hasn't lifted her head from that book you loaned her yesterday. You don't even know how much you've helped our family."

"You're very kind to say that, and I'm glad I could help in some small way. I can't even imagine your daughter's struggle, or yours for that matter. It's hard enough on us adults to accept, never mind trying to explain to a young girl why a man was murdered in cold blood." Rain eyed the woman cautiously before whispering, "Do you know anyone who had an issue with Wallace?" Rain looked over both shoulders to be sure they were out of earshot before leaning closer. "Do you know *why* he was murdered? Why would anyone want to harm him—any idea?"

Melissa leaned in closer and said conspiratorially, "I heard that someone was mad about where his ice shanty landed. I heard it was over an ice-fishing spot, if you can believe it! Men can be so immature!" she scoffed. "Mindboggling." She shook her head in disgust. "They can be so bullheaded and competitive!"

That was exactly *not* what Rain wanted to hear. "I've heard that too," she answered with a nod. "But I must admit, I don't buy it for a second. I don't think this was over a fishing hole; I think it went much deeper than that. I think someone else had a problem with Wallace. I can't fathom this being over a fishing competition, even if there was a great prize at stake. It's just not a strong enough motive for murder, in my opinion." Rain hoped her ramblings would help Melissa see her side. The last thing she wanted was for the people of Lofty Pines to buy into the theory that Nick was guilty.

"Yeah, who knows?" Melissa shrugged. "He was such a quiet man, kept to himself really. I really can't think of anyone else that would want to do him harm." She frowned.

"But you're his neighbor. You must know *someone* who could've had a problem with Wallace? Do you know of anyone? Anyone at all who could've had an issue with him?" Rain pressed. Then she peeped over both shoulders and leaned in even closer. "Enough to kill?"

Melissa hesitated and then scratched her head, leaving her winter hat to teeter on her head. Rain wondered if she should say something so the woman's hat wouldn't fall on the floor but didn't want to break the spell. She could see Melissa was wrestling with something to add to the conversation. It was written all over her face. Rain rolled her bottom lip in her fingers and waited.

"I remember there was that accident over at Smith Brother's Logging with Danny Meyer, but Wallace had shared with my husband that he was trying everything to make things right for Danny's family. In fact, Danny was going to file a civil case, but the case was dropped when they found out it would never stick. Wallace was adamant the accident wasn't his fault, but he still went above and beyond to make it right."

"Really?" The fact that he was trying to make it right was news to Rain. "How so?"

"Because the accident didn't only fall on Wallace's shoulders. Danny contributed to his own negligence too, so the case had to be dropped. Danny never would've won. And anyhow, that happened a while ago, and they seemed to make peace with each other. I can't imagine Danny killing him over it now."

There was a pause, but Rain didn't say a word, in hopes that Melissa would continue, and she did: "Even though my neighbor wasn't officially blamed by OSHA for the accident, and Danny was no longer able to take over the family business like his father had planned, that's just how life goes sometimes. Wallace was a kind and decent man. My neighbor didn't deserve this." Her eyes dropped to the floor, and she shook her head adamantly.

"Of course, no one deserves this. The whole thing is absolutely horrible." Rain bit her lip to stop herself sharing that her own neighbor was the one being blamed for the entire ordeal. But she didn't believe it. Not for one. Single. Second. She wouldn't let her mind go there. She just couldn't.

"In any event, it's totally tragic. And the fact that it happened here in Lofty Pines just sickens me. And my daughter Cassie . . . Wallace was so good to her. He treated her like family, always taking her for rides on the cart of his lawn tractor or letting her tag along behind him while he went about his yard work. She was like his little shadow."

"Yeah, it sickens me too." Rain sighed heavily. "Did Danny's family own the logging business then?"

"Oh no." Melissa shook her head. "Danny's father is a mechanic. Danny had planned on leaving the logging company to take over after he finished the training. He was taking auto classes on the side. But after the accident . . . well, I guess he and his father didn't think he could be a mechanic without two hands, so he went out on disability instead."

Rain grimaced. "That's rough."

"Anyhow, do you think you might have any books that could help Tina? Or me?"

"I'm not sure. It might be too soon for that; I mean for Tina, that is. Personally, I know for me, the first few weeks of letting a new normal sink in made it hard for me to focus on anything, much less reading."

Melissa tilted her head to the side and waited.

Rain continued. "I know how Tina feels, and time and space might be the only comfort for now. In time, maybe, but words on a page might not be what she needs right now." Rain let out a slow breath that came out with more melancholy than she had intended. "What I'm trying to say is that she may not have the wherewithal to focus her mind enough to read."

"And how would you know this?" Melissa's eyes widened "You say it like you have firsthand knowledge. Don't tell me someone you loved was murdered too?"

Rain hesitated and then admitted. "I'm a widow too. Not by murder, so I can't imagine the element that will add to the bereavement process. My husband died in a motorcycle accident over a year ago. So, shock—well, unexpected death? I'm definitely familiar." Rain tugged on her fleece sweater and fingered the soft fabric, bringing her back to the present as the conversation was like a slingshot yanking her back to the moment she had received the horrific news.

"Oh goodness! I'm so sorry. You're so young to have gone through something like that!"

Rain reached out and touched her arm. "Thank you. I think the best thing is to be an ear for your friend. Listen, when's she's ready to talk, and maybe bring over a meal or two. Although she might feel like eating at first, it might be nice to have something in the freezer for when she's up to it. Anyhow, that's the approach I would take for now. Give Tina some time. She'll be okay, and everyone grieves differently. Just try and be aware of her subtle cues—she'll let you know what she needs."

"Maybe, then, you could suggest a book that she might relate to down the line, or better yet, you could talk with her!" Melissa seemed suddenly excited as her tone rose an octave. "Since you've been through the loss of a husband, maybe she'd open up to you? You think? It's always best to confide in someone who has actually been in your shoes, you know?" she pressed. "You could really help."

Rain wasn't sure that would be a good idea, considering the circumstances. Would Tina remember her? Would she remember that Rain had been standing with Nick at the time she'd accused her best friend's husband of murder? How would that go over?

The door opened and a rush of cold air blew into the room. Rain's mouth dropped when she noticed Marge stepping into the library. The older woman brushed the snow from her coat with gloved hands before entering. The minutes their eyes met, Marge's mouth curved into a deep and knowing smile.

"Oh my word! I can't believe it!" Rain returned her attention to Melissa for a moment and said, "Can you excuse me for just a sec? I need to go and greet someone."

"Of course." Melissa smiled. "By the look on your face, it looks like you have an important visitor."

"That I do—a beautiful, totally unexpected surprise," Rain said with a smile before she rushed toward Marge with arms outstretched. "What are you doing here?" she asked, her face muffled against her friend's coat as the two embraced. "I thought you were in Florida for the winter." Rain couldn't get over the shock of seeing her coworker and friend a few feet from her, as she eyed Marge up and down to be sure she wasn't seeing a mirage.

"Well, when I caught wind of what was going on up here, I hopped the first red-eye back! I was lucky too—I got in just before the first wave of snow hit. I heard a bigger storm is coming."

"Yeah, that's what they're sayin.' We just got a little taste of it, but the real deal is on its way soon. It's good you got in when you did. I'm just shocked you left the warm weather for the likes of this."

"What am I going to do down there all winter long, Rain? Knit? Play bingo? Tsk! You know me better than that!" She plucked the hat from her head, revealing a silver head of hair sprinkled with specks of snow where the hat hadn't fully covered. She loosened each finger of her gloves before completely removing them and stuffing them inside her coat pocket.

"I'm guessing you heard, huh?" Rain winced. "That's really what brought you back." She reached out to hold the older woman's hands, knowing full well from experience, despite Marge having arrived with gloves on, her hands would be freezing. And they were, Rain noted, as she rubbed Marge's hands in her own at an attempt to get the blood pumping in them again.

"Of course, dear. Once a Laker, always a Laker! Just because I'm down in the sunshine state, doesn't mean I forget about my good friends up here in the Northwoods! You're all like family to me now." She leaned in and wagged a finger. "You know better than that!"

"You really are a sight for sore eyes." Rain was so elated to see Marge, it was like the first breath of fresh air she'd felt in days. "It's so good to see you. You have no idea how happy I am that you decided to come back. Especially now."

"You know, I got all the way down there and realized how much I was missing you too, my sweet Rainy. You've made me feel something I haven't felt in a long time." Her eyes grew misty.

"And what's that?"

"Needed. Wanted." Marge lifted her chin. "And now that you're keeping the library open all winter, I'm hoping maybe I can even get my old job back?" she asked with a slight lift of her faint brow and a bit of hesitation. "Even if it's not as busy as it is in the summer months. You know me: I'll work for free, if need be!"

"You got it!" Rain said enthusiastically, and leaned down to stroke the older woman lightly on the back. She really needed Marge's help, more than ever, so her friend's return couldn't come at a better time.

Marge straightened her spine and placed her hands on her hips. "Now. Where's Julia?" Her watery blue eyes darted around the room in search of their missing coworker.

"She's back at the cabin taking a nap. She was up most of the night crying, poor thing." Rain stifled a yawn. "And to be honest, I didn't get much sleep either. Marge, I'm worried sick about them."

"Oh, you poor souls." Marge laid a hand on Rain's cheek. "Whatever would lead the police to think Nick had something to do with this?" she added in a hissed whisper. "I don't get it!"

Rain turned to see if Melissa had been paying attention and watching their conversation unfold, but the woman seemed deep into a book she'd plucked from the shelf. She looped her arm into Marge's and led her a few steps farther out of earshot. "They found what they think is the murder weapon. In Nick's own tackle box! What else are they supposed to think?" Rain said in a hushed tone. "Did you know Wallace Benson?" She continued to walk Marge over to the coffee station, thinking a hot cup might help warm the older woman's hands once and for all.

Marge shook her head, and her eyes glazed to a vacant stare until they reached the table with the coffee setup, at which point the older woman's eyes lit animatedly. "What do we have here?"

"Julia's idea to host a coffee station, and it's brilliant! The patrons are loving this new addition to the library, as are we." Rain smiled.

"Oh, it's wonderful!" Marge clasped her hands together and then reached out a hand to Rain. "I just can't imagine what Julia's going through. We're really going to have to be a shoulder for her."

"I'm doing my best to hold it all together for all of us, but I must admit the only refuge I have is when I'm here." Rain waved her hand to gesture at the beloved stacks of books that surrounded them. "Even that isn't doing the job like it normally does," she added dejectedly.

"I believe it." Marge touched a nearby shelf and looked to the leather spines with adoration before returning her gaze to Rain. "Jace must be taking this awfully hard too. Is he on the case? Maybe he can help his brother-in-law out of this mess." She tapped her finger to her temple thoughtfully. "Somebody has to be the brains of this operation."

"No doubt, he's taking it hard. We all are. But in answer to your question, because of the conflict of interest, Jace's officially off the case." Rain removed a mug from the rack and handed it to Marge. "The police aren't letting him anywhere near this."

"I see." Marge's eyes narrowed. "What do we know about our victim? Who on earth wanted the man dead?" she asked as she poured herself a cup of coffee from the carafe. The scent from the steam instantly drifted into the air, and Rain decided to join her.

Rain reached for her own mug and set it on the coffee bar and waited, watching Marge mixing her coffee rhythmically with a spoon. The act almost put Rain into a trance. "I don't know," she admitted. "I'm doing my best to find out. She kneaded her forehead with her fingers. "Unfortunately, Nick seems to be the only one with substantial evidence pointing in his direction. Which is completely absurd."

But someone else had to have a problem with Wallace. Enough to kill. *Someone* had to. Because it could not possibly be Nick who had committed this crime.

It just couldn't.

Chapter Eleven

Rain returned to the main cabin, in search of Julia. She found her friend huddled over a steaming mug of tea with a blanket wrapped around her so tightly only her eyes peeked out. She looked like E.T. when he was riding the bike. The visual almost made Rain chuckle.

"You know, if you're that cold, you could've tossed another log on the fire." Rain looked over at the fireplace and noticed the ash had long cooled, not a hint of warmth left inside of it, or anywhere else in the open concept room, for that matter.

"I wasn't sure what your plans were today. I didn't want to leave a fire roaring if I went home and you were still working in the library. I didn't think leaving a fire unattended would be wise." Julia blew into her steaming mug.

"You're probably right, but you could've at least bumped the heat up—it's freezing in here." Rain rubbed her hands up and down her arms and shivered.

Julia took a sip of tea and said, "If I remember correctly, I think you might have turned the thermostat down last night because we had the fire lit. Anyhow, I didn't really notice how cold it was until you said something." She waved a hand of dismissal. "I guess I'm still a bit out of it."

"Really? How can you say that when you're wrapped up like E.T.?" Rain chuckled. Julia shrugged, and the blanket slipped off her head and onto her shoulders. "I guess this was more for comfort than anything. I'd like to hide away from the world for the rest of my life and pretend I'm not living in a nightmare. If my eyes weren't so gritty, I would've curled up with a good book this morning."

"Ah, I see. Why don't you try going back to bed? You need your rest."

"I can't sleep. Not now. Too much rolling around in my head." Julia swirled a finger around her temple. "What are you doing over here anyway? I'm surprised you left the library unattended. Did you leave a sign on the door? I appreciate you checking in on me, but I'm okay if you need to rush back."

Rain smiled wide, knowing her news would lift Julia's spirits, if even just a little. "You're never gonna guess!"

Julia untangled the blanket from her body and sat upright. "What? Did they let Nick go?" Her eyes widened. "Is he home? Why didn't you come and wake me! Did he stop in the library to find me?" The words came out rapid-fire. It was the first true light in her friend's eyes that Rain had witnessed since the whole mess began.

Rain deflated and bit her lip. "I'm sorry, Julia. It's not that."

"Oh." Julia slumped back in the chair.

"It's still good news, though at least I think you'll be happy to hear it."

Julia remained hunched in the chair, but she lifted her gaze back to Rain. "What is it?"

"Marge is back!"

"Wait. What? From Florida?" Julia's expression turned from confusion to panic. "Oh no! What happened? She's not sick or something, is she?"

"No, it's good. It's really good," Rain confirmed with a smile.

"What brought her back?"

"Two things, really." Rain ticked the numbers off on her fingers. "First, the library is open for the winter, so she wants to get back to work, and second, well . . . she's worried about you, Jules. We all are."

Julia clasped her hands tighter to the mug. "Man, it's good news, but I'm not sure how well she'll fare in another cold Northwoods winter. You know how long it can feel."

"That's true. Selfishly, I didn't even think of that."

"I have missed Marge dearly, though," Julia continued. "So that's the best news I've heard in like . . . forever. Plus maybe it'll give us some time to go and investigate if the library is covered?" Julia hinted with pleading eyes. "Am I right?"

"Actually, I already attempted a bit of investigating back at the library today," Rain admitted, placing a hand on her hip.

Julia's eyes widened. "You did?"

"Uh-huh. I met Wallace's neighbor, Melissa. And she actually thought it might be a good idea for me to go and talk to Tina."

Julia's expression was quizzical as she rested her chin on a closed fist.

"You know, because of Max. I shared that I, for one, know how hard it is to lose a spouse, and she sorta ran with it."

Julia sat up straighter in the chair and eyed Rain expectantly. "What do you think? You think it might work?"

"My *only* hesitation is that she might remember me standing next to . . ." Rain stopped herself short from saying his name.

"Oh, I see." Julia nodded slowly. "You think because you were with Nick, she won't open up. She won't want to talk to a murderer's friend." Julia frowned. "Unless . . ." She snapped her fingers and a new light shone in her eyes.

"Unless what?"

"Unless I go with you and say that I'm on the outs with Nick and I'm going to divorce him over this . . ." Julia flattened her hands against the kitchen table and leaned into it. "That might work," she added, her eyes darting around the room.

Rain rubbed at her throat, her hand then traveling to knead the back of her neck. She blew out a slow breath. "I don't know . . ."

"Come on, Rainy. We have to do something. I can't just sit here waiting. Marge will cover the library. I say we go. What do we have to lose at this point? Seriously? My husband could spend the remainder of his sweet life in jail! You really want that to happen?"

"I guess I'm just afraid something you say to her could maybe implicate Nick even further?" Rain lifted her hands in defense. "Wouldn't you feel awful if that happened?"

"Like what? What could I possibly say that might do that? The police already found the murder weapon in his tackle box. Honestly, it can't get much worse than that, can it?"

"I don't know . . . I feel like it might be a bad idea." Rain chewed the inside of her cheek but stopped when she tasted blood. "Let me think this through."

"Okay. How about this. How about I play the sympathy card and just say I'm considering divorcing my husband over this—and I'm visiting her to confirm her accusations are indeed true. I'll totally play it up big, like I'm on her side. Then I'll leave the rest of the talking to you," Julia added with a decisive nod. She zipped her lips with an imaginary zipper.

"Last time you brought up Tina's name, you were ready to wring her neck. Are you really sure you're up for this? I don't need two of you in jail!"

This flippant comment caused Julia to smirk.

"Or maybe I should go alone? If you come along, you'll need to keep your emotions in check." Rain began to pace the room, then stopped short and said, "Can you promise me you will do that? You'll let me do the talking?"

Julia raised her palm. "I swear."

Rain's eyes scanned the floor as she thought this through. She bit at her thumbnail. "I suppose I could head back to the library and find a book on the five stages of grief. At the very least, it'll give me a reason to show up unannounced at Tina's house. Otherwise, she might think I'm completely off my rocker. I mean, who am I to her? But . . ." She held a palm in the air and hesitated. "If I go bearing a book . . . and say that Melissa had stopped by the library and made the suggestion . . . even though I know full well from experience she probably doesn't have the focus to read right now . . . but that doesn't matter. I just need an *in*.

Julia rose from the chair and rolled her hand in the air as if egging her on. "Yes. Yes! This could work. Right now, Tina is the only one who might give us a morsel of truth. She's the only one who might be able to shed some light on Wallace's life and who might've wanted the man dead. *Besides* Nick. Oh, tiddlywinks." Julia put her head in her hands. "I still can't believe my husband spent the night in jail. I wonder how he's faring. I also wonder how much bail money is going to be required. I'm sure it's more than I have in my checkbook!"

Rain moved over to Julia, placed her arm around her shoulder and gave her friend a comforting squeeze. "We're gonna figure this out. Stop worrying. Worry never leads us anywhere in life. Remember? Instead, we need a plan. And I think we might just have one."

Julia rested her head on Rain's shoulder. "Thanks. I think at least having some sort of plan to move forward sheds a light of hope. And right now, that's the only thing keeping me going. I *need* a glimmer of hope." She added with a sigh. "I'm sorry I'm so completely self-absorbed right now. I just, well . . . I just can't believe the mess we're in."

Rain couldn't speak because inwardly she really hoped this plan would be a good idea. Because at the moment, all she felt was growing apprehension.

Chapter Twelve

"On second thought, maybe you ought to wait in the car," Rain suggested as she maneuvered her SUV through the unplowed driveway. They needed Nick to be released from jail soon, or the two would need to hire the competition to keep up with the relentless snowfall. A fresh few inches every day added up rather quickly, and currently it was up to Rain's knee. If the snow hit her hip, they'd be in real trouble, because Rain was considered tall compared to most women. She stretched up in the driver's seat and craned her neck to look over the drifted pile that sat high on the side of the street, where the road plow had left it behind.

"I'd rather not," Julia said, interrupting Rain's thought. "But if that's the only way you'll bring me with you, I guess I have no other choice."

"Listen. You're my friend, and I love you." Rain lay her hand atop Julia's, which rested on the armrest between them. "But you're emotional right now, *understandably*, and I just don't want to set Tina off if she gets the slightest hint you're not on her side, you know? She thinks your husband murdered the closest person to her. I just don't know if it's a good idea is all." Rain gripped the steering wheel tighter as the main roads weren't much better than her own driveway, and she finally voiced her concern aloud: "If they don't let Nick out soon, the entire town of Lofty Pines is gonna have to shut down! We're headed for a town emergency without your husband!" She chuckled.

This caused Julia's lip to curl upward in a slight smile. "Right? Nick would be so happy if he were out plowing this right now. This is his happy place, and he's totally missing it." Julia abruptly stopped talking as her lip began to quiver. Her friend looked out the passenger side window, and Rain could tell she was trying to keep her emotions in check. Rain tapped her hand again as an act of encouragement but then quickly returned her hands to the steering wheel and held tight. A car passed, kicking up snow, spraying the side of the SUV, and almost bringing them to a grinding halt.

"Did you see that guy!" Rain snapped. "What an idiot! Slow down!" she raised a clenched fist to the air.

The remaining ride was quiet as Rain concentrated on keeping them safe and on the road. Julia seemed to be unusually tight-lipped too, and Rain thought her friend might be trying to prevent her from rethinking the whole idea and doing an about-face for home.

When they finally arrived, Rain immediately noticed a dark truck parked in front of fresh tracks on Tina's driveway. "Someone's here," she whispered, although she had no idea why. It wasn't as if anyone besides Julia could hear her.

"Don't pull in. Let's watch from here," Julia suggested as she tucked deeper into the seat. "Can you park over there by those pine trees?" Julia indicated with a point of her finger, and Rain followed, letting the car slowly roll in that direction.

"Yeah, okay, but I'm not sure if we'll see anything from here. We're too far back from the road. Anyhow, it's probably just a relative or friend offering condolences or dropping off a meal or something. Don't you think?"

"I'm guessing it would have to be someone pretty special in order to take a chance out here in this weather. This snow is unrelenting! I think the storm might be coming earlier than expected." Julia peeked out the windshield where the wipers were having a hard time working at full capacity, and then back to Rain. "I know for a fact you wouldn't be out on the roads if you didn't have to be." She smirked.

"Shoot, this is really a wrench in my plan. I wasn't expecting this. I don't want to show up at Tina's doorstep with someone else inside, do you? I was hoping to have Tina's complete attention. This isn't a good idea. Maybe we ought to turn around and come back later."

"No. I vote we wait. If we go home now, it might be days before we can navigate through the snow to do this. We gotta do it now." Julia removed her seat belt, slumped in the seat, and drummed her fingers along the armrest.

The two sat in silence, but now with the engine turned off, snow began to pile on the windshield, making their ability to see anything almost impossible. The passenger-side windows were beginning to fog as well, and Julia attempted to wipe hers with the back of her arm.

"Now what?" Rain asked.

"We can try and hide over there behind that tree." Julia looked intently at Rain with pleading eyes.

Rain noted the line of trees between Tina's property and the neighbors' but wasn't convinced.

"I say we make a run for it," Julia pressed.

"Great. And what if that's Melissa's house?" Rain flicked a finger toward the neighboring property. "And what if she sees us? How on earth will we explain ourselves?"

"Duh. We won't get caught," Julia teased. "Come on! It wouldn't be the first time we played I Spy behind a tree line!" She grinned. "Besides, if we find out who Tina's talking to, we might be able to interrogate them. Any connection to Wallace at this point is the only lead we have."

Rain rolled her eyes. The more Julia talked, the less she liked the idea.

Julia slipped from the car before Rain had a chance to stop her. She banged her hands against the steering wheel in frustration and watched as her friend darted behind a Jack Pine. Rain tightened her hat on her head and slipped on the leather gloves that lay absently on the dashboard before joining her.

"What now, Sherlock?" Rain smirked as she nudged her friend with an elbow.

Julia peeked through the branch and then eyed Rain knowingly. "I think I know that truck."

"Whose is it?"

Julia put her head in her hands. "I don't know! At the moment it's evading me. I can't place it. But it's familiar to me—I just don't know why. I think it's a company truck—I just can't place the logo, and it's too far to read from here." She slammed closed fists on her legs and gritted her teeth. "Ooh, I hate when this happens! I'm too young to go senile!"

"Shh," Rain put a finger to her lips and whispered. "The door just opened. Someone's coming!"

Julia covered her mouth with her own hand to prove she was doing as ordered and then darted a look to Rain.

"Hey, it's not my fault. I just want you to rip up the paperwork. It's none of your business anyway!" a man said loudly, throwing up his hands. He then backed away from the front door but continued to face his opponent.

"I can't believe you would ask me that at a time like this!" Tina screamed. "Who do you think you are coming here? How insensitive!"

"Damn right I want it, and you better get it to me before the end of this week or I swear!" he yelled.

"Swear all you want, you tactless jerk!"

The man turned, causing Julia to gasp and cover her mouth. The man darted into the truck and screamed out of the driveway, plowing his way through the former tracks that were slowly being covered with fresh snow.

"I can't see!" A branch from the Jack Pine, along with Julia's head, were now impeding Rain's vision, making it impossible to see what her friend had witnessed. "Did you get a good look at him? His voice sounded familiar!"

"It's Seth," Julia said, her head slowly shaking from side to side as if attempting to take the information in. "What the heck is he doing here? I didn't even think he knew Tina."

"Wait. *Seth?* You mean Kim's husband, Seth?"

"The very one."

"Where's Kim then? Why is he here alone? And what was he talking about? I heard yelling! Didn't you hear yelling?"

"These are all very good questions. Especially since Seth acted like he'd never met Tina before Wallace's murder. Didn't he?" Julia's eyes flickered like lightbulbs losing their wattage and then bounced back to Rain. "Apparently they know each other now though, huh? What do you make of that?"

As they were walking back to the safety of the Ford Explorer, a delivery van pulled into Tina's driveway. "This place is like Grand Central Station," Julia said.

"Maybe we ought to rethink this and come back another time. Obviously, Seth upset her. The question is, over what?"

"I don't know, but we're here now. Let's just get it over with. Besides, maybe we can pump Tina to find out why Seth stopped by," Julia added decisively. And Rain knew by her friend's tone she was not going to back down.

A few moments later, Rain and Julia stood at the threshold of Tina's house, but before she gave a knock, Rain elbowed her friend. "Don't forget, I'm doing the talking here," she said out the side of her mouth and then lifted a finger to her lips.

Julia responded by buttoning her lips with her fingers. Meanwhile, Rain noticed her eyeing up the packages that the delivery person had just dropped off.

"I wonder what she ordered?" Julia finally said aloud. "Who would order packages the week her husband dies? That would be the last thing on my mind!"

Rain put her finger to her lips. "Shh. Or you're back in the car," she added through gritted teeth.

"Okay, okay. I get it." Julia locked her mouth with her fingers again dramatically, as if this time she was turning an actual knob.

"She probably ordered a bunch of stuff before Wallace's passing, and the snow hampered delivery. Who knows? In any event." Rain raised her finger to her lips again.

Tina opened the door and seemed as if she was expecting the delivery person to be the one standing there, as she also eyed the packages and then titled her head quizzically. Her hair was neatly combed, and Rain thought she looked a lot prettier than when she'd first met the woman. Of course, the first time she'd encountered Tina, her eyes had been blazing and her hair askew, and she'd been talking crazy.

"Can I help you?"

From the tone of her voice, Rain wondered whether Tina even recognized them. "I'm Rain, and this is my coworker from the library over in Lofty Pines." Rain jutted a thumb in Julia's direction but refrained from saying her name. She didn't want to tip off Tina if she indeed didn't recall Nick's wife. She understood how town gossip worked. If Nick's name was being thrown out there, Julia's wouldn't be far behind, as his better half.

Tina's brow only furrowed deeper. "I think you might have the wrong house." She stepped backward and attempted to close the door, and Rain reached out a hand.

"No, your neighbor—I mean, Melissa—stopped in at the library and suggested I pay you a visit. You see, I know what it's like to lose someone you love. I too lost my husband because of a tragedy, and she thought you might want to talk with someone who has been where you are. When you feel up to talking, that is. I also brought this." Rain handed over a book about the five stages of grief and then waited. "This book has been a lifeline for me. You may not be up for it right now, and that's okay . . . I totally understand."

A knowing expression from Tina followed.

Rain rubbed her hands up and down her arms, hoping the act might prompt an invitation inside, and it did, as Tina said, "Won't you come in out of the cold?"

Julia reached for one of the boxes left by the door. "Can we help you carry these packages inside before they get covered with snow?"

When Julia lifted the box, Tina held the door. "Sure, thank you."

"What's in here? Julia asked. "It weighs a ton." Rain shot her a dagger look to keep quiet.

"I'm assuming it's the ingredients for my plaster molds. I'm an artist," Tina explained.

"How lovely!" Rain interjected and then gave Julia another look that said, *Keep your mouth shut and let me do the talking, as we discussed.*

As soon as they stepped inside and stood on the oversized rubber mat, Tina turned to Julia and said, "You look so familiar to me, but I can't place you. I guess it must be the library, although I haven't been there in quite a while," she added, though she seemed not quite totally convinced.

Rain elbowed Julia as soon as Tina turned her head momentarily, and shot her friend a dagger look. "She gets that all the time, don't you Ju . . . ah, hmm. Come to think of it, I left another book in the car. Can you go get it for me?"

Julia's shoulders slumped before she answered, "Fine," through gritted teeth.

Tina's head snapped around. "Wait. Did you mean to say *Julia*?" Her eyes instantly turned wild and dark.

Rain's heart thumped hard in her chest. "Yes, why?" she asked in the meekest tone she could muster.

"Julia!" Tina hissed. "You mean *Nick's* Julia? You mean the Nick that murdered my husband! You're his wife, aren't you!" Tina leaned toward them with a look so scary, Rain wanted to flee. "That's why you look familiar to me!"

Instead, Julia was the one who took a step backward, and Rain lifted an arm protectively to cover her. She thought Tina was going to either lunge or punch Julia in the face.

"How do you know Nick did this? Huh? How can you be so sure?" Julia's eyes blazed, meeting Tina's match. "It's quite an accusation! You've got my husband in a heap of trouble, lady. Do you know that!"

"Get out of my house!" Tina shrieked. "Now!"

The two turned on their heel for a quick exit, but before they left, Julia spat, "And what was Seth doing over here? Huh? What is my friend's husband doing alone inside your house?"

"Who?" Tina shook her head in dismay, as if she had no idea what Julia had asked.

But Rain didn't give Julia the chance to continue her diatribe. Instead, she caught hold of Julia's coat and yanked until the two were officially back out on the front step. She nearly slipped on a patch of ice hidden beneath the snow and had to grab Julia once again before officially landing on her backside.

"Don't you ever come back here, you hear me? You do, and I'll call the police!" Tina yelled after them before slamming the door shut, sending the welcome sign attached to the door to the ground with a thud. Which was appropriate, since Rain didn't feel welcome at all, not one little bit.

Julia turned and reached as if she was going to knock again, and Rain covered her friend's hand in her own. "No, Julia. Drop it," she said before leading her friend back to the safety of the SUV.

"What are we gonna do now?" Julia asked while she adjusted the seat belt and then folded her arms across her chest in a huff.

Rain slowly shook her head. "I'm not sure, but one thing I think is pretty clear. I doubt she'll drop off the library books that Wallace borrowed, or give back the book on the stages of grief. It'll be a cold day in hell before we see those books on the Lofty Pines library shelves. I guess we might as well order up new ones now. Hopefully, they're not out of print, and we can order another copy."

"No, that's actually good!" Julia straightened in the seat, a new light shining in her eyes.

"What do you mean?"

"I mean, it gives you a perfectly legit reason to come back here!" Julia smiled. "Because this isn't over," she added defiantly. "You're coming back for those books."

Chapter Thirteen

When Rain and Julia returned to the library, they were surprised to find so many patrons perusing the shelves. Marge smiled ear to ear when she noticed Julia walk through the door behind Rain, and rushed over to greet her with a wide embrace. Rex also came to greet them, with tail wagging, and Rain reached down to pet him on the head.

"My dear girl! How're you doin'?" Marge leaned back and studied Julia with furrowed brow. Concern oozed from every pore of the older woman's face.

"Better now, especially since you're here." Julia rested her arm on Marge's shoulder who looked up at her lovingly.

"Looks like the three amigos are back together again." Marge winked playfully. "I see some trouble brewing here with the three of us back together!" she added with a sly smile.

Julia leaned down to pet Rex on the head, and he licked her hand. "Aw, good to see you too, Rexy! How much trouble could us three stir up, huh?" Julia laughed.

The door opened, and with it came a whirl of snow. Rain's jaw dropped when she saw who was standing there. She nudged Julia with her elbow. "Looks like we have company."

"Tina?" Julia whispered. "What is *she* doing here? She actually had the nerve to follow us?"

"I'm not sure, but let's go find out," Rain suggested after alerting Marge that someone was at the checkout desk waiting patiently.

"Tina, welcome," Rain said, in as friendly a tone as she could muster.

"Something we can help you find?" Julia asked, her voice smooth as honey. It was so smooth, in fact, it almost made Rain laugh aloud. Rex followed closely at their heels and jumped on his hind legs, begging for Tina's attention.

She reached down and tapped his head. "Hello, pup— aren't you a cutie?" she said. He sniffed her legs as if she had dog treats in her pockets. Finally, Rain tugged Rex back by the collar and redirected him over to Marge.

"Sorry about that," Rain said.

"No worries, I had a cocker spaniel when I was a kid. I really miss her."

"They make great companions, for sure. Rex comes along with Marge whenever she's on shift at the library. Maybe you ought to think of adopting one?" Julia suggested.

"Yeah, maybe." Tina's gaze fell to the floor. "Anyway, I'm glad I caught you both. I just wanted to apologize for my behavior. I didn't mean to be so rude. It's just this is . . . well, so hard on me."

"It's okay—don't worry about it. We totally understand," Rain said soothingly. "We're all under a great deal of stress, right, Julia?" She nudged her friend.

"Yeah, it's been a lot." Julia kneaded her forehead with her fingers and then forced a friendlier smile.

Tina turned her attention to Rain. "I also wanted to thank you for the book. I realize now that I've been overreacting to the situation through my grieving process. I hope you understand," she reiterated, looking in Julia's direction for confirmation, which Julia gave with a nod.

Someone opened the door to the library, disrupting them. Tina took a step backward in retreat. "I don't want to take up any more of your time. There seems to be a lot happening in here right now so . . . anyhow, thanks again," she said and then spun out the door so fast, neither had a chance to respond.

"What was that about?" Julia whispered.

"Unexpected, right?" Rain said.

"Totally."

Rain looked to the checkout desk and saw a line forming, so she moved to give Marge a hand and let Julia absorb what had just happened. When she arrived at the desk, Marge was deep in conversation with a woman. Soon after, Julia joined them.

"I can't believe you're back in Lofty Pines! It's been ages!"

"And you, Angela, my dear, haven't aged a bit since the last time I saw you."

"Wow, I can't believe how busy it is in here," Rain said, not meaning to, but nevertheless interrupting their reunion. "And warm—it's so warm in here!" she added with a growing smile.

"Yes, I almost forgot! The chimney fella stopped in. He just finished installing the woodstove. And isn't it wonderful!" Marge clasped her hands together in glee.

Despite Marge's enthusiasm, Rain deflated just a little. Something inside her stirred in disappointment, for not having been the one to meet Ryan on his return to the library. "Is he still here?"

"You didn't notice his work truck out front?"

"No. To be honest, I was a bit preoccupied. There were a bunch of cars, and Julia and I were deep in conversation. I must've missed it. He's here, though?" Rain's heart skipped a beat as she rose on her tiptoes in search of him.

"Still lookin' for Mr. Wright?" Rain felt a tap on her shoulder and spun to face Ryan, nose to nose.

Julia hid the look of surprise, which Rain was sure was plastered across her face, by asking, "Mr. Right? Did I miss something?" with a sly smile.

"Julia, this is Ryan Wright from Wright Installation. He's the one who brought the warmth to us. I can't wait to see the new stove! Shall we?"

"You go on ahead," Julia said, giving her a little push. "Marge and I'll have a look in a bit. Go on—we insist. Right, Marge?" She gave a sidelong glance. "Nice to meet you, Ryan."

Marge shared a conspiratorial smile with Julia. "Yes, dear, you go on ahead. You can show us later. Plenty of time for that."

Rain led Ryan by the arm away from the two women before they could do anymore damage to her ego. When they stepped in front of the woodstove, Rain immediately put her hands out to feel the warmth emanating from it. "Oh, this is

117

so nice, Ryan. I think I'll have to move a shelf or two and put chairs next to it so my patrons can really enjoy this."

"I'd be happy to come back and help with that, if you'd like," he offered, rolling up his sleeves to the elbow.

"Thank you, I really appreciate your hard work. This is great."

"No problem." He showed her the basic workings of the woodstove and then said, "Normally, I'd take more time to go through all of this with you, but I only have a few minutes. Dad and I have another stove to drop off today, and he's already waiting for me out in the truck. He had a few phone calls to make."

"That's okay. I'm sure there's nothing to it."

"Really? You don't mind? Just let this fire go out, and I'll come back in the next few days to go over everything thoroughly. I feel bad about leaving you hanging like this . . ."

"Don't." Rain retreated and then led him directly to the door where Julia and Marge were still standing by the desk. "Trust me, I'm fine with it. Again, thanks for your hard work, Ryan. I'm sure the patrons and I will truly enjoy it."

"Okay, I'll see you soon. Ladies," he said with a tip of his head, and then he was off with a backward wave of his hand.

As soon as he was out the door, Julia was at her side. "So, my brother has competition, eh?"

"Knock it off, Julia," Rain said with a laugh. "I'm just glad the stove is installed before Old Man Winter really bears down on us."

"I think Old Man Winter is already upon us." Marge lifted a hand to her cheek and said, "Boy, did I make it back to Wisconsin in the nick of time. Word on the street is that another mammoth storm is blowing in from Canada in the next few days. The storm is expected to be so big, in fact, that there's talk that the schools and other nonessential businesses will be closed for days on end."

"Yeah, we heard. Sounds like I'm gonna be off work again next week," Julia said with a shrug. "Which is fine by me, considering the circumstances I'm finding myself in. I can't imagine facing a room full of kids right now." She scrubbed her hands over her weary face and then kneaded her shoulders with her fingers, as if to ease the kinks.

Marge leaned toward Julia and smiled encouragingly, and Julia responded with a half hug, and then rested an elbow on the bookshelf, as if she needed it to hold her upright.

"I'm really glad to see the library being used. I wasn't entirely sure when I decided to reopen for the winter what I'd encounter. This is actually encouraging." Rain scanned the room, taking it all in.

"I've seen a lot of parents this morning loading up on books so their kids don't drive them bonkers during the upcoming forced hibernation," Marge said as she left the desk. She picked up an abandoned book left on the nearby shelf and reshelved it to its proper location right away.

"Ah." Rain nodded. "Well, it's good to see the library is being put to good use, that's for sure. I guess I'll probably have to close next week too, though, if the roads are going to be that bad," she said, more to herself than the others. "I'm not exactly considered essential either, I don't think. The library is only essential in my own world."

"Oh, for many you are, my dear. One day at a time," Marge said, and Rain wondered if the older woman would rather get stuck in forced hibernation here at the library than be back home alone for days on end.

"You can always stay with me if you want, Marge, so you and Rex don't have to be alone," Rain suggested. "I have plenty of extra room at the main cabin. You're more than welcome."

This brought a smile to Marge's face, and a new light shone in her eyes. "Thank you, my dear, but we'll be just fine. I will check out a few books, though, before I leave. It'll be nice to catch up on my rest and curl up with a book or two."

"Speaking of Rex, where is he?" Julia asked.

"He's over there, getting a lot of lovin' from that little girl," she said, pointing with a broad smile and a nod. Rex was in the process of receiving a belly rub, and the little girl was giggling and cooing over him.

"It's so nice to have him here, the patrons love it when your sweet pup pays us a visit," Rain said. "I'll be sure and buy some dog treats next time I'm at the store."

"No need to spoil him, Rain. Now then," Marge said, lowering her voice and gathering the three of them together, as if she were a sports coach pulling a team together in a huddle. "What did you discover while you were over visiting with Wallace's wife?"

"Well, for one, Seth was over there. *Alone*," Julia added with a hint of disdain.

"Are they friends?" Marge asked. "Maybe there's a perfectly good explanation for why he was there, no?"

"Not to our knowledge," Rain admitted. "Seth certainly didn't act like it when Nick was being questioned at the crime scene. At least, he didn't say anything to us about even knowing the victim. Or his wife for that matter. The whole thing seems odd."

"And Kim wasn't with him either, which I think is totally out of left field," Julia added. "Those two do everything together—it's almost sickening how they're joined at the hip. Although now that they have the twins, I'm not sure that still holds true. It's probably easier sometimes to split up, just so they don't have to bring them along."

"Huh," Marge said, seeming to roll this all over in her mind. "And you didn't call Kim to ask her?"

"I wanted to phone her on the way home, but after talking to Rain about it, we decided it should be a face-to-face conversation. I'm not sure how Kim will respond to this news over the phone, and to be honest, we wanted to see her expression when we ask."

"Well, what are you two waiting for?" Marge's gaze darted between the two and then landed on Rain. "Go over there and find out."

"You sure you can stay a little while longer and cover the library?" Rain asked.

"Absolutely—I've got this. Now go," Marge ordered with a swish of her hands, and then she straightened her spine and gestured a finger in the direction of the door. "Go on—get along now."

"What about Rex?"

"My dog will be fine."

"All right, if you insist. Just let me go and find a few books for her kiddos. I'm sure if a storm is brewing, Kim'll be more than happy to have something to keep them busy too," Rain said as she headed in the direction of the children's section of the library.

Her mind continued to wander back to Seth as she walked down the aisle. More was impending than a huge blizzard.

Chapter Fourteen

As soon as the door opened, Rain and Julia were greeted by a rush of warm air and the smell of freshly baked cookies. Kim stood with one child attached to her hip and the other stuck to her pants leg like superglue. Her red hair was pulled atop her head in a heap, and despite having no makeup on, her eyes were bright and happy. She looked completely in her element.

"What are you guys doing out in this mess?" Kim rose on her tiptoes and attempted a peek above them, as if to verify that it was still snowing. "I figured you'd both be tucked in at the Lofty Pines Library with your eyes deep into the latest release. Or, at the very least, helping a patron find something to weather the storm." She smiled but a slight tease glimmered in her eye. Kim knew them all too well.

"It wasn't easy to leave," Julia admitted. "Rain had a Franklin stove put in. The place is like a storybook log cabin now. I'm sure when word gets out, everyone from town will be stopping in to check it out."

"Sounds lovely!" Kim exclaimed.

"Yeah, I'm pretty excited about it," Rain admitted. "It's really cozy in the library now, that's for sure."

"Hey, cutie pie." Julia reached over to ruffle one of the toddlers on the head. The little boy recoiled and tried to hide behind his mother's legs.

"Don't be shy, Rory." Kim gently pulled on her son's arm to untangle him from her legs and encourage him to greet her friends, but he refused and remained hidden.

"Boy, I still can't get that right. I thought for sure that was Ryder!" Julia chuckled. "One of these days I'll be able to tell them apart."

Kim laughed. "No worries—even my own mother mixes the boys up from time to time, and they're her own grandchildren. If you were around them a lot more, you'd catch it in their personalities. Ryder is my lively one, and Rory is a bit more calm," she said with a hint of pride in her voice, as her eyes passed between her two children.

"They're adorable, Kim," Rain said as she looked on with envy at the matching strawberry-blond heads.

For a brief moment, a wave of jealousy swept over her out of nowhere. She had envisioned she and Max would have kids by now, and yet it had never been in the cards. Now she knew the universe had been looking out for her in the long run, as she'd be a single parent right now if the fertility treatments they'd tried had actually worked.

One of the children coughed, bringing Rain back to the present moment. "It's still snowing, but this is nothing compared to what's coming. Did you hear the news of what's expected to blow in this week from Canada?" Rain asked.

"Oh nooo. Really, more comin'? I haven't exactly been kee- pin' up with the news this week." Kim readjusted her son on her hip and backed up a few steps. The other twin remained stuck tightly to her leg. Meanwhile Kim summoned them inside, onto the oversized rubber mat. "Come in out of that mess."

Rain closed the door behind them, but she and Julia remained planted by the front door. "Yeah, sorry to be the bearer of bad news of more bad weather. We brought books for the kiddos to help, in case you run out of things to do in the next few days." Rain dropped the canvas bookbag to the floor and the child that had been on Kim's hip, reached toward it and wiggled in her arms until Kim placed him safely on the ground. The twins instantly dumped the bag of picture books on the carpet behind them, to rifle through.

Kim looked to her children and said, "Boys? What do you say?"

Four eyes looked up at them and with gleeful expressions the cherub faces said in unison, "t'ank you!"

"Oh, my goodness, thanks for bringing these over. You're a lifesaver." Kim reached out to Rain. "Can I take your coats? Do you want to come in? I can put on a pot of tea or cocoa. And I just baked a fresh batch of peanut butter cookies, if you'd like one."

The boys in unison turned and yelled, "Cookies! Cocoa!" with fists pumping in the air.

"Not for you two—you already had your cookies," Kim cautioned with a stern tone and a warning finger. The two returned to their library books, knowing from the looks of things, their mother wouldn't budge.

Rain looked down to the mat on which they were now dripping snow and creating a wet mess.

Kim must've noticed, as she waved a hand of dismissal. "Don't worry about it. This is where the twins come in after they've been outside to play. I wish we had a mudroom, and every winter I think we should add one on, and every winter we seem to get through it, another year." She chuckled. "Someday . . ."

"Honestly, thanks for the invite, but we can't stay long," Rain admitted. "Marge is back at the library, and I don't want her to have to drive after dark, especially if the roads get too bad. And Rex needs to get home and fed, so she wouldn't be able to stay much longer."

"Totally understand. Well, thanks again, you guys. That was really kind of you to bring these over. Just add them all to my library card, if that's okay?" Kim turned and gestured to the twins. "I doubt I could pry one out of their hands to take back with you at this point." She shrugged. "I guess I'll hold on to all of them."

"Sure." Rain nodded with a smile. "No problem—that's why we brought them. Right, Julia?"

Rain hoped the subtle hint to her friend would get her to open up about the real reason for their visit. It worked too, because Julia stopped making funny faces at the kids and asked, "Where's Seth?"

"Oh, he had to run some errands after work, and we both decided it would be easier if he went alone. He mentioned in passing that he had some stuff to do and that he'd rather not have to bring the twins along if he didn't have to. Also, they just woke from their nap anyway. But I should call him on his cell and have him stop at the store if a storm's brewing," Kim added quietly to herself, as if thinking aloud.

"Oh." Julia's face fell.

"Why do you ask?" Kim folded her hands across her chest and tilted her head.

Rain shot Julia a look before Julia blurted, "We thought we saw his work truck over by Tina's? What do you think he was doing over there?"

Rain interrupted Julia when she noticed Kim's expression turn to one of utter confusion. "But we're probably mistaken," Rain said in a nonchalant tone.

"Tina?" Kim's brow deepened. "Tina, who?"

"You know, Wallace's wife," Julia said, and leaned in expectantly.

"Wallace's wife?" Kim took a step backward. "Nah, Seth doesn't even know Tina. There'd be no reason he'd be over that way. But what were you two doing over there?" Kim's arms dropped from her chest and landed on her hips. "You really think that's wise, Julia? I mean, considering?"

"Considering?" Rain asked.

Julia looked at Rain and said, "Since Kim and I last spoke, I think she's implying my husband's situation is worsening by the minute." Julia blew out a breath and let it out slowly. "Let's just call it what it is. What you mean is, considering Nick's arrest for the murder, I shouldn't be caught dead over there. Am I right?"

Kim reached out and touched Julia on the arm. "I'm sorry. I can't even imagine what you're going through right now. I wish there was something I could do to help." Kim's shoulders slumped, and her smile morphed to a look of concern.

"It is what it is," Julia said with candor, surprising Rain that she would be so blunt.

"Is there anything? Anything at all I can do? Do you need bail money or something like that?"

"Wait. You already knew about Nick's arrest?" Rain whispered for fear the children might overhear, but they seemed preoccupied flipping through the stack of picture books to give them the time of day."

"Yep." Julia's gaze dropped to the floor. "Kim already knows."

"I wish there was something I could do to help, Julia. I just don't know what we could do. I feel like our hands are tied," Kim said, ringing her hands. "But to answer your question, I'm sure Seth wouldn't be caught dead at Tina's, not after everything that woman has put your husband through. Of that, I'm certain!" Kim stated with conviction and a curt nod. "I'm sure you must be mistaken."

Rain and Julia shared a look. This was going to be a little more complicated than they had anticipated.

Chapter Fifteen

Rain and Julia arrived back at the library, but after a strong nudging, Julia had finally acquiesced and returned home for a hot bath and an early bedtime. It was obvious that her friend needed the rest, and there wasn't much either of them could do but continue to roll over scenarios in their mind. Both needed a serious mind break. Clearly, they wanted desperately to clear Nick of this crime; they just needed the clarity of mind to do so.

After Julia's departure, Rain immediately went in search of Marge. She found the older woman tidying a stack of returned books and organizing them into genre as Rain noticed a stack of young adult books in one pile and a subsequent pile of mysteries set to the other side of the floor. Marge smiled and immediately dropped what she was doing and moved quickly toward her as soon as she'd noticed Rain approach. "Any news?" Marge asked.

"Nothing. Except the fact that, according to Kim, Seth doesn't know Tina." Rain shrugged and blew out a slow breath. "None of this is making sense."

"What would Seth be doing over at Tina's house if he didn't know her?" Marge's eyes narrowed. She removed her glasses, putting one arm in her mouth as she studied Rain.

"That, my friend, is the question we keep rolling in our minds." Rain sighed and rubbed at her eyes, an attempt to remove the grit. Unfortunately for her, it did little to ease the discomfort.

Marge frowned but didn't reply. Instead, she set her glasses back on and turned her attention back to the books. It was then that Rain noticed how quiet the library was. "Are we alone?" Rain asked. "I don't hear a peep in here. Are things finally slowing down?"

"Yes, dear, the last patron left about fifteen minutes ago. It's well after five o'clock," Marge said, peeking over the top of her reading glasses and pointing to the large clock that hung on the wall above one of the shorter bookshelves.

"Oh no. It can't be already!" Rain threw a hand to her cheek. "It gets dark so early this time of year. I guess I lost track of time, I didn't realize it had gotten so late. I'm so sorry, Marge—please forgive me."

"It's no bother." Marge waved her off with a dismissive hand. "I probably need to get Rexy home, though." She frowned. "See him over there, curled up under the desk? I hate to go and wake him—he looks so peaceful, but it is a little past feeding time. My poor little Rexy." Marge looked at him with pity before removing her reading glasses and setting them down on the desk.

"Please. Let me drive you home. It's dark out, and it's still snowing pretty heavily. I know you don't like driving this late, and it's my fault you're here after sunset. I'll come and pick you up tomorrow first thing, and then you can get your car back. How does that sound?"

Marge thought a minute and then agreed with a nod. "I suppose that would probably be wise. I really need to have that cataract surgery soon. It's so hard for me to see at night, especially out of my right eye. Besides, the last patron that stopped in mentioned in passing that they had interrupted her afternoon TV programing for the newscaster to officially declare people should stay off the roads." She groaned. "Just let me put away the rest of these returns so we're ready for tomorrow. We might be in for another busy day in preparation of the storm." She lifted a few books and tucked them in the crook of her arm. "By the way, everyone that checked out books today reiterated how thankful they are that you've decided to keep the library open year-round. It looks like you made a wise choice." Her eyes lit with fresh enthusiasm, and she smiled warmly.

Rain didn't think it was necessary to put away all the returns right that second, because it seemed the storm had already arrived, but she knew Marge needed to have her way and finish the job before leaving. "Let me help you then, so I can get you home. As you said, Rexy needs to eat." Rain too was growing weary from the lack of sleep and stifled a yawn with the back of her hand.

"I'll take care of these, dear, if you wouldn't mind checking the drop box outside. I didn't get to that yet." Marge shuffled back to the desk, where another pile she had stacked had been abandoned, waiting to be reshelved. "Then we'll be all set for tomorrow," Marge said, jutting her chin and then moving along with her duties.

Rain knew from Marge's body language that her coworker wouldn't let it go. *All* the returned books would have to be put safely back on the shelf. Including the ones left in the drop box. So she headed back out into the snow. She didn't bother with a coat, but plucked the key to the box from the desk drawer before stepping out the door. Rain thought of Nick and all the workmanship he'd put into the lovely box. She reverently ran her hand along the top to remove the snow and shook her hand loose of the wet slop before jamming the key into the lock. When she opened the door, her jaw fell. The only books left inside the drop box were cookbooks. The two cookbooks that Wallace Benson had borrowed before his death.

Rain plucked them from the box, locked it, and rushed back inside. She closed the door behind her to keep the snow where it belonged—outdoors. She stood at the threshold with the books held to her heart, unable to move from the gravity of the situation. A man had lost his life the day after he'd stepped into her library and spoke so casually with her, as if they'd both live forever. And now he was gone, and all that remained was the memory and the books in her hand, reminding her of how fleeting life could be.

Marge turned from the bookshelf and inched in her direction. "Dear, what is it? You look upset. Is something wrong?"

Rain held up the books for demonstration. "We only had a few left behind in the box, and it's the books Wallace borrowed. I have no idea how they got in there. I'm sure Tina didn't drop them off. Certainly she would've brought them inside when she stopped in and not left them in the drop box. Besides, I think cookbooks are the very last thing on her mind right now."

"I think there's something sticking out of it." Marge pointed to a corner of lined yellow paper that protruded from the bottom.

"What in the world?" Rain opened the cover, and the lined yellow sheet of notepad paper fluttered in the air. She reached to grasp it before it fell to the ground, and caught it expertly with one hand. She then read the handwritten note aloud:

Dear Rain,

Thank you. Meeting you at the library gave me the courage to move forward and do what I must do. Know that your little library is worth far more than books. I see you're a wise ole soul. Thank you for your kindness.

P.S. I'll be sure and drop off a few perch and walleye filets for your freezer after the jamboree so you can try your hand at that fish fry. Maybe we'll both learn something new.

P.S.S. I have successfully made my first batch of chili and look forward to making many more. See, I guess it's not too late for this old man.

Kindest regards,

Wallace Benson

Rain set the cookbook down on the desk and scratched her head.

"Well, now. I see I'm not the only one that sees a treasure in you." Marge winked. "That's pretty special. Pretty special indeed."

"Marge, I have no idea what he's talking about. I didn't give him any advice." Rain dropped the note to her side, and then had to reread it silently once again to confirm that she'd indeed read the words correctly. She then handed the note to Marge for her own inspection. "What is he talking about, me giving him the courage to"—she threw her hands up in air quotes—'do what I must do'?"

"Ah, my sweet Rain, you don't even know you're doing it. You encourage everyone you greet, and they feel better just from meeting you," Marge said knowingly, patting her on the hand. She then plucked her glasses from the desk and examined the note carefully. When her eyes finally returned to Rain, she beamed a smile.

"I'm guessing he dropped the book off before the ice-fishing tournament," Rain said and then looked down at Marge for verification. "Neither you nor Julia had checked Nick's box for returns yet, had you?"

"I, for one, did not." Marge jutted a thumb to her chest. "And I'm pretty sure Julia has been too preoccupied to think about reshelving books."

"I'm sure you're right," Rain agreed with a nod.

She wondered what advice she'd sublimely given and whether it had had any influence on why the man was murdered. She could almost feel the blood dripping from her own hands. As if maybe, just maybe, she could've done something, *anything*, to stop it.

Chapter Sixteen

"Thank you so much for driving me home. You're right, my dear girl—I don't think I would've made it very far in this mess." Marge pressed her hands on the dashboard and looked out of the windshield. "I think the storm they predicted from Canada might be coming early. What I'm seeing out the window is frightening if it's a precursor of things to come." She huffed as she sat back in the passenger seat and readjusted the seat belt around her waist, pulling it tighter. Rex hung his head between them, from the back seat, and Rain reached out and scratched him under the neck.

"It's no problem. I'm having a hard enough time driving in the dark, and I don't have an eye that needs surgery. I wouldn't even consider letting you navigate these roads yourself." Rain squinted and leaned closer to the steering wheel, where she kept her grip tight and attempted to keep her foot steady on the gas pedal. "And if it weren't for Rex needing his food, I would've convinced you to spend the night," she added with a smile. "I'm going to have to keep dog food on hand in case this happens again."

"Yes, I do need to get Rexy home. I wouldn't sleep a wink if he didn't have his dog bed, his toys, and all his other things too. Thank you for being patient with me, dear."

"Oh, I know, I totally understand," Rain said as she readjusted her grip on the steering wheel. "If I had a pup like Rex to care for, I'd be the same way, I promise you that," she added, taking a quick peek via the rearview mirror and finding him settled down on the backseat.

"Have you thought about a rescue dog?" Marge asked with a gleam in her eye.

"I have, actually," Rain said with a slow nod. "Especially up here in the Northwoods, since we have the acreage for a dog to run. I'll definitely think about it."

"Good, my dear. A dog can provide such good company." Marge drummed her fingers on the console. "What do you think Wallace meant by that note he left behind? You must've told him something of value for him to leave a note like that. Have you thought on it some more? You clearly touched him deeply."

"I haven't a clue. In fact, I'm replaying it over and over, and I just don't know. The only thing I recall is encouraging him to try a recipe or two because he mentioned he hadn't done much cooking in the past. I remember telling him to hold on to the cookbooks as he might want to try something else besides chili. Actually, I'd made the assumption that his wife was deceased, from the way he talked with me. But you know what they say about assuming," Rain added with a chuckle.

"You know that's a gift, right?" Marge shifted in her seat, held her seat belt away from her, and turned toward Rain.

"What's that?" Rain quickly glanced at Marge again, and then her eyes immediately turned back to the road in front of them. Snow sprayed the windshield so quickly that the wipers were barely keeping up. The wiper on the driver's side seemed wonky somehow. She needed to stay focused or else they'd land in a snowbank, and she couldn't imagine either of them attempting to walk the rest of the way home.

"You're a very sensitive woman, Rain, and you exude such empathy. Unfortunately, that doesn't come without much pain. Wallace noticed it too. You're not just loaning library books back there; you're loaning wisdom," Marge said softly as she folded her hands in her lap.

"Really?"

"Yes, dear. I'm sorry to say, but great wisdom comes from great sorrow. The loss of your husband so young . . . Well. You've experienced a deep sadness, my sweet, and that sadness has changed you. How could it not?" She paused before adding, "Some choose to wallow in their grief while others choose to encourage others in similar pain. You've chosen wisely. You've chosen the latter."

"You really think so?"

"I know so. I've witnessed it myself on more than one occasion," Marge said with conviction. "A few patrons even asked specifically for you today. Said you'd given them some very good advice, and I could tell they were hungry for more than just books. I know that being able to give good advice doesn't come without much pain, however, and I'm sorry you're having to walk through it." Marge reached out and patted Rain on the hand. "A blessing and I curse, I might imagine," she added thoughtfully.

"Huh. I wasn't even aware I'd been given a gift. Or that I'd even been using it. To be honest, I thought I'd been pretty self-absorbed in my grief."

"Oh, my sweet dear. Many blessings come from pain, you know. But some don't seize hold of it." Marge raised a clenched fist in the air. "Some let the grief overtake them. But you, my dear, you have held strong. You're well on your way to becoming an empath. Pain is pain. It may come from a different source, but pain feels the same for most people, and now you can see it just as clear as we can see this snow falling. It's palpable to you now."

Rain thought about this as she navigated her SUV into Marge's driveway, which she noticed had been recently plowed. She turned to Marge quizzically when the vehicle came to a complete stop.

"It must've been my neighbors. I tell you, Rick and Janice are the best!" Marge said with a raised finger, answering Rain's question of who had attacked the driveway with a snowblower, as the imprints were still evident. "And it's a little karma. Whatever you give out to the world comes back to you. Believe me, I cleared my share of driveways for the old folks back in the day. Now, I can't believe I'm one of them!" Marge said with a twinkle in her eye. "More than you can imagine, I wish I still had that kind of physical strength back again," she added wistfully. "Ah, yes, I'd do anything to have that back."

"Would you like me to walk you to the door?" Rain asked, already unclicking her seat belt in anticipation of doing just that.

Marge laughed and held up a hand to stop her. "My dear. Please. I'm old, but not dead yet. I've got this," she said as she opened the door to exit and headed out with a grunt. "Take some time to think about that note, okay? We need to get Nick out of this horrible trouble. We all know he didn't do it—he just couldn't have. In any event, that note might lead us to something," she said, wagging her finger. "A clue perhaps," she added before closing the door, letting Rex out the back door, and shuffling through the snow to the front of her house. Marge turned and waved before she and Rex slipped inside.

Rain was paralyzed by what Marge had said. Had there been something deeper to the conversation she'd shared with Wallace? Something that she'd perhaps missed? If only she could remember and make sense of it. And Marge had reminded her of karma. Had Wallace gotten what he deserved because of the pain Danny had endured? Losing a limb because of an accident caused by another could certainly spur on bad blood. Is that what this was about? Retribution? Was that really the motive?

Rain backed the SUV out of Marge's driveway and noted the road ahead of her was completely void of cars. The only light above was from the neighborhood streetlights that failed to do the job, as they were caked in snow and ice, and barely glowed. Citizens must've heeded the warning given on the evening news—to avoid going out unless completely necessary— as the place looked like a ghost town. Nick behind bars and not being on call to help plow the roads was having an impact on the town of Lofty Pines, no doubt about that. It was quite amazing how one person could create such an impact. Like a ripple in the water, its widening circles reaching unimaginable lengths. Marge's wisdom still rang in her ears.

The one thing that bothered Rain immensely was that a bloody knife had been found inside Nick's tackle box. It was too easy. The timing too perfect. If her friend had indeed committed this crime, he wouldn't have hung on to the murder weapon. Nick would be smarter than that. Besides, she was absolutely sure he hadn't done it, despite the cut on his hand. Nick hadn't cut his hand on the murder weapon; he'd cut it on fishing tackle, just as he'd said. But she'd be lying if she didn't realize that didn't add up either. She knew that he wasn't usually that careless, he'd said as much. Rain hadn't voiced any of this to Julia, because, after all, this part of the discussion seemed off limits. If she dared express any questions about Nick, even the slightest question, Julia might assume she thought Nick had sealed his fate, but that wasn't the case. Rain didn't believe Nick was a killer. Not for a single second. She believed someone had purposely planted that knife inside his gear. The question was, who and *when*? It wasn't adding up. Had someone planted the knife in his gear *after* Wallace was killed? Was that even possible?

As these musings plagued Rain's mind, the snow continued to fall heavily from the sky. The wiper on the driver's side began to stick, and then flop, and then not work at all. She tried to squirt fluid across the windshield, but the sprayer must've been blocked with ice, because it too wasn't working. She remembered she had topped it off, as she'd used an entire bottle of windshield washer fluid when she'd refilled it. All of this couldn't have happened at a worse time, because the window was being pelted with snow. Rain checked the rearview mirror before flicking on her hazard lights, to pull off to the side of the road. When she felt safe enough to do so, she hopped out of the vehicle and reached out to wipe the snow off the wiper that was giving her trouble. A brilliant light unexpectedly blinded her, and she shook her head to regain her vision, and then lifted her forearm to cover her eyes. Her teeth clenched as she couldn't understand why the oncoming vehicle hadn't turned off their brights. When the lights only grew stronger, she kicked the door shut and leapt backward, behind her vehicle for safety. But it was too late. The brilliant lights continued toward her at high speed, leaving her defenseless. That was the last thing Rain remembered before flying backward into the snow.

Chapter Seventeen

"Rain. Rainy!"

The sound of her name and the feel of a warm, ungloved hand aside her cheek, caused Rain to blink several times.

"Rain, Rainy, it's me! You okay?"

When her eyes finally came into focus, she noted red and blue lights swirling around the white blanket of snow like a disco ball, and fat flakes stuck to her eyelashes. Snow was falling peacefully now, and a quiet lull ensued, as if she were watching a shaken snow globe. She shivered and quickly realized her jeans were wet, and they stuck to her legs like cellophane.

"Hey, Rain, can you hear me?"

"Uh-huh." She squeezed her eyelids tight and then refocused before pushing herself up on her elbow. A strong arm reached out and lifted her to her feet, as if she were weightless. She found herself eye to eye with Jace, who was looking her over from head to toe with a furrowed brow. The nerve in his temple was bulging, and she wondered if she should be the one to ask if *he* was all right.

"Are you okay? What in the world happened here?" Jace asked, brushing the snow from her arm.

This caused Rain to wince.

"Oh no, I didn't mean to hurt you. Maybe I shouldn't have moved you." Jace cringed. "Can you move your arm? It isn't broken, is it?" Jace watched while Rain extended her arm back and forth a few times, checking.

"I don't think so. I think I just bruised it." Rain ran her hand up and down her arm and felt the muscles in her legs suddenly tense up. Her stomach flip-flopped for a second too.

"What are you doing out here in the ravine? Did something make you slip and fall? Why did you get out of the car? Did a deer run in front of you or something? That's it—you hit one, didn't you?" He looked around as if searching for animal tracks in the snow, and then his eyes met hers again in question. When she didn't reply, he looked her over once again with a worried expression. "My guess is you were trying to help an injured animal. Where is it?"

Jace's words had fired off like a rifle, and Rain placed her wet hand to her forehead to center herself. All the questions made her head spin. *Boy,* she thought, *he is so like his sister—he sure can fire off the questions.* She attempted to plant her feet in one place so she wouldn't fall again.

"Did you hit your head? Did you black out?"

"Nooo. I don't think so—just stunned mainly. I think I broke the fall with my arm." Rain caught her breath after rubbing her arm again. She shook her head slightly to rid the cobwebs and said, "The last thing I remember was headlights heading in my direction, and the next thing I knew I was in the ditch." Rain pointed to the flattened snow where she'd apparently rolled until she'd hit the bottom. Just looking at the drop made her wince in pain again. If she felt pain now, she could only imagine what she'd feel like tomorrow.

"Hang on a second. You mean someone tried to deliberately hit you?" Jace leaned in closer and held her by the arm to keep her steady on her feet.

"I don't know . . . I-I," she stuttered. "I'm really not sure . . . I couldn't see, and then headlights were coming at me , and I couldn't understand why . . . why would someone do that and not stop?"

"What were you doing out of the vehicle? And what are you doing out on a night like this anyhow? You should be home with the rest of Lofty Pines, safe and warm, tucked in front of a hot fire." His mood was a little more demanding than Rain appreciated.

"I was taking Marge home from the library so she wouldn't have to drive in this mess." Rain's tone was a little sharper than she'd meant it to be, but she didn't appreciate the interrogational tone from Jace right off the bat. As if she was the one causing trouble for no reason. It wasn't like she'd chosen to go out on a joy ride in a snowstorm.

"You're lucky I was out on patrol and found you out here. The snow's getting thicker. Let's get you back to your vehicle, where it's warm," Jace encouraged, leading her gently by the elbow, slowly back up the small embankment. "Can you walk? Does anything else hurt?"

"Besides my ego?" Rain chuckled, and this finally brought a smile to the officer's lips.

"I'm just wondering if you're okay to drive." He hovered over her as if he were a parent caring for a sick child.

"I'm fine, Jace, really. I'll be just fine." Rain huffed a breath, sending a puff of hot air out front of her. She was more embarrassed than anything—and ticked. She was definitely ticked. *Why would someone do that?*

Jace opened the driver's side door to her SUV and then must've noted the problem, as he said. "Oh, I see now. Your wiper's broken. Is that why you pulled over?"

Rain nodded after slipping into the driver's seat. Every muscle in her body was starting to throb like a dull toothache. She couldn't wait to slip into a nice hot bubble bath.

"Anyhow," he continued, "it didn't take long for me to see the flattened snow and follow it to where you landed. I was more concerned with where you were, so I didn't notice this."

Rain agreed with a nod and then kneaded her forehead with her fingers. "Notice what exactly?"

Jace moved over to examine the wiper closely. "Did you do this?" he asked, peeking at her over the doorframe to maintain direct eye contact.

"Do what?"

"Unclip the wiper blade."

"Now why would I do that on a night like this?" Rain said sarcastically. "I wouldn't even know how to do that." And then it hit her like a bolt of lightning. If she hadn't . . . who had? Her heart began to thump erratically in her chest. "Jace?"

"No. Hang on, Rain." He lifted a hand to stop her. "It looks like someone unclipped the wiper blade. It's loose, and a twist tie just fell on the ground." He looked at his feet and picked up what looked like a tattered string. "I think somebody tampered with this. Probably the twist tie held on just enough for you to go a few miles, and then it would break away completely." He frowned.

Rain did a double take.

"This isn't right." Jace raked his hand through his hair. "Not right at all."

"No, it certainly isn't, because I had new wipers put on the last time the car went in for an oil change. How about the sprayer for the window washer fluid? It's clogged with ice, right?" Rain asked, her adrenaline now in overdrive. She already knew the answer before the words came out of Jace's mouth.

"Nope. Not that I can see. It's perfectly clear." His eyes scanned the windshield, and he rubbed his hand along the area, wiped off a bit of wet snow, slapped it to the ground, and then shrugged. "Why?"

Rain knew she had filled the windshield washer tank; she was sure of it. "Can you please back away from the windshield for a minute?"

Jace took a step back from the SUV and placed his hands on his hips. He watched from a safe distance, as if to not get wet.

When Rain attempted to squirt the fluid, nothing came out. "It's acting like it's empty, but I filled it to the top." She kept at it with more and more vigor to the point of frustration, but continued to come up empty. Nothing sprayed as it was supposed to.

"Pop the hood." Jace removed a pencil flashlight from his police belt and shined it beneath the hood while Rain waited. When Jace's head popped up, he said, "Rain, the window washer tank is dry as a bone. I don't see any evidence of any kind of liquid in here."

"That's impossible!" Rain banged her hands on the steering wheel and then exited the car to see for herself.

Jace shined a beam of light on the tank, and sure enough, it was empty.

"Jace, I promise you, and as Julia is my witness, I filled that fluid to the top!" She held up a hand as if she was on the witness stand, holding her hand above a Bible.

"I could crawl underneath to verify, but I'm not sure either of us needs to see that to know that someone must've poked a hole to drain the fluid. If the wiper hadn't been meddled with, I might think you were off your rocker, but add two and two together, and you don't have to be a rocket scientist to figure out what happened here," Jace said grimly.

Rain gasped because she knew the implication. Someone had purposely tried to run her off the road. She could've been killed! Someone was trying to sabotage her investigation of this case. Someone knew she would be on the road and would have to pull over. Someone had been watching them leave the library. It was the only explanation. Because only someone involved in the murder investigation would want her to stop trying to clear Nick's name. And that person would surely be the killer.

Chapter Eighteen

After shedding her wet clothes and changing into fleece-lined leggings and a hoodie, Rain was huddled near the fireplace, wrapped in an oversized Sherpa throw. The rocking chair was pulled close enough to the hearth that if she wanted to, she could rest her stocking feet on it. Her hands were tightly woven around a hot mug of herbal tea.

Jace had insisted that he stay with her back at the cabin for at least a half hour, as Rain had refused to go to the hospital to be checked out. As tired as she was, the last thing she wanted was to sit in a waiting room for hours on end, waiting to be seen by a doctor. She knew tomorrow she'd most likely be covered in black and blue, but she figured her ego would be bruised the most. When she'd seen the headlights coming toward her, she should've hopped back into the safety of the car. Why had she allowed someone to intimidate her like that? Was it because she couldn't fathom another human attempting to run her off the road? A sliver of anger ran through her mind before her musings were interrupted when Jace spoke.

"I'm glad you're okay, Rain. I have to admit, you really had me freaked out back there, finding you lying in the ditch. I didn't know what I was gonna find," Jace said with a shake of his head, his back to her. "It could've been so much worse," he added under his breath.

Jace was busy hustling about, loading the stacked stone fireplace with logs. He lit a match and tossed it near the kindling stick that he'd previously added to the middle of the pile. Rain watched as he crouched down, his hands on his knees, and blew into the fireplace before standing back to admire his handiwork.

Rain appreciated his concern but didn't want any additional mothering from the man. She was afraid if she even hinted at a sore muscle, he'd insist again that she stop in at the Emergency Room, so instead she changed the subject entirely. "The chief had you out on patrol tonight, huh? Seems like they're keeping you out of the police station and as far away as possible from the murder investigation? Is that your take? You think they're purposely keeping your nose out of it?"

Jace turned to her and shrugged, leaving his hands in a defensive stance. "Maybe. Probably. Heck if I know," he said before returning to watch the flames, It seemed he was not quite sure the kindling would take over to his liking, because Rain noticed him prodding the log with the cast-iron poker.

"I really appreciate your offer to take care of my car, but I can have it towed tomorrow if need be . . ."

Rain wasn't finished speaking before Jace interrupted. "It's no worry at all. I'll stop in at the auto dealer and pick up a new set of wipers. Hopefully, it won't be snowing too hard for me to get 'em on for ya. Really. It'll take me, like, two seconds to do."

"If you're sure." Rain hesitated. She wasn't used to depending on anyone else besides Nick to help her out from time to time. She didn't even realize how much she'd relied on Julia's husband until Nick was in a world of hurt of his own. "Well, I sure do appreciate it."

"No, problem, I'll take care of it," he said casually. He turned to face her directly and asked, "How's Julia?"

"Dead tired. I don't know how she's standing up straight," Rain admitted. "I sent her home for a hot bath and early to bed, and I haven't heard a peep from her since. If she were awake, she would've texted me by now. I told her to keep in touch. I made her promise, if she woke up, she'd come back over here to spend the night. The last thing I want is for her to feel alone right now."

"Thanks for looking out for her. Now let me return the favor and tell you how much I appreciate it." He grinned, tucking a thumb to his chest.

Rain returned the smile but hesitated before adding, "You know, Jace, I care about your sister just as much as you do. I'm worried sick over this." She took a sip of tea and returned the mug to her lap. The liquid warmed her from the inside out, and she was thankful to be home.

Jace nodded in agreement. "Yeah, I know. I was just wondering how she was holding up. She tries to put on a brave face for my behalf, but I know Nick's arrest is killing her. It's killing all of us." He raked a hand through his hair, and the muscles on his jaw tightened. "I can't even believe this is happening to our family. It's awful."

"Me neither. We need to solve this case and get him outta there," Rain said with renewed resolve.

"Do you have any idea who would've wanted to hurt you?" he asked her pointedly. His eyes were eager and expecting. "Been on a bad date lately? Any ticked-off guys you left hanging in the wings that I need to know about? Trust me, I'll go after 'em like a bull!"

From the sound of his tone, Rain didn't doubt him for one second. She tilted her head back in mock laughter. "Now, that's a funny one, Jace. No, I haven't been dating."

He raised a brow, as if interested in this fact.

Rain grew serious. "I don't have a clue. But I'm pretty sure this has to do with Nick somehow, or me digging into the case. It has to be—I don't have any enemies in this town," she answered before taking another sip of tea.

"Hey, I just want to make sure I'm ruling everything out here and not jumping to any conclusions."

"I understand." The chamomile filled her nostrils, and she took in the scent to calm her stomach and her nerves. "Are you sure you don't want tea? Coffee? Something?"

"Nah, I'm good, thanks." Jace shook his head before he turned completely away from the licking flames and took a seat on the hearth, facing her.

His sitting so close caused Rain to cross her feet beneath the rocking chair instead of extending them onto the hearth. Despite socks, her feet were still like cubes of brittle ice.

"I can't help but agree with you that this attempt to run you off the road has to do with the murder investigation. You say you've been digging. Who've you been talking to?" He laced his fingers together and leaned toward her, resting his arms on his thighs. There was only about two feet between them. Instead of this making her uncomfortable, she felt safe in his presence.

When she didn't answer, he pressed, "Come on, what have you got?"

From Jace's demeanor, Rain didn't think he was upset that she'd been sticking her nose into the investigation. On the contrary, he seemed to want to collaborate. She thought she'd test this theory a little further by asking him a few pointed questions.

"Anything new come to light on your end that I might've not heard yet?" Rain lowered the mug of tea to her lap and held it with both hands. The warmth from the steaming cup kept her hands comfortably warm. "I mean, any of your buddies down at the station filling you in on the sly? I know they're not supposed to, but you've got to have at least someone on the force who's in your favor."

Jace turned to stoke the fire and poked around until the logs were ablaze. The flames reflected off the side of his face when he turned back to face her. "I caught wind of a few preliminary results that came back from the autopsy."

"Besides what might have caused the fatal wound, you mean?"

"Yeah."

"Well, what is it?"

"There was a substance around Wallace's mouth that the coroner can't quite put his finger on. Preliminary results show it could potentially be chloroform and another unidentified substance."

"Chloroform?"

"Yeah. It's highly toxic when inhaled, and since the substance was found around his mouth, they're concluding that it must've been used as a sedative to knock Wallace out. The killer must've stuffed his mouth with a rag and then removed it before abandoning the body. In order to knock someone completely cold, the perp would've had it in his mouth at least five minutes. Anyhow, the police are a bit intrigued about this discovery. As am I," he added with raised brows.

"What do you think it means?"

"I think it means this was premeditated."

Rain cocked her head and waited.

"In other words, who had access to the knife *and* the chloroform? If it were an impulse crime—say, by one of the fishermen, as suspected—then access to chloroform would be an issue. Someone thought about this and used the event as a way to throw off suspicion.

"Yeah, you're right. Sounds to me like the killer wanted to be sure the deed was done and had this planned all along. Why else would someone use both the chemical *and* a knife?"

"Exactly," Jace said as he turned to stoke the fire, causing it to reignite with fresh flames. "In any event, we need to find out who had access to chloroform. Certainly not Nick. I guess this is the only thing giving me a gleam of hope at the moment."

"Yeah, we find the chloroform, we find our killer," Rain said pensively. "Where would someone get something like chloroform? Where is it used?"

"In the olden days, it was used as an anesthetic for surgery or dental appointments. That sort of thing. Believe it or not, there're YouTube videos of how to make it. So, technically, anyone could give it a go."

"Really?" Rain scrunched her nose in disbelief. "You're kidding."

"I'm not."

"That's crazy."

"Yep, you betcha. You'd be amazed what you can find out there."

"And the government doesn't shut these videos down?"

"I'm sure it's not from a lack of trying."

"What about the knife? Who had access to Nick's gear? Certainly the knife was planted. The question is, when? That's been bothering me all along."

Jace turned and slowly nodded his head, then lifted his hand to his chin. "I like the angle you're going with here, Rain. I was so fixated on who had access to Wallace, I didn't even think to consider things backward. He tapped a finger to her temple. "You're not just beautiful, you're a pretty smart cookie." For a second, the look on his face was one of shock, and Rain was aware the beautiful comment had leaked out entirely by accident. It warmed her, though. As did his shyness about it.

"I'm just trying to prove to you I didn't hit my head in the ditch and that my noggin is still in perfect working order so you don't drag me to the hospital." Rain chuckled.

This caused Jace to throw his chin back in a laugh. "Nice one. Don't worry—I won't drag you to the Emergency Room if you don't want to go. I sense there is a stubbornness about you." He grinned. "You're as bad as my sister."

"You think?" she teased.

Jace's demeanor returned to bleak. "We need to get Nick out of this mess," he said, rubbing his temples and closing his eyes momentarily. "I can't have my bro spend a life sentence behind bars for something he didn't do."

"And you're gonna let Julia and I dig our teeth into this investigation without stopping us?" Rain leaned forward in expectation of him to tell her to back off.

He surprised her by saying, "As long as you keep me in the loop for anything you find out. We're gonna need to band together on this one, because I get the impression my buddies down at the station seem to think they already have the right guy, and they have this case closed. They couldn't be further from the truth," Jace added with conviction. "It's almost like they're mocking me with it. For some of them, it's like they want my brother-in-law to be the bad guy," he confided.

"Jealousy, you think? Someone out for your job?"

Jace shrugged. "I dunno. Rumor has it Bentley thinks he should get it. That is, despite the fact he's a new hire up here. There was talk of a promotion for me before all this started. I'm not sure how that's gonna go down now, with my family member being the main suspect in a murder investigation. I'm guessing my hopes for promotion are a lost cause. Maybe that's what Bentley is hoping for."

Just then, Rain's phone buzzed on the table, alerting her that a text had come in. She reluctantly tossed the throw blanket aside, rose from the comfort of the rocking chair, and moved to pick up the message.

"Julia's up, and she says she has some new information, but it's too important to share via text. She's on her way over."

"That's great news!" Jace leapt to his feet and reached for Rain in an unexpected hug. The two shared a grin before retreating to their respective seats.

Rain couldn't help but feel she had taken a large step closer to Julia's brother. In a way, she was bummed their embrace had ended so suddenly, and she found herself wondering when he might hold her again. And she wondered, too, if she'd have to be the one to instigate that in order for their relationship to progress. The way Jace had quickly retreated for his seat made her think it was all up to her.

Chapter Nineteen

Julia pushed through the back door, removed her boots and set them aside, before rubbing her hands together to warm them. "It's colder than a penguin's foot out there. I think the Northwoods has turned colder than the dang Yukon!"

Hearing the door open, Rain had rushed to greet her. She noticed by Julia's fresh and chipper tone, that her friend must've caught up on some sleep. She summoned Julia to follow her into the great room.

"Come, the fire's going, and it'll warm you back up after that nasty trip across the yard."

Julia stopped short when she entered the room, put her hands to her hips and said, "Jace? What the Sam hill are you doing here?"

"Didn't you see his cruiser parked out front?"

"No, I came over through the path, instead of climbing the banks to the road." Julia's eyes travelled between the two of them before landing on her brother. "Oh." She covered her mouth with her hand before uttering, "Oh no. No no . . . Oh boy . . ." Julia clasped her hands together and slowly backed out of the room. "I'm interrupting something. I didn't mean . . ."

"Not at all, Julia. You're not interrupting a thing," Jace said, a little too quickly for Rain's liking. She'd hoped he'd felt something earlier too.

"I'm not? It's looking very cozy in here," Julia said accusingly as she replaced her hands to her hips. "Wait. You two aren't plotting strategy without me? Are you? Why didn't you wake me! There better not be any more meetings of the minds without me. Do you hear loud and clear?"

"No, I was in an accident," Rain admitted. "Jace just happened to be my rescue."

"Wait. What?" Julia's eyes doubled in size. "Come again?" she cuffed a hand to her ear.

"To be fair, it wasn't exactly an accident, more like I was run off the road tonight."

Julia reached out a hand to comfort her. "Oh no! Are you okay?"

"Yeah, yeah," Rain deflected by reaching for the Sherpa throw and wrapping it around Julia's shoulders. "Here. This oughta help warm you up too."

Julia clasped the throw to her neck and gripped it tight. "Wait a minute. Back the train up. You said someone ran you off the road? Like on purpose? Who would do something like that?"

Rain and Jace shared a glance before Jace said, "That's the million-dollar question."

"You didn't see the car?"

"Nope. All I saw was headlights beaming in my direction, and I couldn't understand what was happening, until after I landed in the ditch. My brain just couldn't compute it, for the life of me, I couldn't understand why someone would intentionally try and hurt me."

"You did *what*? You landed in the ditch? What were you doing out of the car?" Julia exclaimed.

"Yeah, and she wouldn't let me take her to the emergency room either. You two knuckleheads are like clones." Jace scoffed. "Between you passing out when Nick was arrested, and now finding Rain in the ditch, you two are gonna be the death of me, I swear." He held up Scout fingers.

"Rainy," Julia said in a tone of deep empathy.

Rain spun on her heels to demonstrate all her body parts were in working order. "It's okay—I survived, see?" She pasted on an Academy Award–winning smile and tried hard not to flinch.

"Ah, I get it now . . . so that's why my overprotective brother is still here. Why wouldn't you go get checked out, though?"

"And spend the entire night in a waiting room when I can be here, sitting by the fire? I think not! You two are like mother hens. I'm fine." Rain waved them off with a flick of her hand, growing more annoyed by the minute.

Julia shot her a look that said *I don't believe it.*

"Seriously, Jules. I'm fine." Rain folded her arms against her chest and winced. The arm that she'd fallen on had a dull throb that might require ibuprofen at the very least. Now that was something she could agree to.

Julia pointed to her arm. "See? you're not fine! You scrunched your face!"

"Oh, good grief. Enough already. What news do you have that caused you to trudge across the yard in the cold and snow? It must be something good. Spill."

"Yeah, what've you got?" Jace took a seat on the sofa and patted his hand for Julia to join him.

Instead, Julia gestured for Rain to take that seat, and she sat across from them, dragging over the rocking chair. "Nick called and asked if I could find him an attorney, but when I had him on the phone, I asked him about Seth."

"Seth?" Jace leaned forward, rested his arms on his thighs, and clasped his hands together.

Julia looked to Rain. "You didn't tell him?"

Rain shook her head. "We didn't get that far. I was gonna bring it up for discussion, but then you walked in."

Jace turned his attention to Rain, shifting his body to face her. "What am I missing here? You didn't tell me what?"

"When you questioned Seth at the crime scene, what exactly did he tell you?" Rain asked. "Did he tell you how he knew Wallace?"

"No. He told me he didn't know the victim. Why?"

"Aha!" Julia said, raising a finger and causing the blanket to drop from her shoulders.

Jace sat up straighter. "What the heck is going on? Why did you bring up Seth anyway?" His stare lasered between them.

"First of all, we saw him over at Tina Benson's house," Rain said before Jace suddenly switched to officer interrogation mode.

"Wait. Let me get this straight. You mean to tell me you two went over to talk to Tina?" Jace dropped his head in his hands, shook his head in dismay, then looked to his sister. "Julia, come on! Your husband is the number-one suspect. And you went to talk to his *wife*. This isn't gonna help Nick one bit!" He slammed his fist against his leg. "What were you thinking?" he said with a sigh.

"Hang on a second there, bro." Julia held up a hand to stop him. "Don't get your panties in a knot. You're getting off course here. We saw Seth coming out of her house, and *you* said Seth told you he never met Wallace or his wife. Kim said the exact same thing, swears up and down her husband doesn't know them. Never mind *me*, what was Seth doing over at Tina's? Huh? Can you explain that!"

"I'm not sure, but is this really where you're going? You want the heat off Nick, and you want to pin this on Seth now?" Jace rose from the sofa and raked his hand through his hair, causing Rain and Julia to look up at him with a worried expression.

Julia shrank back in the chair. "That's not at all what I'm saying."

"What are you saying then?" Jace began to pace in front of the fireplace like an excited dog. "What *exactly* are you getting at, Julia?" his voice escalated and he halted his pace. "'Cause it sounds to me like you want to pin this crime on another one of our friends!"

"That's not what I'm saying at all," Julia said defensively. "I'm saying, for some reason, Seth lied to you. I don't know why, and I'm sure there's a perfectly good explanation. But it needs to be *explained*. That's all." She sat back defiantly in the chair. "I'm only implying that there's a bit of information that he's holding back from the police. Something he's not telling you," she added quietly.

"Great. And that's supposed to make me feel better. That a good friend of ours is now on the hook for this. Gimmie a break, Julia!" he huffed.

"Hey, don't shoot the messenger! I'm just sayin'—"

Rain stood up and put her hands between them like an umpire. "I know this is emotional for everyone involved. We need to keep our wits about us, okay? Let's just take a deep breath here," she said, taking a full breath herself and letting it out slowly, demonstrating.

Julia slumped back in the chair, and Jace returned to his seat on the sofa.

"Hang on—I've got an idea." Rain moved away from the warmth of the fire into the crispness of the bedroom, where she brought back a whiteboard and marker that she'd resurrected from underneath the bed. She shook the dust bunnies off along the way.

"What is that?" Julia asked as Rain set the whiteboard against the hearth to balance it and then uncapped the marker, using her teeth.

"It's gonna be our crime board. Our family used it for Pictionary back in the day, but I think it would be perfect if we share all our information right here. Seems like we need to get our suspect list out in front of us and hammer out all the details. Whaddya say?"

"I think it's brilliant since you two seem to hold back information from me. I'm the cop but seemingly the last to find out anything around here," Jace said with a hint of annoyance.

"Which, by the way, is wrong on so many levels." His eyes narrowed and he glanced between them accusingly.

Rain let his comments slide. She could understand Jace's frustration. Nick was the closest thing he had to a biological brother, his closest *bro*, and he was currently behind bars. And Seth was like their third musketeer. It must've been hard for him that the two people closest to him were the top suspects on the list, and Rain hoped to fix that. "Okay, here we go. First of all, there's the missing piece of Seth's information, so we'll just put him down on the board for starters." Rain wrote down Seth's name and put a question mark next to it.

Julia leaned forward in the rocking chair and pointed to the board. "Add on Danny." She nodded. "There's potential motive there."

"Who's Danny?" Jace's glance ping-ponged between them, like a volley, until it finally landed on his sister with a frown.

"'Cause of an accident, Danny lost a limb. Talk around town is that Wallace was blamed for the accident, until OSHA let him off," Julia answered.

"Yes, and there was a civil suit started and dropped by Danny. Maybe he's still ticked about that." Rain wrote down *Danny* and put *revenge/justice* as a motive next to his name.

"How'd you hear that?" Jace leaned back in surprise.

"Greg Benson," Rain and Julia said in unison, and then shared a smile.

"Greg?"

"Yeah, he worked with Danny and Wallace over at Smith Brothers Logging," Julia said. "That is, before Wallace quit his job. Should we add him to the board?"

"Where was Wallace working? I mean, before he died?" Jace asked.

Rain and Julia shrugged, then Julia said, "Not sure it's relevant, but we didn't hear what he'd been doing for employment since he quit."

"Oh."

"Anyhow, Greg is no relation to Wallace Benson if that's what you're thinking," Rain said as she watched Jace shake his head in bewilderment and then roll his eyes as if trying to keep up.

"You two have been busy!" he said with what Rain thought might have been a hint of admiration beneath the underlying frustration. "I have no idea how you've gotten this far already, nor do I want to know, but do any of these motives actually stick?"

"I think one of us needs to talk to Danny and get a feel for the situation. That would be our best bet." Rain clicked the marker against his name on the board.

"Well, I for one don't think it should be you, Julia. You could get Nick in a heap of trouble if the guys at the station catch wind that you're messing with the investigation. You're gonna have to hop on the back burner for this one and ease up on your sleuthing. Brains only from here on out in this part of the process, you hear?" he said, lightly bopping her on the head, as if they were back to grade school and not grown adults. "Rain and I'll handle the rest."

Rain nodded. "I hate to admit it, Julia, but your brother's right. If the police think you're meddling in their investigation, things could get awfully sticky. You could end up making things a lot worse for Nick. Let us handle the conversations, okay? But I promise, we'll bring you everything we know just as soon as we know . . . right, Jace?"

"Right."

Julia sank back in the chair and fiddled with her hair, defeat written all over her face.

"Look, it's not as if you're not going to help. We'll use the whiteboard to gather intel, and that intelligent brain of yours will be the one to crack this wide open, you hear?" Rain encouraged.

Julia didn't respond verbally. Instead she laced her fingers together and placed her hands atop her head, leaned back in the chair, kicking one foot on the hearth and allowing herself to half face them.

"Speaking of brains, Rain was onto something earlier," Jace said, looking to his sister. "Who had access to Nick's gear? Who could've potentially slipped the murder weapon inside his tackle? Anyone?"

"I can think of one person, and one person alone," Julia said with a smirk.

"Who?" Rain and Jace asked simultaneously, and then shared a laugh before returning their attention to Julia.

"Neither of you are gonna like my answer. But the only one I can think of that would've been familiar with Nick's gear is Seth."

Chapter Twenty

The library was bustling, with books flying off the shelves faster than Rain and Marge could loan them out. The snowstorm was having a wild effect on patrons' behavior. As if they'd be stuck indoors for the remainder of winter and not merely a few days. Rain silently wondered if the library would feel like an empty tomb when the storm finally paralyzed the community. After all the hustle and bustle, it was sure to become unnervingly quiet. If she were honest, Rain noticed a change within herself. She no longer wanted silence and time alone to wallow in her grief, but instead longed to be surrounded by people and feel the joy of existence and fellowship again. She was finding more acceptance of her place within her community and found herself no longer wanting to be a mere spectator, but an active participant in life.

Rain peeked over at the circulation desk to see Marge smiling ear to ear, completely in her element, checking out books. The line was growing, but no one seemed to care, as the older woman kept the patrons entertained with her animated smile and banter. Rain was so thankful for Marge's return from Florida. Without her, she wasn't sure if she would've been able to keep up. And she loved the older woman like a surrogate grandmother, who made her feel as if they were truly extended family.

Julia was off from substitute teaching at the local school, and Rain had sent her on an errand to the grocery store to pick up extra coffee to keep up with the expanding library crowd. Rain had also given her a short list from Marge for any last-minute items the older woman might need should they be snowed in for the foreseeable future. She hoped for Julia's sake she'd be able to navigate Nick's truck with the plow attachment. Her mechanically deficient friend had only been given instructions on how to run the plow attachment fewer than a handful of times and had shared with Rain that she never really recalled how to do it. Julia would ask her husband to reteach her every time she was expected to use it again. Rain wished again for Nick's release, as she'd probably need to close the library soon because she wouldn't be able to keep up with the plowing either. The last thing she needed was having a patron get stuck or be unable to navigate out of the driveway. But all the wishing and willing wasn't going to release her friend's husband from jail. Only narrowing in on a suspect and bringing the real perpetrator to justice for Wallace's family could prove just that. And Rain couldn't determine, as her mind waffled on the options left behind on the crime board, just who that might be.

The encouraging thing was, Rain didn't have to go far in order to question one of those whose names was penned on their makeshift board. Danny had entered the library, seeking her out, and when he'd found her, he asked kindly,

"Rain Wilmot? I hear you're looking for me. Name's Danny Meyer." He stood proud, his stance solid, as if nothing in the world could phase him. A strength that Rain could only envy seemed to surround him like a protective armor.

"Looking for you? What do you mean, where'd you hear that?" Rain asked.

It was impossible not to notice the empty sleeve hanging from his coat, evidence of a lost limb. A pang of regret surged through her for the pain the man must've endured. And the things one takes for granted. She clasped the book she held tighter in both hands, as if reminding herself how blessed she was that she still had two arms. Even though her own was still sore and bruised from her recent fall, at least her limbs were still attached to her body. How difficult it must be to lose one.

"Doesn't matter, the usual town gossip. But I'm here to tell you, I had nothing to do with Wallace's murder. As a matter of fact, I'm saddened by it. It's awful to hear something like that could happen to one of our own in our community. It bothers me." Danny jutted out his sharp chin. Rain found herself imagining that he'd be a great fit for a Carhartt ad. He had strong features and a rugged complexion, as if he spent long hours outdoors doing hard labor. His honey-colored hair was neatly combed, and his ears were reddened from the cold and lack of winter headwear.

Rain reshelved the book she was holding and leaned against the bookcase. "It bothers me too. Just so you're aware, I never accused you of anything or pointed a finger in your direction, if that's what you've heard. I don't even know you, so how could I accuse you?" she studied him, but his gaze was unwavering.

"I know, people like to talk. But I promise you, I didn't hurt the man. I couldn't hurt a fly." His hazel eyes held an expression Rain couldn't quite calculate.

"Well, if you're saying people like to talk, what have you heard? Sounds like Wallace burned a few bridges at work. Not a lot of friends on the job?" Rain folded her hands across her chest and watched him intently.

"I don't know if I would say it quite like that. Wallace kinda kept to himself, is all, didn't get into the politics of the job—if you know what I mean."

"What about Greg? Did he work with him?"

"You mean Greg Benson?"

Rain nodded.

"I don't know. I didn't really work closely with either of them. I only worked with Wallace the day of my accident, 'cause the guy that I usually harvest wood with was out having surgery. But it was my impression that Greg tried to distance himself from Wallace. A lot of people thought they were related since they shared the same last name, and Greg didn't seem to like that much." Danny leaned into the bookshelf and rested his elbow on it, facing her. He seemed so self-assured, and for some reason Rain continued to be surprised by his demeanor and level of confidence. He was borderline cocky.

"He didn't? Why?"

"Because Greg was always trying to make a name for himself. Trying to climb the corporate ladder. Heaven forbid anything that might tarnish his reputation," he said dismissively.

"He's more of the white-collar type. I don't think the guy did a day of hard work in his life," Danny mocked, flipping his hand and looking at his fingernails. His fingers were cracked and callused, as if he never wore a set of gloves outside in the cold.

"Ah, I see."

"Besides, Greg was the one who rushed to judgement and brought OSHA out to hang the guy out to dry. Listen, what we do out there is dangerous, everybody knows that. There are multiple fatalities every year. I was one of the lucky ones. It was pretty obvious Greg wanted Wallace out. Wallace ended up quitting not long after that," Danny continued with a shrug. "He should've just left it alone."

Rain didn't speak for fear he might halt his loose lips.

Danny looked down at his jacket that held the phantom arm. "It was an accident, plain as that. Accidents happen, and then you need to learn to live with the consequences. We all have our cross to bear, don't we? Like I said, I'm one of the lucky ones. I survived."

"So true, we all have our cross to bear," Rain said with a puff, and this caused Danny to crack a smile. There was a friendliness about him she couldn't help but warm to. She used this opening to dig further but hoped it wouldn't trip up the conversation. "What about the civil case? You dropped it?"

"You heard about that too, eh?" He raised one light brow. "Boy, you can't keep secrets in this town, not a one," he added with a chuckle.

Rain shrugged and smiled weakly.

"You know, initially, I was mad, real mad. I was angry at the whole world. But then, reality sank in. My wife was the one pushing for the civil case. She thought it might help us somehow financially, but then Wallace started giving us checks on the side to help us out. I could tell he really wanted to help my family at that point."

"He paid you?"

"Right up to the day he died," Danny admitted with a slow whistle.

This news came as a surprise to Rain. Instead of letting it rattle her though, she asked, "Do you happen to know a guy named Seth Rogers?"

"Can't say I do. Why?"

"Nah, it's nothing. I was just curious about something, but never mind." Rain chewed her cheek to stop her from sharing anything that might implicate another friend. She almost wished she could unsay Seth's name, but the horse was already out of the barn.

The spell between them was broken when a woman approached. Her winter hat was caked in fresh snow that dripped on her furrowed brow. She said, "I'm looking for something, but I can't find it over on the new release shelf. Can you help me?"

Rain felt a sense of relief for the digression that forced Seth's name out of the conversation. Maybe Danny would forget she'd asked.

The woman inquired if the library had a copy of the latest Nick Sparks novel, which they had on order but hadn't received yet.

The library patron walked away disheartened, and Danny said, "Anyhow, I didn't just come here to bear witness of my innocence. I figured I'd kill two birds with one stone. I hear you've got a knack for picking out books. I have a few youngsters at home that could use something to keep 'em busy this week. Sounds like school is going to be closed due to the weather. Can you give a guy a hand?"

"Yeah, sounds like we have another heck of a storm blowing in," Rain said, moving away from the Nonfiction section and leading him to where she'd housed the children's books. "Now this is something I can certainly help you with. Hopefully we still have something left on the shelves, they're pretty picked over. We've been busy this week for that very reason, but here you go." She gestured a hand to the remaining books and added, "They're marked by age group, so hopefully you'll find something your kids would like."

"I do appreciate it."

"No problem," Rain said, and then hurried away from him. Something about Danny's demeanor and his desire to clear his name to a perfect stranger made her feel mildly uncomfortable. And she could hardly wait to get Julia's take on it.

Chapter
Twenty-One

When Julia returned, she pushed into the library with grocery bags dangling from each arm. Dropping them beside the circulation desk, she removed her hat and mittens and set them atop the wet bags. Rain rushed over to give her a hand, releasing the books she'd held in the crook of her arms, to the desk.

"Marge," Julia said, setting her hand lightly on the older woman's shoulder, "Janice is waiting outside to pick you up. I put your groceries in the backseat of her car."

"Oh, heavens, already? It's so good of her to pick me up. I don't want to keep my neighbor waiting, but . . ." Marge looked to Rain for approval, and Rain replied by retrieving Marge's coat from the hanger beside the door and holding the garment open so that the older woman could easily slide her arms inside it.

"But what about the books? I didn't get a chance to clean up the mess yet. People never reshelve what they're looking at. It drives me batty!" Marge said with a scowl, removing her hat and gloves from the depths of her coat pockets.

"Go on now—we're finally winding down here. I wouldn't bank on coming in tomorrow either. From the sounds of things, due to the weather, I'm thinking we'll probably be closed," Rain said. "I'll have all the time in the world in the next few days to clean up any messes left behind. No need to worry about that."

Marge's typically bright demeanor dimmed. "Oh, dear. I suppose you're right." She blew out a resigned sigh. "You know how I hate to leave a mess, though. I don't feel right leaving you girls to do it all by yourselves." Her brows came together in deep crevices showing her age. Rain thought the older woman looked a bit more tired than usual. She understood, though, as Marge had traveled quite a distance to get back to Lofty Pines and hadn't had a minute's peace since her arrival. She was quite a trouper.

"No worries—we've got it, I promise," Rain said, patting the older woman on the back.

"Yeah, listen to Rainy. Don't worry about that now. Janice is waiting, and if she waits much longer, she'll have to clean her car off again because it's snowing like a banshee. You best hurry," Julia piped up.

"How much do I owe you for the groceries?" Marge asked Julia politely, turning toward her, as she began to dig into her purse that now hung from her arm.

"We'll catch up on it later." Using a slight nudge of her hand, Julia spun Marge back in the direction of the door.

Even though they were alone, Marge lowered her voice to a whisper. "If you girls need any help with the investigation, you just give me a call, you hear?" Taking Julia's hand in hers and tapping her lightly she said, "I'm only a phone call away if you need me."

Rain and Julia nodded.

"All right, get going now—the roads are getting worse by the second." Julia's expression pinched with worry before she and Rain, like a set of bookends, walked Marge over to the door. "It was even a bit treacherous for me getting back here, and I was driving the truck. Give one of us a call when you get home so we know you arrived safe, okay?"

"All right, my dear." Marge hurried then, squashing her hat on her head and lacing her fingers into gloves. She gave them each a quick squeeze before officially heading out the door. The howling wind blew indoors along with a tornado of flakes, and Rain reached to close the door behind their coworker after a quick and final wave goodbye.

"I have some news for you too, lady. Anyone still here?" Julia asked, lifting on her tiptoes, and then eyeing the tall shelves of books that surrounded them like a hidden fortress.

"I'm pretty sure Marge checked out the last patron right before you walked in. I was just down there and didn't see anybody," Rain answered, flicking a finger in the direction of the center aisle. "Why? What's up?"

"We need to close up shop and go pick up your car before we settle in for the night. Jace called, and he's totally swamped at work. Apparently, he's working overtime with all the cars that are landing in the ditch." Julia rolled her eyes and added through the side of her mouth, "It's like the people of Lofty Pines have completely forgotten how to drive in bad weather.

He asked me to take you over to the service station. He had your car towed there this afternoon."

"Oh, he did? He didn't have to do that." Rain frowned. "I could've taken care of it."

"He had hoped to change out the wipers himself, but as you know, duty calls."

"Oh, I know. Not his fault. I get it," Rain agreed with a quick nod. "We'd better hurry, though, if the roads are getting that bad. I don't think I want to leave my car at the service station overnight or for days on end."

"Hang on—there's more." Julia grinned. "My brother is brilliant!"

"Whaddya mean more? How can there be more to it than that?"

"He didn't have your car sent to just *any* service station. He had it sent over to Meyer's!"

Rain scrunched her nose. "Meyer's? I'm still not following Julia."

"The one Danny's father owns!" Julia looked smug. "Jace had your car sent there so we could do a little digging about his son. Isn't that brilliant!"

"Ah, I see what you're sayin.' Right, Danny Meyer. I see now what you're getting at."

"Why aren't you jumping out of your skin? It's fantastic! We have a reason to prod the guy about Danny!" Julia jutted a thumb to her chest. "I for one, think this is a terrific idea."

"I already talked to Danny," Rain said flatly.

"Pardon?"

"He came into the library, looking for me."

"Hang on, did you just say you talked with him?" Julia held her hands up as if she were a crossing guard not allowing the kids to cross the street. "Danny came here looking specifically for *you*?" Her voice rose an octave. "Why would he do that? That makes no sense whatsoever."

"If we hurry up, I can tell you all about it on the ride over."

"Fine, I'll wait." Julia pouted and then smiled. "But I'm not happy about it. You'll need to bring the groceries back to the main cabin before we go. There're a few items that might need refrigeration in case we're gone longer than expected."

"Julia, you're a lifesaver. Thanks for picking up a few things for me."

"Hey, it was a selfish gesture. If we end up snowed in together, I bought some rocky road ice cream and the fixings to make chocolate chip cookies too," Julia said, laughing. "We might need a bit of comfort food. At least I will. Until I get Nick home, nothing will be the same." Her smile faded, and she puffed out a resounding sigh.

"I promise you, we'll get him out of this," Rain said with a conviction she was trying really hard to hold onto as she dug around inside the shopping bag, looking for the coffee. When she found something else, she looked up at Julia and winked. "Thanks for remembering to pick up herbal tea. I'm almost out."

"No problem." Julia removed a can of coffee from the bag and a bag of marshmallows. "Is this what you're looking for? Here's the bag of stuff for the library. I tried to keep it all together in one bag. And hurry up—I'm dying to know why

Danny came over here looking for you," she said, abandoning the full bag on the floor. "I'll go warm up the truck if you want to quick run the rest of your groceries home.

"Perfect," Rain said, grasping the bag handles in her hands. "I'll meet you outside."

After dropping off the groceries and locking up the main cabin, she noticed Ryan walking toward the library door, and stopped him with a shout of his name.

He turned and gave her a wide smile, and lifted a hand in greeting. When she met him by the door, he said, "I was hoping to show you the complete workings of the woodstove before the storm gets any worse, but it looks like you've already locked up for the night."

"Raincheck?" Rain asked.

"Sure, it's no problem."

"Honestly, I'd go over it now with you, but Julia is waiting for me. She's taking me to the shop to pick up my car. I had an incident this week."

"An incident?" His brow furrowed, and he leaned in closer, so close she could feel his breath on her face.

Rain jutted a thumb toward the parking lot. "I'm really sorry . . . Julia's waiting." She turned away from him and looked out to the parking lot and held up a finger for her friend, in hopes that Julia could see her asking for a moment.

"You mean you were in an accident?" His tone was filled with growing concern.

"I really gotta go."

"Of course, for sure." Ryan took a step backward and nodded slowly. "Just want to make sure you're okay."

"Yep, I'm fine. Really, I'm good." Rain smiled to encourage him. "We'll get to that woodstove. Um, for now, I'll just keep the furnace running. It's okay, Ryan, really. I do appreciate you taking time out of your day and stopping by, though."

"Yeah, no problem. Anything you need, you know I'm here to help." He unzipped his coat and pulled out a business card from an inside pocket. "My cell phone is on there. Why don't you give me a call, and I can stop by when you're ready?"

"Sure, thanks," Rain said, looking at the card before putting it in her pocket. "Yeah, I just have the number to your office, so this is great."

"Well, now you can get ahold of me any time you want to," he said, with intensity growing in his eyes. "Anytime at all," he repeated with a smile.

"Hey, on second thought, before you take off . . . any chance you know how to run a snowplow? Julia could really use some help with the controls. But only if you have a minute."

"Absolutely," he said, turning on his heel and heading in the direction of the driveway. And after a quick refresher course from Ryan, Julia felt confident she could use the equipment, in a pinch.

"Ryan, you're a lifesaver!" Julia said gratefully. "Thanks a lot!"

"Not a problem. You ladies have a great evening."

"You too," Rain said before he backed away from them, and then she watched as he jogged through the snow toward a blue truck and disappeared from sight.

After Rain was settled next to Julia, and they were rolling down the road, Julia said, "Ahh. So, what was that about back there?"

"Oh, that? Ryan stopped by to go over the workings of the stove. We still haven't gone through it all yet."

"Uh-huh."

"What?"

"It's very convenient that he keeps having to stop in, don't ya think?" Julia's eyes left the windshield, and she looked at Rain accusingly. "You two were standing awfully close to one another if you ask me. Something you're not telling me?"

"Actually, I don't remember asking you." Rain smirked. "He's very busy, Julia. Swamped actually. With this weather, everyone and their brother is putting in a Franklin stove. Business is hoppin'!"

"Uh-huh," Julia said with a sly smile.

"Whatever," Rain said with an eyeroll. "Let's just get back to the investigation, shall we?" She was happy to dodge the current topic and finally fill Julia in about her conversation with Danny.

"Don't you think it's a little weird that he came to the library seeking you out? To me, it's almost more an admission of guilt than anything. It's like the guy is totally overcompensating, right?" Julia pointed out. "Who does that? It's weird."

"Honestly, I didn't get that impression," Rain admitted. "He seemed genuine. Besides, there's another little tidbit I gathered."

"I dunno—seems odd to me." Julia blew out a breath. "Wait, what? Tidbit? Now I'm intrigued. Do tell!"

"Maybe Danny's just tired of being the talk around town. I'm sure the loss of his arm is something he's weary of discussing. You know how Lofty Pines can be sometimes—too many gossips to count on one hand." Rain shrugged.

"That's your tidbit?"

Rain smiled. "No, that's not it. Danny told me that Wallace was paying him. Sounded sort of like a guilt payment, to help out his family. I guess he started paying him around the time Danny dropped the civil case against him."

"Ohh, really? Now that *is* interesting. Especially since the payments would stop now that Wallace isn't around anymore. Perhaps you're right. It sounds like Wallace was worth more to Danny alive than dead? I'm not exactly sure that helps our case against him," Julia added with a grunt. "Fudge popsicles!"

The snow was coming down sideways in sheets, hitting the side of the truck and at times making a pelting sound.

"Hail?" Rain asked.

"Sounds like it. They're even talking a chance of thundersnow later tonight."

"Thundersnow? You must be joking." Rain laughed.

"Actually, I'm not."

"I didn't even know that was a thing. Are you serious?"

"It sure is. It doesn't happen very often, but when it does, it can be pretty dangerous."

"How so?" Rain couldn't believe in all her life spent in Wisconsin she'd never encountered it.

"Well, besides the thunder and lightning like a regular storm, it can cause extremely low wind chills, leading to frostbite if you're stuck outdoors in it. It can even cause property damage like a regular storm."

"I swear, I've never heard of such a thing! Learn something new every day," Rain added under her breath.

"It's pretty rare, but sometimes we have just the right conditions in the Northwoods for crazy stuff like this to happen. Especially now," Julia said, leaning closer to the steering wheel and looking out the windshield. "Let's just hope we don't get stuck in it before we get your car home."

"Yeah, no kidding. I've had my share of ditch rolling for one lifetime, thank you very much." Rain chuckled.

"Are you still sore?" Julia looked over, cringing.

"If I was, I'd never admit it to you *or* your brother," Rain said teasingly. "Otherwise, you'd be trying to convince me to see a doctor, and clearly all my limbs are still in working order. See?" Rain wiggled her arms, but she should've held back as it actually didn't feel all that great to do so.

Julia cleared her throat. "Speaking of Jace . . ."

"Yeah?"

"Anything else happen between you guys before I arrived? Despite what you think, his overprotective nature is just his way. I get the feeling he has a real soft spot for you, Rainy."

"And I for him," Rain admitted. But that was as far as she would take the conversation. She was thankful Julia was navigating the truck into the parking lot of the service station, and she could squelch the topic here and now. "Ah, look, we made it. And all in one piece too."

Julia unclicked her seat belt. "I'm coming with you. Heck if I'm going to lose an opportunity to talk with Danny's father, even if you don't question his son's motives. I'm gonna need a lot more convincing. I wanna hear this for myself."

"Suit yourself," Rain said as she hopped from the warmth of the truck into the pelting graupel that looked suddenly like

Dippin' Dots ice cream. She stuck out her tongue and let the water instantly dissolve.

Julia looped her by the arm and said, "Wouldn't it be cool if God did us a solid and sent out flavors of the snow? Like chocolate or cookies and cream?" She giggled like a schoolgirl, and for Rain, the sudden sound of her friend's silliness and lightness in her tone, was music to her ears. Unfortunately, it didn't last.

Before they could take another step, Julia's name was called out, causing them both to spin on their heel, in an about-face.

Officer Bentley approached and looked them both over sternly.

"Something wrong, Officer?" Julia asked.

"Yeah, something's wrong," he said, leaning toward them with his hands firmly planted on his hips.

"What is it?" Rain asked.

"You have a commercial driver's license to run that plow?" He flung a hand in the direction of Nick's vehicle and then studied Julia with the demeanor of a hall monitor.

"No. But I just drove the truck over. I didn't even lower it," Julia defended. "I'm just trying to help my friend pick her car up from the service station. That's it." She shrugged innocently.

Officer Bentley grunted. He adjusted the hat on his head, revealing a military-style buzz cut, as if he'd just been released from basic training. Rain wondered if he'd was currently in the Reserves or had been a member before joining their local police department.

"What is with you? Seems to me, since the day you showed up at my house, you have it out for my family for some reason. What did we ever do to you? That knife was planted!"

"Watch your tone," the officer warned. "In the state of Wisconsin, a CDL is mandatory to run that plow. I should issue you a citation right here and now. Maybe I will," he taunted.

"*Actually*, maybe you should be out looking for Wallace's killer and doing your job instead of arresting my husband, who I promise you isn't your perp! Stop wasting your time issuing me and everyone else in this county citations!" Julia's eyes widened as she seemed to realize how far she'd crossed the line.

"I'm warning you—you'd better watch it," he cautioned, wagging his finger. Then, turning on his heel, he sunk behind the wheel of the cruiser and took off.

"What on earth was that about?"

"Something fishy is goin' on in this town," Julia said. "And I don't like it . . . not one little bit."

Chapter Twenty-Two

A man Rain could only conclude was Danny's father met them at the entrance counter of the service station. He shared the same honey-colored hair, and his eyes, shaped like half-moons at the slightest smile, were almost identical to Danny's. The father's eyes, however, were the color of speckled green grass, not at all the color of Danny's.

"Can I help you?"

"Mr. Meyer?" Rain asked, her eyes rising to the sign above the man's head that read "Meyer's Garage: Happily Servicing the Community for three generations!"

"The very one. But you can call me Doug. 'Mr. Meyer' makes me sound like an old man, and although I am, I hate to be reminded of it," he said with a deep voice and a slight smile. "You lookin' for me? Or you need a tow?" His eyebrows narrowed. "We're kinda backed up at the moment."

"Her car was already towed here this afternoon," Julia said, leaning her elbow against the counter. "She's the one with the broken windshield wiper."

"Got it. We've had a slew of 'em today. Seems everyone has forgotten how to drive out there again," he said gruffly, looking at his hands, which were slathered in dark grease that lined the stubs of his fingernails. "I just assumed you were another one of those that needed to be hauled in."

"That's exactly what I said!" Julia smiled. "It's not like it's our first rodeo! How is it people forget how to drive at the sight of the first big snowstorm?"

"Beats the heck outta me. I wish everyone would just slow down." Doug shook his head before he crouched behind the counter and returned with a familiar set of keys. He then walked from behind the counter out onto the service station floor, where Rain's car was nowhere to be seen. He handed her the keys. "Your car is parked outside. Sorry, you'll have to clean the snow off again, but I didn't have any room in here to keep it dry. As you can see, we're packed."

"I appreciate the fix. What do I owe you?"

"Already paid for."

"Huh?"

"Your boyfriend paid for it over the phone with a credit card."

Rain's face turned scarlet. She knew it because she could feel the instant burn as if the sun were beating directly on her.

Julia laughed. "Oh, that's my brother—not her boyfriend," she said, but then she gave Rain that look. The one that made Rain want to slap her best friend.

"Anyhow," Doug said, "you're all set. Be careful out there."

Rain was surprised Julia hadn't prodded Doug at this point. She wondered if they'd get out the door before either of them said a thing.

"By the way, how'd you do it?" Doug asked.

"Do what?"

"Break your wiper clear off like that?"

Rain wondered if Jace had ripped off the blade so as not to alert the mechanic that it'd been tampered with. So, she said lightly, "I guess it's a woman thing. I'm talented that way."

Doug grinned knowingly.

Rain saw this as an opening. "Three generations of Meyers have worked here, huh? I'm surprised we haven't met before, but up until now I was just a weekend visitor to the Northwoods. I'm now living up here full-time, so it's nice to know that you're here in case I need a mechanic again. I'm sure I'll be back."

Doug sighed and his friendly smile turned downcast. "Well, unfortunately this business ends with me. And I'm not getting any younger. In fact, I was due to retire three years ago, but I held out because my son was planning to take over. That's not gonna happen now."

"Really? Why not? Your son not into fixing cars like you had hoped?" Julia asked after sharing a sideways glance with Rain.

"No, it's not that." Doug's shoulders slumped, and his voice turned so soft Rain barely heard him add, "Some bastard ruined it for me."

"So, are you saying this service station is gonna close down? That's awful! Where will everyone go for repairs?" Julia asked desperately. "I'm guessing it would have to be outside Lofty Pines." Her smile faded.

"Your son refuses to take it over?" Rain asked, already knowing the answer.

"My son's unable because of his handicap," he muttered. "And I can't keep this place goin' forever." The frustration in his voice was clear as day.

"I'm sorry to hear about your son. Has he been sick long?" Rain asked, darting a look to Julia when Doug had turned his head to see someone else enter the garage.

"He's not sick. His life was taken from him by a jerk who stole it from him. And now, thankfully, he's gotten his comeuppance. Can you excuse me?" Doug looked over at the entrance, where Danny was waiting by the counter. "I need to get back to work."

When Danny saw that it was Rain that had been talking to his father, he rushed in her direction.

"What are you doing?" he asked.

"I'm just—" Rain started, and then Danny interrupted her by flicking her shoulder.

"Hey! Watch it!" Julia said.

Danny ignored Julia, instead laser-focusing his attention on Rain. "Who do you think you are, coming here and questioning my father? Huh?" His eyes narrowed, and there was a hint of venom to his words. "Did anything I say to you at the library have any merit? Any merit at all?"

"What do you mean?" Rain said softly in an effort to calm him, but it did little to de-escalate the situation. "I—"

"You have some nerve showing up here and asking my father about Wallace's murder. He's already been questioned by the police. That was harsh enough. And now you think you should come here to his place of business and pester him?"

"No, I—" Rain began, but he wouldn't let her get a word in edgewise.

"I don't see a badge on your shoulder!" His eyes toured Rain's body as if looking for one. He poked a strong finger to her chest. "This town gossip needs to stop. And I'm gonna squelch it right here and now. It's people like you—"

"Hold up, buddy," Julia interrupted. "You got it all wrong here."

"Oh, really? I do, eh? And are you a member of the police department? 'Cause I don't see a badge on your shoulder either!" he said sarcastically.

"Actually, my brother Jace Lowe is a police officer for Lofty Pines—"

"Jace? Jace is your brother? Ohh, I see . . . this is just great! You must be Julia! *Nick's* Julia," he added with disdain. "I see what this is all about now. You're just trying to get the heat off your husband's back! You'll put the blame on anyone, is that it?" He leaned in toward Julia and interrogated her with his eyes. It was almost an act of intimidation.

This immediately put Julia's back up, because she straightened her spine and held his gaze like a boxing match was about to occur. She pointed a finger to his nose. "Actually, *buddy*. You're the one who has it all wrong. We're here to pick up her car. *Not* to interrogate anyone. But it seems to me one of you has a guilty conscience, because your attitude sucks! So, was it you? Or your father? Which one of you?"

Danny took a step closer to Julia, and Rain wondered if he was going to swat her.

"And guess what?" Julia added through gritted teeth. "My husband is innocent, and I have every right to get to the bottom of this."

Rain squeezed between the two of them and parted them with her hands. "I think we all need to calm down. This is getting a bit outta hand."

"Yeah, I agree," Julia said, taking a step backward. She gave Danny a once-over before ripping the car keys from Rain's hand and dangling them in front of his eyes as if to prove why they were standing in his father's garage.

Rain quietly took the keys back and nudged Julia toward the door, but she stood like a bull ready to charge again. For a woman of such short stature, she sure could hold her own.

"Get outta here," Danny said, officially dismissing them, turning his back on them and walking away with a backward wave of his hand.

When they were back to the safety of Rain's car, Julia slipped into the passenger side while they both waited for their cars to warm up. They had cleared the snow off both vehicles but wanted to be sure the windshield was completely clean before taking off.

Julia put her head in her hands, and Rain stroked her back encouragingly.

"Well, that certainly didn't go as planned," Rain said.

Julia turned to her and apologized with sad eyes. "I know, and I'm sorry for losing my cool back there. I need an attitude adjustment. Do chiropractors do that? Or do they just manipulate the spine?" she teased with a chuckle.

Rain giggled. "Now wouldn't that be somethin'? The line would probably be out the door. You're not the only one to lose it sometimes," Rain added, patting her friend's leg. "You're going through a lot, Jules."

Julia gave Rain's hand a quick squeeze before releasing it. "Yeah, but that's no excuse."

"It's okay, my friend. We're gonna get you through this."

"Why do you think Danny got so upset back there? You think he or his father had something to do with this?" Julia asked.

"Anything's possible. Honestly, I'm not sure, but either way, we'll keep digging."

Chapter
Twenty-Three

The land was white. The sky was white. Everything Rain saw outside of the log cabin window was white, as if Benjamin Moore had dipped the town of Lofty Pines in Chantilly Lace. The snow continued to fall, each flake further cutting them off from the roads—and the rest of the world, for that matter. Earlier, Rain had shoveled a path from the log cabin to the driveway, knowing full well, as soon as she had done so, that her effort was in vain. Because soon the gravel path would be covered in a blanket of white yet again. She sighed heavily and turned her attention to Julia, who was wrapped tightly inside a blanket, lying prostrate on the sofa. Her eyes were closed, and Rain did her best to remain quiet as a mouse, as she knew her friend needed to catch up on some much-needed rest. The only sound to be heard was the eerie noise of the log walls, popping and cracking under the pressure of the bitter cold. Decades after the cabin had been erected, the sturdy ten-inch pine logs seemed to groan with age.

Rain stepped in front of the fireplace to warm her chilled hands by the licking flames once again. After jabbing the poker straight through the crumbling wood, she realized she'd need to add another log soon. When she returned to retrieve more wood, she frowned as she looked at what had been left behind from the pile of logs, which was now merely bark crumbs. Knowing that the wood pile was officially depleted, she groaned inwardly at the prospect of having to venture outdoors to replace it. But she didn't have much choice. If they lost power from the storm, it would be their only heat source, and for that reason, and that reason alone, she needed to keep the fire burning.

Rain donned her hat and coat to prepare herself for the elements. She reached for the empty wood bin, located by the back door, before stepping outside. The minute she swung open the door, the wind blew flakes around her head like a cyclone, and she had to blink several times to catch her bearings. She glanced toward the frozen lake and noticed a trail of smoke billowing from one of the ice shanties, planted not too far from the shoreline. She rolled her eyes, wondering what kind of idiot would be out fishing in the middle of a snowstorm. Only a diehard Wisconsinite for sure! And she wasn't sure she fell into that category, she thought, as she was already shivering after being outdoors for mere seconds.

Wallace's place remained forlorn, completely void of smoke since his death, and she wondered when the vacant shanty would be removed from the lake. The mere site of it brought everything to the forefront of her mind once again. Jace had mentioned to Julia that he might stop over, after a long day at work, to check on them, and so far, they hadn't heard a peep. Rain wondered if he was catching up on missed sleep too, or still assisting cars out of the ditch. Or giving out citations for needless car accidents that could've easily been avoided if people would just slow down and take their time.

Rain plodded over to the woodshed, on the far side of the yard, with the oversized plastic storage bin dangling from one hand. She pushed her boots through the deep snow along the way, to make a wider path. When she arrived at her destination, her eyes studied the peeling structure that leaned to one side like the leaning tower of Pisa. Rain wondered if the woodshed that protected their main heat source would make it through another winter. Spending this season in the Northwoods had opened her eyes to things that needed to be fixed around the property. Things that one didn't notice on a quick weekend trip up north in the warmer months now seemed glaringly obvious. *The wood shed is one more thing to add to a growing list,* she thought with a sigh.

Rain tossed in as many logs as would fit inside the bin and hoped her slender arms could carry the lot. Then she back-tracked along her original path, returning to the cabin. When she walked into the great room, huffing and puffing, she was greeted by Julia, who yawned widely, stretching both arms over her head.

"Where'd you go?"

Rain set the wet bin on the fireplace hearth. "We ran out of wood. And honestly, it's gonna take a few more trips before we have enough to last us a few days. I'm thinking of putting a pile out by the back door and covering it with a tarp to keep the wood somewhat dry. The woodshed is doing a good job keeping it that way, but I don't want to trudge through snow drifts every time we need wood for the fireplace. Whaddya think?"

Echoing Rain's earlier actions, Julia ran her hands up and down her arms and said, "You're probably right. If we lose power, and the fire goes out, we could freeze to death. As it stands, it's nice and toasty in here."

"My thoughts exactly, and I'd like to keep it that way," Rain said. She tossed a few logs onto the fire and waited for them to catch before asking, "Wanna help? Maybe we could use a sled to drag it over. I'm sure there's one in the shed or the back of the boathouse that I can dig out."

"Absolutely, I'm on it. I'm not gonna make you do all the grunt work. I have to earn my keep around here, don't I?" Julia said with a yawn. She looked like a languid cat stretching after a long winter's nap.

"You don't have to earn a thing," Rain laughed lightly and then lifted her arm to show her muscle. "Besides, this is a good workout while the gyms are closed. Trust me, I'm feeling the burn." She was feeling even more than that, with the bruises beneath her shirt, but refused to admit it.

Julia snorted. "You don't need a gym, you skinny little thing. What you need is to dig into that rocky road ice cream I bought," she teased, and then turned serious. "Hey, Rainy, thanks again for letting me ride out the storm with you here. I really appreciate it."

"I wouldn't have it any other way. And besides, I really don't want to be alone during this storm any more than you do."

"It's sooo cozy being surrounded by these log walls during a storm. I feel like I'm in one of those movies or books and we're lost somewhere deep in the woods. Honestly, it's making me want to tear down our house and replace it with a log cabin,"

Julia said thoughtfully. "Hey, a girl can dream, right? But it's not something I would ever consider doing alone, and with Nick gone . . ." Julia's stare turned vacant, and Rain refused to let her friend dwell on such negative thoughts.

"Speaking of which, I wonder how Marge is holding up. I think she was bummed we weren't opening the library today. She really loves coming to work." Rain emptied the last of the logs beside the hearth and noticed how small a pile she'd created. What she'd brought in from the woodshed wouldn't keep them warm for very long.

Julia must've agreed as she said, "We should give her a call after we load up on more wood." Julia tossed the blanket off herself and threw it on the back of the sofa before rising to her feet. "I'm sure Rex is keeping her company, and Janice is right next door. She might even be over there by them. My bet, she is. They're probably deep into playing cards or a board game."

"That's true," Rain agreed with a nod. "Like me, she's blessed with great neighbors." Rain grinned and nudged Julia on the shoulder. "And if she wants company, she surely won't need to be alone."

"And I did tell her that I could pick her up in the truck and she could hang out with us if she got lonely."

"You did? Thank you for that."

"Of course! She's like family to me too, Rain. I know for a fact that Nick and I are one of the main reasons for her return from down south. I'm very grateful to both of you, for your support. I'd be lost without you. Especially now," Julia added under her breath, running her hands through her hair, seemingly to untangle it after her nap, and then tucking a strand neatly behind her ear.

"Don't go getting misty on me," Rain teased. "I love ya, Julia, but you already know that." She added seriously, "You'd do the same for me."

"I do know that. Right back atcha, sistah. Now let's go get that wood before I change my mind about helping." Julia grinned and threw her arm over her friends' shoulder as the two headed toward the door.

Just as Rain removed Julia's coat from the hook and was about to hand it to her, a chime from a cell phone alerted them that a text or an email had come through.

"You or me?" Rain asked, handing Julia her coat, and then patting the pockets of her jeans, back and front, in search of her phone.

"I think it's me, hang on a second in case it's Jace," Julia said backtracking into the living room while Rain followed.

Julia's gaze clouded, and she looked up at Rain with a blank stare. "It's Kim. She said Seth's been missing for hours, and she wondered if either of us has seen him?"

"Seth? He's missing?"

"I wonder where he is." Julia bit her lip. "It's not like him to leave her for hours on end. Especially in a storm like this . . . and with the kids . . . alone?"

"Call her," Rain demanded. "Don't do this via text. Just give her a call."

"You're right." Julia hit the button on speed dial and when they heard a frantic hello, Julia said, "Hey, Kimmy, you're on speaker. I'm over at Rainy's riding out the storm. What's goin' on?"

"I fell asleep on the couch when the twins took a nap, and Seth's truck is gone. He mentioned in passing that he wanted to go fishing, but I told him not to, because of the weather. I can't imagine that he would've gone, after I said he shouldn't. That was hours ago . . ." Kim's voice trailed to barely a whisper.

"Maybe he ran to the store for something?" Julia suggested, as she held the phone between her and Rain, so they both could participate in the call.

"Yeah, I'm sure there's a perfectly good explanation," Rain added.

"But he's not answering his texts or his calls. He always texts me right back. It's been a few hours now, and he hasn't not responded. I'm worried."

Julia and Rain shared a grimace.

"I also texted Jace, and he hasn't answered me either. You don't suppose they're together?" Kim rambled on. "I'll have their hides."

"No, I don't think so," Julia said. "Jace is either still on an overtime shift or sleeping. He's been straight out since the storm began. We haven't heard from him either."

"Oh."

The sound of deflation in Kim's voice caused Julia to look at Rain alarmed.

"Wait a minute. He mentioned he might be fishing?" Rain asked.

"Yeah."

"Where's Seth parked, do you know? Maybe he's out on the lake? I saw smoke out there . . ."

"Ugh," Kim grunted. "Stupid man. If he's fishing and that's the reason he isn't texting me back, I swear I'll ring his neck when I see him!"

"Wait." Rain held up a finger and paused. "Didn't he park his shanty in front of your property?"

"No, he didn't. We don't have good fishing over here. He's parked over by the weed line, as he had hoped to have a better chance at winning the Jamboree there."

Rain covered the speaker with her hand and mouthed to Julia, "The weed line is right over here."

Julia looked at Rain perplexed, and Rain said into the speaker. "Kim, we'll go have a look, and get back to you. Hang tight okay?"

"Yeah, sure. Thanks for your help."

"No problem," Rain and Julia said in unison and then shared a grin.

When Julia ended the call with Kim, she waited for Rain to explain.

"When I was outside, I noticed smoke comin' out of one of the shanties not far from my shoreline. It didn't even cross my mind that someone we knew had parked there, never mind that it was Seth."

"Oh, gotcha."

Julia turned and started walking toward the door, and Rain reached for her shoulder to hold her back. "Hang on a sec. What I don't understand is why Seth never mentioned to us that he was parked so close to Wallace."

Julia's brow furrowed.

"What I'm trying to say is, why are we just *now* learning where Seth was parked? The day of the murder, he didn't mention a thing. I automatically assumed his shanty was parked way down the lake," Rain said, waving a hand dramatically as if to demonstrate just how far. "Way, way, way over there, in front of their house. I mean, I certainly did, didn't you?"

"Ohh dear."

"Yeah. You catchin' what I'm castin'?" Rain threw an arm over her shoulder as if she was casting an imaginary fishing line.

"I think so," Julia said, her eyes now darting across the floor, as if seeking answers. "But Jace won't be happy to hear it. Not one bit."

"You wanna know what I think? I think we may have just found opportunity. Now, we just have to finds means and motive, and we might have our killer."

Julia let out a long slow breath and shook her head. "Oh no, Rainy, it can't be, can it?" she asked as her whole body deflated. "It can't be Seth who committed this crime. It just can't be."

"Hey, I don't want to believe it any more than you do. I'm just following the evidence here," Rain whispered, as she didn't even want to utter the words aloud. "First, we see him over at Tina's after he acts like he's never met the woman in his life, and then we find out his shanty is parked not far from Wallace's? Things are starting to add up here. Things that aren't lookin' good for our fellow Laker."

Chapter Twenty-Four

"What should we do? Now, that we know Seth seems to be hiding even more relevant information that could be detrimental to solving the murder investigation," Julia asked, throwing her hands to her hips. "His stinkin' fish shack is parked next to Wallace's . . . and he never mentions it? *Really?* It just keeps piling on!" Julia pressed her lips together in a thin line. "Why wouldn't he tell us where his shanty was parked? It's like he purposely didn't mention where he just happened to be fishing the day of the jamboree. It doesn't make sense. And now I'm angry because, as I remember it, he was the one who was insinuating Nick actually did this. I thought he was our friend!"

"There's either a perfectly good reason he's withholding information, or he's involved somehow. Those really are the only two scenarios we've got to go on. Right?" Rain threw the number two in the air with her fingers, then dropped her hand to her side. "I agree, it doesn't make sense," Rain said, lifting her hand once again to chew on her thumbnail.

"True friends don't hide this kinda stuff from each other. Friends should be open and honest. Unless he's hiding something big, there's just no reason for his lack of transparency. That's what I think anyhow." Julia puffed her mouth up like a blowfish and let the air out slowly. "If we could only get to the bottom of what the flapjack he was hiding."

"Yeah, it sure would be nice to get to the bottom of it."

"The frustrating part is, I don't even know where to go with any of this information." Julia dug her fingers into her forehead, rubbing hard, and then looked to Rain for an answer. "If I'm the one to bring up all these inconsistencies to the authorities, everyone will think I'm just looking for a scapegoat to free my own husband. I can't say a fish-flappin' thing! Even Jace was upset at me for the mere *suggestion* that Seth could be involved somehow." Julia threw her hands to her head and laced her fingers there, closing her eyes momentarily, as if trying to regroup.

Rain remained quiet, allowing her friend to have a moment.

"Ugh, I hate this. I hate even questioning this stuff in my mind . . . one of our own, a Laker . . . someone this close to us. Not to mention one of my husband's closest friends up here in the Northwoods." Julia gripped her hand to her heart and thumped her closed fist there. "The thought that anyone I know could actually do something as heinous as this makes me feel sick to my stomach."

"Trust me, I understand what it's like to completely lose your faith in a person. Someone you *think* you really know."

Julia looked at Rain knowingly. "You mean Max? Right?"

"Yep. I understand this is different—my late husband didn't go so far as to kill a man, but his indiscretion destroyed my heart. He hurt me badly, Julia. And here we go again." Rain rolled her hand in the air. "Here we go with another man testing my faith in humanity. My issue of lack of trust biting me in the butt once again. I think what I'm trying to say is, I don't trust easily anymore, and maybe you shouldn't either. Maybe you don't know Seth as well as you thought you did."

Julia sighed heavily. Rain hesitated, wondering if she should even say it aloud, but she had to know. "Forgive me for even bringing this up, Julia, but has your belief in Nick ever wavered? Even for a second?"

"You mean about this? About Wallace's murder?" Her eyes narrowed.

Rain nodded and held her breath as she waited for an answer.

"It's not like I was happy seeing the murder weapon removed from his tackle box. If you remember correctly, I about fainted. Actually, I did faint, but that's beside the point," Julia added out of the side of her mouth and waved her hand dismissively. She turned to Rain and faced her squarely. "But do I think my husband could commit murder? That's a bit of a leap for me. Someone most definitely planted the murder weapon in his gear. I'm ninety-nine percent positive about that," she declared.

"I'm so glad to hear it."

"Why? Have your thoughts about Nick's innocence changed? Even just a little? You can tell me, Rain. Honestly, with everything that has gone down I would understand . . ."

Rain placed her hands firmly on her friend's shoulders and met her eyes directly. "Not for a second do I think your husband had anything to do with this. Not for one. Measly. Second. Nick's not ninety-nine percent innocent; he's one hundred percent innocent."

This made Julia smile. "Thank you for that."

"Of course. Don't mention it." Rain grinned.

"But you don't trust anyone, yet you trust Nick on this. Why?"

"Besides the fact that I love and adore your husband, I think it's too clean. The evidence found in his tackle box is just too planned . . . too planted for me. If Nick did the deed, he'd be smart enough to make the murder weapon disappear. Your husband is not that stupid."

That comment made Julia smile. "Yeah, he's a kinda smart guy. Even though at times a smartass too." She grinned. "God, I miss him."

"I do too. I especially miss his snowplow services! Just kiddin'. I miss my favorite couple together, that's what I really miss."

"Now that we've both cleared my husband from the roster, that doesn't really mean squat or help the investigation one bit, does it?" Julia chuckled. "People could care less what we think, it's what we can *prove*." She tapped her foot impatiently to the floor. "So, now what?" she pressed. "What do you think we should do to get the love of my life out of this mess?"

"Right now, let's just stick to what we know and put this puzzle together one piece at a time. First, though, I suggest we help Kim locate Seth. And then we share whatever findings we come across with Jace, just as soon as we hear from your brother. At the moment, that's the best we can do. Besides, we could be jumping to a lot of conclusions here. We still don't have all the facts. All we have is a whole lot of theories that don't add up to squat. We need answers from Seth. If we get a chance to speak to him alone, I say we call him out on it, and ask him a few pointed questions. He's a fellow Laker and a good friend. We have the right to ask, don't we?"

"You're absolutely right."

"Because we don't have anything concrete anyway. Let's just get past the speculations at this point and flat-out ask him. I'm tired of tiptoeing around this," Rain said while starting to pace the room. "But I do think all these little secrets that Seth seems to be keeping add up to a whole lot of somethin' . . . I just don't know what yet. We'll be able to tell if he's lying to us or holding back. We're pretty good at reading people. Especially after all the time we spend in the library. Pun intended," Rain added with a light laugh to lift the mood.

"Yeah, I agree. All this speculation adding up to a whole lot of nothin' is just piling on the frustration." Julia huffed. "All Seth has to do is man up and explain why he's been hiding pertinent information. It's that simple. Why would he act like he never met Tina if he had, and why didn't he tell us his shanty was parked so close to Wallace's to begin with? Holding all of this back just seems suspicious, and I'm tired of it too. It needs to stop."

"I say we go over to the shanty and talk with him. Maybe he'll leak a bit of information by accident, and we'll have more to go on. We need to officially eliminate him as a suspect once and for all and move on—crouton. Or collect the evidence that we need to implicate him for this. Either way, we need answers. Besides, we have a perfectly good explanation of why we're going there. His own wife is looking for him!" Rain stopped pacing and held Julia again by the shoulders so she had her friend's full attention. "We just have to keep the conversation light and nonconfrontational. Agree?"

"Totally agree," Julia said, turning on her heel and heading toward the door. "You lead, I'll follow," she said, slipping her arms into her coat and then pulling her winter hat tight to her ears. "I won't say a combative word," she added, zipping her lips with gloved fingers. "After what happened when we went to visit Meyer's service station, I officially learned my lesson."

Rain found that hard to believe. Julia had a way of not being able to hold her tongue in the best of circumstances. She hoped, for both their sakes, this time she'd be wrong.

*   *   *

The biting wind and bitter flakes stung Rain's cheeks as they trekked across the yard and down to the frozen shoreline. The snow was growing deep in spots, and she reached out to give assistance when she noticed Julia had hit a thigh-high drift that seemed to be an impenetrable wall for her height-challenged friend. In that moment, all she could think about was Marge and wondering if their coworker had made the right choice by returning from Florida. She couldn't fathom why anyone would overwinter in the Northwoods if given a choice. Of course, if it weren't for Nick's arrest, maybe Marge wouldn't have made the decision to return.

Rain tossed the hood of her coat up over her knit hat and pulled the garment closer to her neck, squeezing it tight. She cowered under the weight of the storm as it whipped and thrashed around them.

"Wow. This is incredible, eh? I haven't seen Old Man Winter this bad in years," Julia said through chattering teeth. She reached out to grab Rain by the shoulder to catch up and shuffled to her side. As they approached to within a few yards of their destination, Julia stopped short. She titled her head to the side and eyed the ground beneath them. "Something's missing here."

"What's that? Warmth?" Rain said with a chuckle. "It's freezing out here. We're gonna have to work on fillin' that woodpile by the back door just as soon as we get back to the cabin. That outta be a picnic," she added sarcastically under her breath. "It might take us all night."

"No. Look." Julia pointed to the shanty that had smoke billowing from its roof and then back to the ground. "There's no footprints going to or from here. Or anywhere around, for that matter." Julia spun on her heel one complete turn. "Seth must've started fishing in there hours ago! Oh, Kim's really gonna have his hide." She grimaced. "He could've at least shot her a text, instead of letting his wife worry to death while he's out here playin' around."

"Maybe he lost cell reception out here. With the freezing air, nothing would surprise me." Rain licked her chapped lips.

"It might be cold out here, but I doubt it's cold in there," Julia said, lifting her finger to point out the gray cloud coming from the smokestack. "What's that noise? You hear that?"

Rain zeroed in on the buzzing sound and said, "Sounds like a chainsaw, but I can't imagine anyone would be outside cutting wood today!"

"No, I think it's coming from inside the shanty. Listen."

They both cupped gloved hands to their ears and waited.

When the whistling wind finally subsided and she could clarify what she was hearing, Rain said, "Must be the ice auger. But I have no clue why Seth would be cutting another hole inside the shanty. Wouldn't he already have one cut if he'd been out here for hours fishing already?"

"Maybe he got it stuck? Or he caught something really big that won't fit through the hole."

"Yeah, maybe."

Rain approached and kicked the deepening snow away from the entrance with her boot. She pounded on the door of the shanty with a closed fist, wondering the entire time if Seth would even be able to hear them over the roaring engine. She hoped they wouldn't startle him with their unexpected visit. She also hoped it was indeed Seth's shanty and not some other crazy fisherman who chose to hide away from his family in a freakin' blizzard. But as she turned her head and noticed Wallace's vacant shanty a few yards away, she confirmed that this one was the only one in sight that had smoke billowing from its roof. They had to have the right location.

"Why isn't he answering," Julia closed both her hands into fists and joined Rain in pounding on the door.

"He probably can't hear us," Rain said raising her own voice to compensate for the loud buzzing sound from the motor emanating from the ice shanty.

Julia put her hand on the doorknob and Rain made a face. She hoped for both their sakes they wouldn't startle Seth. Instead, Rain was the one who was startled when Julia thew open the door. The smell of exhaust hit them like a ton of bricks, and Rain waved her hand in front of her face to clear the smell, then blinked her eyes that instantly started to burn. After the smoke had cleared, her eyes refocused. It was then she noticed Seth lying motionless on the icy floor.

Chapter
Twenty-Five

"Seth!" Rain and Julia screamed in unison.

Rain shrieked again, and when their friend didn't flinch from all their commotion, panic rose in her throat.

Please God, tell me we're not too late.

Julia ripped off her gloves and checked his wrist for a pulse. "It's weak, but there's something there, unless it's only blood pumping through my own finger," she added, lifting her glance, to meet Rain's. "My heart is beating a mile a minute—it's hard to tell."

All Rain could think about was Kim and those adorable twins. The image of the three of them standing by the door flashed before her eyes. Rain begged quietly in her mind, *Please, God. Please, please, don't let him die! Not on our watch! Please, God, no!*

The ice auger was set to idle, the blade resting halfway in a newly cut hole of ice, as exhaust plumed the area. Rain rushed to turn it off.

"We gotta get him outta here!" Julia shouted, coughing through the exhaust. "Hurry, help me!"

With Samson-like strength and the power of adrenaline, Rain and Julia lifted Seth beneath his underarms. After a count of three, they gave a momentous tug toward the open door. Although Seth was larger than both of them put together, the bare ice floor of the shanty allowed them to drag his body across the floor and closer to the door.

"Let's get his head outside at least, so he can breathe!" Julia exclaimed, panting from exertion. Neither of them let go, but Rain could feel Seth's dead weight making every muscle in her arms throb.

They pulled and panted but managed to drag Seth's body to the door opening. Rain returned inside and picked up a blanket that had been tossed haphazardly on a wooden stool, and tucked it underneath his head, resting on the snow. She leaned closer and noticed Seth's breath was shallow, but at least there was a hint of something, leaving her with a glimmer of hope. She slapped his cheeks and screamed his name to revive him, but he didn't respond.

"Do you have your phone?" Julia shrieked. "Where's your phone?"

"It's back at the cabin," Rain answered frantically, touching all her pockets to double-check. "I didn't want to drop it in the snow!"

Julia's eyes were wide and wild with frenzy. "Go! Go call for help. I'll stay with him! Go—and hurry!" Julia added, before turning back to Seth, and saying his name repeatedly, "Seth, you with me? Come on, Seth!"

Tears brought on by the wind and cold, and probably fear as well, slid down Rain's face, burning her cheeks. In spite of the cold temperature, she was overheated from the supreme effort required to lift their friend to safety. Her arms still trembled from the exertion, and her legs felt like wobbly Jell-O as she pushed ahead and navigated the path back to the cabin.

This was the last thing she'd expected when they'd gone out in search of Seth. How would she tell Kim? With two small children at home? That her husband might not . . . Rain shook her head anxiously and gulped and choked, fighting for her next breath as the snow kept relentlessly falling. No. She wouldn't let her mind go there . . . With renewed resolve, she squared her shoulders and tripped her way through the snow, moving as fast as humanly possible. When she arrived back at the cabin, she immediately noticed a car was parked in the driveway. She could tell the automobile was still warm, as it wasn't covered in fresh snow. Like a white knight, Jace suddenly appeared at her side. Without a second thought, she threw her arms around his neck, and her whole body started to tremble uncontrollably.

"Rain! What's wrong?" He smoothed her hair away from her eyes and regarded her tenderly.

"It's Seth," she choked out breathlessly. "There's been an accident!" Tears came now, fully running down her face in streams. "He's hurt, I dunno if he's gonna make it." Rain feverishly wiped the tears from her eyes. "We need to call an ambulance!"

Jace ripped his cell from his back pocket and called it in to dispatch. As soon as the call ended, he asked, "Where is he?" His eyes darted the area around them anxiously.

"He's out by his ice shanty, not far from the shoreline. You can't miss it, it's the only one with smoke coming from the roof." Rain pointed to the faint gray line in the sky that looked as if it had been painted there with the stroke of a brush. "Julia's with him now."

Jace glanced to the sky and then quickly turned onto the recent trail of flattened snow Rain had left in her wake.

She followed.

Jace stopped short and put a hand firmly out behind him, as if instructing her to halt, and ordered over his shoulder, "Stay back at the cabin where it's warm."

"No! I will do no such thing! I'm coming with you!"

When he turned back to fully face her, Rain noticed Jace wasn't dressed in his official uniform. Instead, he wore faded jeans and a hunting jacket. She also noticed the shadow beneath his eyes and the fatigue that suffused his face.

"You stay here and wait for the ambulance. Can you do that for me?" he lifted her chin for verification.

Rain nodded. Selfishly, she wished they could stay together; she didn't want to leave his side. But he was right: someone needed to stay back to direct the ambulance personnel where to go.

Jace wiped the tears from her eyes with his thumb. He wasn't wearing gloves, and Rain reached for his hand and squeezed it tight. She was surprised to feel it was still warm. "You need to cover these hands. You can't go down there and wait for an ambulance like that. You'll get frostbite. And your ears . . . they're all red." She reached out to touch one, and it was ice cold.

"I wasn't exactly expecting to stay outside," he said with a slight shrug, quickly digging deep into his pockets and plucking out winter gloves. "I was hoping for a beer by the fire, if I'm being honest."

"Wait here," Rain demanded. She ran through the snow as if she was running in a triple jump race. Only it wasn't hurdles she was navigating but snow piles. She threw open the door to the main cabin and hurried to the closet, not caring that she was leaving a wet mess in her wake. She snatched a winter hat from her father's collection and rushed back out the door. "Here," she said, tossing the hat toward Jace, who caught it with one hand.

His hair was already covered in wet flakes, but he did what she asked and pulled the knit hat tight to his head. "Don't be surprised if it takes the ambulance a bit of extra time, okay? It's brutal out on the roads. Plows are having a hard time keeping up." For a moment, their eyes locked. It was as if he saw her raw fear and wanted to cure it. He reached out a hand to smooth the hair away from her eyes.

"I'm scared, Jace." She blurted. She could feel her lip tremble, and it wasn't from the cold.

He folded her into his arms. "It's going to be okay," he whispered softly into her ear as he stroked her hair. His tenderness was like a soothing balm. He leaned back to verify that she felt safe before he let her go.

He turned on his heel, but Rain stopped him when she hollered, "Wait! What about Kim? What do I tell her?"

Jace turned back to face her as he continued backward down the path. "Don't call her yet. I don't want her out in this weather or out on the roads with the boys. I'll handle it when the ambulance comes. Sit tight on that, okay? We'll call her, I promise—just not yet."

"Yeah, sure, I'll wait on that then," she hollered after him.

Jace left her alone, and all she could do was stand and watch him rush to the shoreline. Rain wrapped her arms protectively around herself, but it did little to relax her. If something happened to Seth, there would be two little orphans left behind in Lofty Pines. And she just wasn't sure she could handle that. But she was forced to think, since their burning questions had yet to be answered, that he might be leaving two little kids behind anyway. Not by his death, but by a life sentence in prison for murder.

Chapter
Twenty-Six

After directing the EMTs where to go, Rain watched the drama unfold from the cabin window as they hurried to retrieve Seth. She observed, via binoculars, the EMTs working quickly to wrap him in blankets and move him carefully to a sled. Then they transported him across the snow, and Rain's heart caught in her throat when she witnessed them pass by her window. His body was so eerily still. Jace and Julia followed numbly behind, shoulders slumped and wearied. Rain rushed out the door in slippered feet to greet them, not caring that her house shoes would be soaked in seconds.

"Is he gonna be okay?" Rain asked, throwing her hands to her heart, and holding clenched hands in anticipation.

"Yeah, they think he'll pull through. He started mumbling down there, so . . ." Julia answered.

"Mumbling?"

"Yeah, a bunch of words that didn't make sense. Mostly moaning sounds," Jace said.

"Except, I swore he said Danny's name once, but Jace didn't hear it, so I can't be sure."

"Oh?" Rain ran her hands up and down her arms, but because of the seriousness of situation, she didn't even feel the cold. "That's interesting."

"That's what I thought," Julia said.

The ambulance pulled out of the driveway, and all that was left in its wake of red flashing lights were three shocked faces. Rain looked down to see the snow seeping past the rubber of her slippers but still didn't feel the cold.

"I still can't believe it," Jace said, removing the winter hat he had borrowed and returning it to Rain. He raked his hand through sweat-soaked hair. "It's not like Seth to be so careless. I just don't understand it."

"I have to agree with you there—it makes no sense," Julia agreed with a downcast shake of her head. "No sense at all."

"Thanks to Julia and her immediate reaction for us to drag him outta there, there's a real good chance he'll pull through this. We have to have faith," Rain reminded them. "He'll be okay," she added, breathing deeply. "I'm just glad we found him when we did. What if we hadn't? I can't even let my mind go there."

"Yeah," Jace put a hand on his sister's shoulder, gave a quick squeeze, and agreed with a look of pride. "Awesome job, Jules."

Julia's response was a heavy sigh and a dismissive wave with her hand. "You better hurry over to Kim's. Are you sure you don't want us to come with you?"

Jace vehemently shook his head and put up a firm hand. "Please stay here. I really don't want anyone else on the roads unless it's absolutely necessary. As much as you'd like to be there for Kim, I think it's safer for you to stay back. And to be frank, I don't need any more worry on my head," Jace added wearily, wiping his hand over his face like a washcloth. "I've had about enough for one day."

"What about the twins?" Rain asked, her glance darting between them. "They can't spend the night at the hospital. Maybe you ought to bring them back here, and Julia and I can watch them."

"That's very kind, but I'm sure Kim's mother can take them. No doubt her parents will be stickin' close to home because of the storm. We'll drop them off when I take Kim over to the hospital," Jace confirmed with a nod. "If we need a plan B, I'll be sure and give you guys a call."

"I wish we could be there when you give her the news. But I agree, telling her over the phone, while she's home alone with the kids, isn't a good idea. She must be frantic by now, not hearing from us." Julia gave her brother a slight nudge toward his car and then opened the driver's side door. "Keep us posted, will you?"

"You bet." Jace lifted his hand in a thumbs-up and then ducked behind the wheel. "Now, get inside before you both freeze to death," he ordered before closing the door.

They watched as he backed his car out of the driveway, following the path that the ambulance had left, so he could navigate between the growing snowdrifts. "We're gonna have to shovel again soon," Rain said heavily. "Look, he can barely get outta there."

"Um, I think you're forgetting something a little more important than that?"

"What's that?"

"The wood pile." Julia frowned.

"Oh, crud." Rain slapped a glove to her forehead. "You're right," she said with a disappointed sigh. "Well, since we're already wet and cold, we may as well do it now."

The two headed in the direction of the woodshed, and Rain veered off toward the boathouse. "I'm gonna go pick up the sled. I'll be right there."

When Rain returned with the sled in tow, she noticed Julia curled over and vomiting in the snow, "Are you okay?"

Julia stood, wiped her mouth, and said, "Yeah. I'm guessing it's just all the stress hitting me hard."

"Oh, my dear friend, I'm sorry. I have to admit, I'm feeling it a bit too. My body is starting to feel like we were in a car accident." Rain noticed a look of guilt wash over Julia's face and prodded for more. "What?"

"Rain, I thought we were gonna lose him! I feel like such a jerk! The whole time all I could think about was what if Seth was involved in Wallace's murder and he doesn't make it? What then? How would we prove Nick is innocent? That's the last thing I should've been thinking when a dear friend is lying lifeless in the snow! I'm a horrible person," she added, as her shoulders sank, and she covered her eyes with her hands.

"Oh Julia, you're not a horrible person. You're just in a difficult situation, and it's starting to wear on you. Go on and head inside. I've got this."

Fat tears began to form in Julia's eyes.

"Maybe some peppermint tea might help. Or I have ginger root in the fridge, if you want to cut a slice and put it in hot water," Rain suggested. "It works for me when I'm feeling sick."

"Are you sure you don't want me to stay out here and help with the wood?"

"Positive! It won't take me long, and I'll be right behind you."

Julia didn't move.

"Go on—get inside where it's warm." Rain waved at Julia with both hands, indicating she should back away from the wood pile. "A hot shower might do you some good. If you decide to go that route, I'll have the tea ready when you get out."

Julia reluctantly turned away from her, but then followed orders and walked slowly toward the cabin.

Rain hurried to do the job, silently crossing her fingers that there would still be a few burning embers inside the fireplace when they returned.

When she finally arrived back inside, she noted that Julia had used the last of the wood that she'd brought in on the first load, and it was roaring inside a cozy fire. Julia rounded the corner with her hair wrapped in a towel.

"That felt amazing," Julia admitted.

"Oh good. I'm glad you're feeling a little better."

"I held off on the tea. I wanted to wait until I got out of the shower so the kettle wouldn't be screaming unattended."

"No worries," Rain said, filling the kettle to reheat on the stove. "Thanks for putting a few logs on."

"Yeah, we arrived in the nick of time. The fire was burning pretty low when I came in. Thanks for bringing a full sled back. You did, didn't you?"

"Uh-huh. But instead of unloading the wood by the door, I just covered the sled with a tarp and left it there. It's not like it's a trip hazard. I doubt we'll have any company tonight."

"That'll work. Besides, I'm not sure about you, but my arms are killing me. I don't even know how you loaded wood right now. I think I used muscles that I didn't even know existed on this body, getting Seth out of that fishing shack."

"Yeah, especially after my fall, my arms still haven't really fully recovered yet either. Honestly, for a second there, I didn't think we'd be able to pull Seth's weight," Rain said with a shudder. "Did you?"

"Let's try not to relive it and just thank our lucky stars we got him out in time. At least, I hope so. Why don't you go and take a shower? I'll watch the kettle."

"You sure? You feel up for that?"

Julia chuckled, "Yeah, I don't think there's much left in my stomach, but I actually feel better."

"Saltines in the cabinet," Rain directed before hitting the bathroom.

Steam filled the shower, and Rain massaged her shoulders as the hot water ran down her back. If Julia hadn't been in the next room, she probably would've opted for a hot bath, but she didn't want to linger, as she wanted to be sure her friend was truly okay. She hadn't admitted it, but the same thought as Julia's had crossed her own mind. If Seth did have something to do with Wallace's death and he died, what then? Would having him in the hospital bring them any closer to the truth? It certainly created a wrinkle to their plan to question him. She dried off and donned a pair of fleece pajamas and a plush robe. She dried her long dark hair by pulling it straight and shimmery with the hairdryer. She no longer wanted to feel even a hint of chill in her bones. By the time she joined Julia by the fire, she was nice and toasty.

"I brought your tea over," Julia said, pointing to the hearth, where a mug sat on a coaster. "I hope you wanted peppermint."

"Sounds perfect," Rain said lifting the mug to her lips.

"I was gonna suggest we head over to the library and pick out a few books for the night, but I don't think I want to venture back out into the cold to get there," Julia said, wrapping a blanket tighter around her shoulders.

"I agree. I think we'll have to stick to what I have over on the shelf, at least for tonight." Rain pointed to a nearby bookshelf where she'd been slowly accumulating her own private collection of favorites. Only books that she would ever choose to reread made the cut.

When Julia stepped over to peruse the shelf, Rain asked. "You want me to whip up something to eat?"

"I think I'll stick to saltines for now."

"Yeah, I don't have much of an appetite either."

"Rain?"

"Yeah?"

"I'm disappointed we didn't get a chance to question Seth."

"Yeah, me too."

"I don't even know where to go from here. It's not like we can question him at the hospital. Especially knowing Kim like I do—she won't leave his side. We might have lost our chance." Julia sounded deflated.

"Maybe not. We'll figure it out," Rain soothed.

Julia's cell phone rang out in song, interrupting them. "It's Jace."

"Put him on speaker."

Julia pressed the button and stood close to Rain. "We're both here. What's the good word? Seth gonna be okay?"

"Yeah, yeah. He'll pull through. And Kim told me to pass on that she thanks you for your heroic efforts. Because according to what the doctor told her, Seth wouldn't have made it if weren't for you two. The doctor said that a few more minutes of exposure to the carbon monoxide would've killed him."

Rain and Julia released their jointly held breath, and Rain clutched her heart before uttering, "Oh, thank God."

"That's not the only reason I called, though."

"You need someone to come and take charge of the twins?" Rain interrupted.

"No. Not that either."

Rain and Julia shared a look of confusion.

"I'm calling to tell you that what happened to Seth was no accident."

"Huh?" Julia asked.

They heard a rustling sound as if Jace had been adjusting something, and then his voice became a mere whisper. "They're doing testing now, but they think a toxic substance was found around his mouth."

Rain and Julia gasped.

Jace continued, "The doctor told Kim that Seth said someone came up behind him and put a rag over his face. That's the last thing he remembered. The idling ice auger was just a ruse, to make it look like an accident."

"Someone wanted to kill him with carbon monoxide!" Julia said, the shock leaving her mouth hanging open.

"And tried to make it look like an accident," Rain added.

"Exactly," Julia and Jace said in unison.

Now more than ever, Rain wondered if Julia had been right and Seth *had* mumbled Danny's name. And what would that mean?

Chapter
Twenty-Seven

Morning streams of light penetrated the window like an unwanted guest, and Rain held the blanket over her eyes for a second to block it. The scent of bacon caught her attention, and she threw back the covers. She slid her feet into fuzzy socks and wrapped herself in a fleece robe to investigate. When she entered the kitchen, she noticed Jace bent over the frying pan and Julia missing from the scene.

He turned upon hearing her feet patter across the wood floor.

"Mornin'."

"Mornin'," Rain said as she self-consciously ran her fingers through her tangled hair. He was the last person on earth she'd expected to find making breakfast in her kitchen. She kinda liked it.

"Julia's in the shower, so I took over the stove. Hope you don't mind," he said, as if reading her thoughts.

"Mind? Why would I mind? I'm starving and it smells so good in here!" she said, moving closer to his side to get a better whiff. Rain held her hair in a makeshift ponytail at the nape of her neck, but she lacked a hairband, so she twisted it up and held it there while she breathed in the smoky scent.

Jace set down a fork aside the stove, and turned to her fully. "I hope I didn't wake you," he said with a slight hesitation that surprised her. "You look beautiful first thing in the morning, by the way."

Rain blushed. He must've noticed her surprise and, embarrassed by his show of feelings, overcompensated by ruffling the top of her head as if she were his sister.

Part of her wanted to lean into him and linger there, to feel his warm body next to hers. One of the things she'd missed the most since losing Max was the feeling of being held protectively by strong, solid arms.

"When did you get in?"

Jace's eyes glanced over to the digital numbers on the microwave. "Looks like I've been here for about a half hour. Spent the night in a hospital chair, until Kim convinced me to go home. But I came here instead."

"You haven't slept?"

"I think I may have caught a few hours in the chair at the hospital," he said with a slight smile, and then rubbed his eyes with one hand.

Rain noticed the weariness in his eyes and the deep furrow to his forehead, and gestured for him to take a seat. "Let me take over. I didn't even know I had bacon; Julia must've bought it when she picked up a few things," she said over her shoulder. Jace acquiesced, and she took over tending the stove.

"Actually, I brought the bacon. I stopped for a few essentials because I wasn't sure what you had on hand—or if you two would be able to get out," he said, plopping onto the kitchen stool that flanked the island. "But when I pulled into the driveway, I realized it was the right move. You're buried out there."

"You're unbelievable," Rain mumbled, shaking her head.

"What?" Jace defended. "You're mad I didn't plow you out—on top of everything else?"

"No, on the contrary." Rain turned from the stove to face him and held out a warning finger. "You need to take care of yourself, Jace. Haven't you heard about putting your own oxygen mask on first? You should be home, getting some rest. Instead, you're over here making breakfast. I'm afraid you're gonna crash!"

Jace chuckled, "How about' that . . . worried about little ole me?" he teased. Which made Rain's face flush again, so she returned her attention to the bacon, to hide her feelings.

"Any change in Seth's condition? He still holdin' up all right? I should've asked straight off, but forgive me. I'm not much good before my first cup of coffee," Rain admitted with a yawn. She reached for a coffee pod and popped it into the machine. "You want a cup?"

"Actually, I'll have decaf tea if you've got any."

"Tea, huh? Interesting. I wouldn't have taken you for a tea guy," Rain said under her breath as she opened the cabinet to share the options. "Learn something new about a person every day." She looked at him, and they shared a grin.

"I'll take the chamomile," he said, pointing his finger.

Rain removed a teabag and tossed it into an oversized mug while waiting for the water to reheat.

"I kinda overdid the coffee intake at the hospital," he confessed as he held out his hand, which showed a bit of tremor. "Another reason, it'll take me a few more hours before I can get some real shut-eye." He chuckled.

"I just want you to know, I appreciate your service. I know nowadays that seems to go unnoticed from the general public. But I notice." Rain jutted a thumb to her chest. "I can't imagine choosing to put your life on the line day after day when people can be so thankless. What you do out there is admirable."

"Mornin'," Julia said, interrupting them when she walked into the kitchen. "You didn't share any news with her yet, did you?" she asked accusingly, with her eye lasered in on her brother. "You said you wouldn't share a *thing* until we were all here together."

"I just woke up," Rain answered as she removed the bacon from the stove and placed it on a paper towel–lined plate that one of them had already placed there. "Would you like your eggs sunny-side up?"

Both Jace and Julia agreed with a nod. "Whatever's quick and easy," Jace said, lifting from the stool and stealing a piece of bacon from the plate.

Rain cracked a few eggs into the hot pan, directly into the bacon grease, and Jace approved with a clap of his hands. "Bravo, my girl. I would've thought you wouldn't dare cook those eggs in grease," he said with a laugh.

Julia added in a teasing tone. "I know, right? It's sickening how she stays thin. After breakfast, I'll immediately have already gained five pounds!"

"You do like your donuts," Jace reminded her.

"Yeah, I most certainly do," Julia admitted with a giggle as she took the spatula from Rain's hand and took over flipping the eggs. "But this protein is better for me than all that powdered sugar."

"Thanks—I always break the yolks when I try to turn the eggs over," Rain admitted, pointing to the eggs Julia had expertly flipped inside the pan.

"All right, fill us in now. How's Seth?" Julia asked over her shoulder. "All I got outta you on your arrival was that he's alive, and strict orders from you to go take a shower." She grinned. "Look, I'm all dressed and ready for the day."

"He's okay. I didn't get to talk to him, if that's what you were counting on. I know you were expecting me to interrogate him, but I never got the chance."

"Rats," Julia said, deflated. Then she slid the eggs onto plates, balanced them on her arms like an experienced waitress, and brought them over to the table. Rain followed with the platter of bacon and cutlery. The three took a seat and immediately dug into the food like a hungry pack of wolves.

"He was in the pressurized oxygen chamber until I left," Jace said between bites. "At least, that's what the doctor told me. He wasn't allowed visitors."

"How scary!" Julia grimaced. "I hate hospitals."

"We know," Rain and Jace said in unison, sharing an amused, conspiratorial look.

"Well, listen to you two!" Julia teased. "You're starting to sound like Rainy and me." Julia winked at her brother, and then her gaze dropped back to her plate of food.

"How long does he have to be in there?" Rain asked.

"I'm not sure, but supposedly it helps the heart and brain, which are particularly vulnerable after experiencing carbon monoxide poisoning. But the doctor thinks Seth'll make a full recovery. Thanks to you two," Jace said with a smile. "Otherwise"—his smile faded, and he took another bite of egg—"things could've ended badly."

"I'm still pretty shook up over it," Rain admitted. "I kept going over it in my mind every time I rolled over last night." She cracked her neck from side to side and then rolled her head in one continuous circle. Her body ached from every muscle being on high alert the previous day.

"Me too. All I kept picturing was Seth lying on the ground, so lifeless," Julia said with a shudder, and then turned her attention on her brother. "You mentioned this was no accident. What are the police doing? I'm guessing they're investigating this as a crime now too?" she asked.

"Yeah, you bet they are. That was another reason I hung around the hospital last night. I wanted to get their take on it."

"And?" Julia rolled her hand in the air impatiently.

"Clearly they think it's connected. The evidence certainly seems to point in that direction."

"How so?" Rain asked. "I mean, did they test Seth for chloroform too, since they found it on Wallace, to see if there's a connection?"

"Yeah, but the results aren't in yet. However, Seth told the doctor that a figure wearing a dark ski mask entered his shanty and put a rag over his mouth, and that's the last thing he remembers. Sounds like chloroform to me, or some other substance that would render someone unconscious. If we find out it was indeed chloroform, we'd have to conclude it was Wallace's killer. It's just a little too coincidental, don't you think?" he added with a lift of his brow.

"Ski mask is all he remembers. So, he didn't say, tall, short, stocky—one arm maybe?" Julia asked, and Jace replied with a disapproving stare.

"Hey, I'm not trying to be rude at all. Scratch that. I'm just trying to find out if Danny had anything to do with this?" Julia said defensively as she leaned in closer. "Did he?"

"Nope. Seth didn't say. But again, the police weren't able to question him fully yet. Doctor's orders," he said, lifting another piece of bacon from the plate and chewing on it contemplatively.

Rain looked at Julia and she could tell by the look on her friend's face, she wasn't buying it. They both wondered about the rumored mumblings of Danny's name.

"How's Kim holdin' up?" Rain asked.

"About as good as can be expected. Obviously, she's freaked out by the whole ordeal."

"Yeah, we'll have to call her soon," Julia said, "Or better yet, if the storm lays off, maybe we should go see her."

Jace's cell phone buzzed from his pocket, and he reviewed the caller before telling them, "It's the station. I have to take this."

Chapter
Twenty-Eight

Julia drummed her fingers atop the kitchen table as they waited for Jace to finish his phone call, and Rain felt every bit of anxiety oozing from her friend. The two watched attentively as his face morphed from confusion to elation and then back to a furrowed brow. The wait was excruciating. Julia seemed like she could hardly wait another second as she abandoned her spot at the table and paced a hole in the floor, waiting for answers. Rain decided she'd be more productive with her nervous energy by removing their empty plates and loading them into the dishwasher. But she, too, was compelled to try and gauge the updated news from Jace's one-sided answers. There were a lot of *uh-huh's* and *yeah's*, and *okay's* before he finally ended the call. Julia immediately halted her pacing, and Jace summoned Rain back over to the table, where the three huddled together. Rain could hardly wait for him to speak.

"Good news!" Jace broke out in a wide grin as he wiped his hands vigorously together as if anticipation of something big. "I can't tell you what a huge relief this is!"

"What?" Julia said impatiently, sitting higher in the chair and flattening her hands against the table. She leaned in closer to her brother, as if not to miss a single beat.

"Nick's being released!"

"Whoop!" Julia raised a clenched fist and then started punching the air above her head while she continued to squeal in delight. "Yes! Yes! Yes!" she said, rising from the chair, and pushing it aside, as if she could no longer sit and contain her excitement.

Rain was relieved but also cautious. She hoped Nick's release wasn't only to appease the district attorney and give the police more time to continue to collect evidence against him and solidify the case even further. She'd seen stuff like that happening on crime shows, where they'd let the suspect go, but then continue to trail him everywhere. That's the last thing she wanted, for Julia to have such high hopes, thinking that Nick was totally in the clear, and then to be slammed back to harsh reality again.

"So, apparently, the murder weapon was tested, and only one DNA sample of human blood was found . . . and that was Nick's. The rest of the blood found on the knife was fish blood."

Julia halted her happy dance, and then Rain and Julia shared a look of confusion.

Jace continued with a roll of his hand, "Meaning, neither Wallace's blood nor a speck of his DNA was found anywhere on the blade of the knife. The police don't think the knife the police found in Nick's gear is the murder weapon. We all know there's a chance someone planted it there anyhow. Especially when Nick has been claiming all along that he never had seen that fillet knife in his life, I think the police are starting to believe him. He's always used the same brand of fish gutting knife, which is a Smith and Wesson Extreme Ops. I should know—I bought it for him for his birthday last year. And the one they found in his gear, well . . . that one's not it. So, there's that in his favor too." He lifted a hand in defense. "Maybe my buddies down at the station will actually believe me now."

This information allowed Rain to relax a bit, knowing Nick's freedom was more secure than she'd originally thought.

Julia jumped up and down, and jubilation filled her face as if she'd just won a lottery jackpot. "I knew it! I just knew it!"

"Well, not to be a killjoy here, but if Nick was planning on killing someone, I think he'd be smarter than to use his own Smith and Wesson fillet knife. Wouldn't he?"

Julia stopped her animated dance and squarely faced Rain. "What are you saying?"

Rain put her hands up in defense. "Julia. You know for a fact that I don't believe Nick committed this crime. I'm merely saying that it's hard to prove someone planted it in his tackle box. It's a proof issue, is what I'm getting at. How are we gonna find this person, and furthermore *prove* the knife was planted."

"She's right, Jules. The knife handle was wiped clean of prints. Only Nick's blood was found on the blade. Which again, is in Nick's favor as his prints weren't found on the handle either."

"Well, you two certainly know how to kill a party!" Julia's hands landed on her hips and she stuck her tongue out teasingly at them. "You're still looking at Nick as a potential suspect? When your own department is ready to release him?" She shot a look at her brother. "Seriously?"

"No, that's not what he's saying. Look. I'm only playing devil's advocate here. I don't want them to release Nick on lack of evidence and then turn around and bring him right back in after digging for more, you know? I just want him to come home and never go back there again. *Ever!*" Rain added with emphasis as she slammed a commanding fist to the table. "The point is, we still need to solve this case."

"So, what do we do now?" Julia folded her hands across her chest and waited. "How do we make sure Nick stays in the clear?"

"The police are surmising that a duplicate knife was used, as the blade found in Nick's tackle is the same size as the one that made the fatal wound, and they can't figure this part out yet. They're checking all stores within a fifty-mile radius to see if matching knives were purchased, but that takes time. If they can find a store that carries this particular fillet knife, and two that were purchased under one receipt, they're hoping maybe we'd get closer to our killer. They're figuring maybe the murder weapon was tossed down the fishing hole. There's talk they might even send out a dive team to look for it."

"A dive team?" Rain asked. "Wow, I wouldn't want to be the one diving under the ice right about now," she added with a shiver. "That sounds miserable."

"Yeah, no kiddin'. That'll take a bit of time too. We don't have anyone that's qualified to do that here in Lofty Pines. I'm sure it'll take at least a few days to round up a crew. Especially, like you say, in the weather conditions we're facing here." Jace frowned. "The bummer is, the longer this goes unsolved, the harder it is to find the actual killer," he added with a hint of discouragement. "And like you said, Rain, it doesn't completely remove Nick from the suspect list. As of right now, they just don't have enough to hold him. But that could change . . . we just have to clear him of this once and for all."

Rain moved over to the fireplace and returned with their crime board and set it down on the kitchen table. "We need to figure this out then. Who's left on our suspect list? Do we take Seth off because he was attacked and therefore another victim in this case? Or should we wait?"

"Not so fast, my friend," Julia answered. "Seth's still got some explainin' to do."

"Yeah, I have to agree with you there. We still need to talk to him, to rule him out completely. And maybe something he shares could tip us off to more." Rain turned her attention to Jace. "Any chance the doctor will let him have visitors today? Maybe we should give the hospital a call?"

"I have no idea, but Kim did mention that if all went well, the doc would probably be willing to release him as early as tomorrow . . . which, by the way, is now today," Jace said with a chuckle and a stifled yawn.

"That's good news." Rain tapped a finger to her lips. "I'm thinking we should make a casserole or something to bring over to their house. It might make him feel better. Besides, it'll help out Kim a ton, I'm sure."

"Or soup!" Julia piped up. "Let's deliver him some chicken soup. Oh, and one more thing?"

"Yeah?" Rain asked.

"Can you take the enchilada lasagna back out of the freezer? My husband's coming home!" Julia pumped her fists in excitement. "And nothin' either one of you say is gonna rain on my parade!" Julia squealed and then clasped her hands to her heart. Her grin was radiant and contagious.

"You bet." Rain winked. She wished she could feel as elated as her best friend regarding Nick's release. But without another suspect in custody, or even one on the horizon, she still felt the storm clouds looming overhead. Like another round of thundersnow might just be on its way.

Chapter Twenty-Nine

Because of the limited resources of the Lofty Pines police department, Jace had no other choice than to go home, grab some quick shut-eye, and prepare for another looming beat shift. After he dropped Nick off at the cabin, Rain watched as husband and wife reunited.

Julia and Nick clung to each other until Rain teased, "All right already, get a room, will ya?"

They both turned to her and grinned but remained attached, with Nick's arm hanging loosely over his wife's shoulder.

"Honestly, babe, if I wasn't so doggone tired, I'd have to agree with Rainy." He wiped a hand across his face wearily. The bags under his eyes were evident, and his complexion was pale, as if he were getting sick.

"Plenty of time for that," Julia soothed.

"Yeah, it sure looks like you could use a little rest," Rain said.

"I don't think I've had a decent night's sleep since this whole ordeal began," he admitted easily with a chuckle.

"We're heading over to see how Seth is doing. You wanna stay here and go to bed?" Julia asked.

Nick waffled by shaking his head back and forth before saying, "Yeah, I'm gonna have to hold off on that for now. I'm worried about him, but I'm a little ticked at the moment that Seth threw me under the bus. I think it would be smart if I rested up before I see him face to face. I might not handle myself well otherwise."

"Totally understand," Julia said with a quick glance to Rain. "She's seen me lose it a few times now already."

"It's all good," Rain said before they accompanied Nick to the door.

Nick turned to Rain and the two embraced. "Good to have you home, my friend," she said, holding him at arm's length.

"I can't even express how good it is to be home! And thanks for taking care of this one for me," Nick said with a nod to his wife. "I'll see you back at the house. I'm hitting the hay, like immediately. Wake me when you get back, okay?"

Julia nodded and then they watched as Nick trudged across the snow to home. A sigh of relief to have him finally heading safely where he belonged. *Home.*

* * *

Rain and Julia stood on the threshold of Seth and Kim's house. When their friend opened the door, Rain took a step backward. Kim was dressed in stained sweats, her hair was tucked randomly into an old baseball hat, and the dark circles around her eyes were so sunken, it made her look like a racoon. Kim always looked so put together that Rain's attention was drawn to the drastic change.

"Hey, thanks for checking in on us," Kim said as she opened the door wider and helped them inside by removing a grocery bag from each of their hands.

"We weren't sure what the kids like to eat, but we picked up fixings for peanut butter and jelly or grilled cheese," Julia said, lifting the other bag.

"Sounds perfect, I can't thank you enough."

"We also made some soup. It's still warm, if you're hungry." Rain pointed to the paper bag that held the thermos.

Seth lay on the couch with the TV remote dangling from one hand. He turned his head and greeted them with a slight smile. After lowering the volume to the television to silent, he said, "I guess I owe you guys my life." He set the remote on the carpeted floor and slowly lifted himself up to a seated position, with a grunt.

"You don't have to get up for us—just relax," Julia said, putting out a hand to encourage him to do just that.

"Where are the boys?" Rain asked.

"I just put them down for a nap, which is where I'm headed soon too." Kim answered with a long sigh, and then her gaze landed on her husband. "Just as soon as I get this guy something to eat."

"Go now," Rain encouraged. "Let us take care of him for a bit. As I said, we already have soup made. Just show me to the kitchen, for a bowl, and we'll take over."

Kim looked wearily at her husband for permission, and he replied with a wave of his hand. "Yeah, go get some rest, hon, I'll be fine. As a matter of fact, I can take care of myself. None of you need to hover."

"Are you sure? I feel like I'm being totally rude."

Rain rushed to Kim's side and removed the grocery bags from her hands. "On second thought, let me take that to the kitchen. I'm sure you haven't slept, and if the boys just went down, you should grab your chance. Go on—we got this," she encouraged.

Kim nodded resignedly. "Thanks for understanding. I'm about ready to pass out," she admitted with a slight smile.

"Go," Julia ordered. "We'll take care of your husband," she said as she shot Rain a conspiratorial smile before heading in the direction of the kitchen. Kim, on the other hand, headed the opposite direction toward her bedroom, leaving Rain alone with Seth.

"How ya feeling?"

"Grateful to be alive." He grunted, then looked appreciatively in her direction. "I can't thank you enough."

"Do you have any idea who would've wanted to do this?"

"Nah, but I know the police think it has something to do with Wallace's murder. Which has nothing to do with me, I can promise you that," he said, scratching the back of his neck. "I don't get it."

"Do you remember mumbling Danny's name? Did he do it?"

"I don't exactly remember mumbling Danny's name, but I do remember him stopping by my fishing hole. He wanted me to make him a box of my specialty fishing lures. The rest of the day is a blur, I can't remember nothin'."

"Nothing?" Rain repeated, and moved to sit across from him in a recliner. She clasped her hands in front of her and leaned forward expectantly. "Are you sure about that?" She purposely softened her tone. "Look, Seth, we all know there's something you're not telling us. You can trust us. We're your friends!"

"What do you mean?"

"I mean, Wallace wasn't a stranger to you, was he?"

Julia entered the room, carrying a bowl of soup and a spoon. "Here we are," she said, and Rain rushed to find a nearby TV tray for her to set it down on. Julia placed the soup directly in front of Seth, and he settled in front of it.

"Thanks," he said appreciatively. "I'm hungry, but I didn't dare ask Kim to do another thing for me. She literally worried herself sick. This whole ordeal has really freaked her out," he said, and then immediately lifted the spoon to his mouth, blowing softly on the hot liquid.

"I was just asking Seth here about his relationship with Wallace."

"I didn't have a relationship with the guy," Seth defended. "I only met him a handful of times."

"Why didn't you say that when Jace questioned you?" Julia pressed.

"He never asked!" Seth answered before putting the spoon down to rest beside the bowl on the tray table. He wafted his hand over the steaming bowl, to cool the soup down.

"He never *asked*. And you didn't think to mention it?" Julia said sarcastically, throwing up her hands as her eyes rose to the ceiling.

"Yeah, okay, I never offered it up," he admitted.

"Why?" Rain asked.

"I wasn't about to do that"—he lowered his voice to a whisper, his eyes darting around the space, seemingly to be certain

Kim hadn't returned—"so I could be accused of murder too. Not a chance."

"Instead, you let Nick take the hit," Julia said with a sigh of resignation.

"No. Hey. Wait a minute." Seth put up a hand in defense and sat up straighter. "Look Julia, I have two small kids and a wife to support. I'm sorry but—"

"So did you do it?"

Rain couldn't believe Julia's bluntness. Her mouth dropped open, and stunned silence ensued.

Finally, Seth rallied. "Yeah, and I knocked myself out with chloroform too, and then I attempted suicide with my own ice auger. Really, Julia? You have some nerve."

Rain cleared her throat. "I think she's just upset because of everything Nick has gone through. She didn't mean it. Right, Julia?" Rain elbowed her friend, who now stood next to her with closed fists by her sides.

"I thought you were our friend," Julia said as her eyes suddenly filled, and she momentarily turned away from him, as if she couldn't tolerate another second of this conversation.

"I *am* your friend. And I'm sorry I never told you or Jace, or anyone. I was only trying to protect my family."

"Then how does Kim not know Wallace? Or Tina? Or is she lying to us too?" Julia asked, her tone now morphing from anger to sadness.

"I've never met Tina before," Seth said.

"Try again, Seth," Julia said with an eyeroll. "We saw you coming out of her house the other day. Don't even try and hide it."

The look of shock on his face did not go unnoticed. He turned ashen. "You don't understand."

Rain thought he looked defeated, like he was a husband caught with his pants down around his ankles.

"Try me." Julia softened.

"It's not what you think. I wasn't having an affair or anything like that."

This caused Julia to smile and shake her head disapprovingly. "That was the absolute last thing that crossed my mind! But you were *there*, at Tina's house, and we want to know why." She folded her arms across her chest and then took a seat beside him on the couch. "Come on—spill it, Seth."

Seth took a deep breath and then let the air out slowly. "Remember a few months ago when Kim went to visit her sister down in Milwaukee with the kids, and I stayed back to fix the roof?"

"Yeah." Julia's brows furrowed, and she threw an incredulous look to Rain. "What does that have to do with anything?"

"Let him finish," Rain said.

"I hired someone to fix the roof, and I went fishing with a few buddies instead."

"Still not following," Julia said impatiently, tapping her foot on the floor.

"My buddy Travis had heard Wallace was outta work and was picking up odd jobs. Travis convinced me to have Wallace do the work. And I never paid him for it."

"You didn't? Why not?" Rain asked.

"'Cause he wouldn't take cash. Wallace said he was trying to establish a new handyman business and he wanted to be on the up-and-up. But I told him I refused to pay with a check because I didn't want Kim to know. We argued about it for months, the self-righteous jerk."

"But you went to Tina's . . . why? The man's dead. I doubt he'd be sending you a bill," Julia said with a mocking laugh.

"Worse. He said he was putting a lien on our property! I went over there looking for the paperwork, to verify if he had. Because if he did, I'd have some serious explaining to do to my wife."

"And did he?" Rain asked.

"I don't know. Tina kicked me out before I got an answer."

Julia put her head in her hands and wiped her eyes. "So, instead, you let Nick get arrested," she finally said, shaking her head in disapproval. "When you were clearly the one with the stronger motive."

"It's not like I was intentionally trying to get Nick in trouble, Julia. I just knew what it looked like, so I kept my mouth shut. I understand people might see it as a motive to hurt someone, but I did no such thing."

"You think?" Julia said, huffing out a breath.

"You're mad at me," Seth said, looking at Julia with puppy-dog eyes.

"I'm not mad at you, I understand why you did what you did. I'm just frustrated with the situation," Julia said as her body deflated like a popped balloon.

"You're not gonna tell Kim about this, are you?" Seth asked sheepishly.

"It doesn't matter now. What matters is that the same person who tried to hurt you also murdered Wallace, so we need to find the common denominator," Rain said, breathing deeply. "That, my dear friends, is what we need to focus on."

"What about Danny? I swore I heard you say his name when you were hurt. Why would you bring up his name? Did you?" Julia asked.

"Yeah, we already spoke about that. He was making Danny a set of lures," Rain said.

"Well, if we're being totally honest, there's a little more to it than that," Seth said with a resounding sigh.

"What did I miss here?" Rain asked.

Seth cleared his throat. "I had gone over to speak with Wallace a few weeks before he was murdered and parked out on the road. Their garage was open, and I overheard Tina telling Wallace to stop paying him."

"Stop paying him? You mean *Danny*?" Julia asked.

"Yeah, I don't know what he was paying the guy for, but it was clearly a hot button between them. I walked back to my car and got outta there. Look, I wasn't about to get into the middle of a heated argument between husband and wife. Trust me, I've learned from my own experience when to keep my mouth shut."

Rain looked to Julia for wordless confirmation, because in her mind that piece of information changed everything. If Danny was no longer going to receive a payoff from Wallace, maybe he did have a motive for murder after all.

Chapter Thirty

The snow had finally stopped, and an icy coat covered the road like a glazed donut, leaving ruts in spots, that made the ride a rocky one. Rain looked out the window, searching for answers, and then back to her friend. "I don't even know where to go from here. Do you?"

"I agree. I feel like we're right back to square one in this investigation," Julia said with a hint of frustration as she navigated the truck around a large chunk of snow that was evidently leftover from a neighboring driveway, because the heap of snow was abandoned clearly in the road. They had left Seth and Kim's house in a haze of disappointment. Although they'd had a chance to question their friend, it had led them nowhere closer to the perpetrator. If anything, it had only brought on more dead-end leads—not to mention their disappointment in Seth, as he had basically thrown Nick under the bus.

"The only thing that's crossed my mind is if Wallace thought he might put a lien on Seth and Kim's property, maybe there's someone else in Lofty Pines that he threatened with that? Could that be possible? I wish we could dig into his paperwork and see."

"But that would require us to go back to Tina's, and I don't see how we'd even get past the front step. Just because she apologized, it doesn't exactly mean the three of us are friends." Julia said, finishing Rain's thought for her.

"Yep."

"Unless . . ."

"Unless what?"

"We break in," Julia said defiantly. "At night, after Tina's asleep."

Rain cleared her throat, "You want to do *what*? I think you've officially lost your mind, my friend."

"Hey, it's like you said. Unless we find out who's behind this, Nick will always have a target on his back. Not to mention, everyone in Lofty Pines will think my husband got away with murder. He'll always be accused in everyone's mind, even if he hasn't been convicted for this. It'll never go away."

"I said that?" Rain asked, turning to her.

"Maybe not in so many words," Julia said, gripping her hands tighter on the steering wheel.

"I'm not sure breaking and entering is such a hot idea. You're gonna have to come up with a plan B."

"You have any other ideas? 'Cause I'm out!" Julia said with a resounding sigh.

Rain put her head in her hands and rubbed her eyes. "Now that Nick has been released, maybe Tina would be open to talking to us again. I mean, why wouldn't she? Especially if she thinks we're on her side—which we are. We all want the same thing . . . don't we? And that's justice for Wallace. Besides, she took the first step by coming to the library. Maybe we're totally overthinking this."

"I suppose. All we can do is try, right?"

"Right—what do we have to lose? Who knows? Maybe she'll open up like a flower this time."

"Highly unlikely." Julia looked out the rearview mirror and then pulled a U-turn in the middle of the road.

"What are you doing?"

"Going to Tina's house," Julia said adamantly. "No time like the present."

"Indeed," Rain said, breathing deeply. She knew in that moment Julia's mind was made.

*　*　*

When they arrived at their destination, it was evident that either no one was home or Tina hadn't been outdoors in quite a while, as snowdrifts blanketed her driveway. Julia kept the truck in idle while she seemed to weigh the option of whether she should just drive right over the drift.

"How about we start off on the right foot by helping her out? You remember how to run that thing?" Rain pointed to the plow control located on the floor between the two seats. "Maybe she'll approach us in a better mood if she knows we did her a solid."

Julia pushed forward on the lever to drop the plow. "Voilà!" she said with a grin. "I'm actually getting used to this thing, thanks to Ryan's lesson. He's a much better teacher than my impatient husband. I'll be an expert before long," she added before making swipes across the driveway.

As the plow continued to hit the ground, Rain was surprised Tina hadn't come to the front door to see who was doing the work. Maybe she was in the back of the house and couldn't hear? Or maybe she wasn't home after all? Although Rain couldn't understand where she could've possibly gone in a blizzard. Julia finished the entire driveway after a few sweeps, and there was still no sign of Tina.

"Do you think she'll be a little more gracious this time, since we plowed her out?" Julia lifted the plow via the lever and then jammed the truck into park. "Maybe now she'll consider us friends?" Julia grinned.

"One can only hope," Rain said as she opened the door and a rush of cold wind filled the truck. "Don't go telling me you're getting cold feet now that we're here."

"She was a little scary the other day," Julia admitted before joining Rain outside. "It's like she has multiple personalities and you're never really sure who you're gonna get."

"I don't suppose you have a shovel in the back?" Rain noticed the steps leading to Tina's steps had snow that was deeper than Julia's knees in spots, and she wasn't sure if she should carry her friend piggyback, to avoid it.

"No such luck," Julia frowned, and then plowed right through, using her feet. After she arrived at the top step, where the drifts hadn't quite reached, she immediately brushed the snow from her jeans and then hit the doorbell.

When Rain joined her on the step and stomped the snow from her own boots, she noticed Julia still fumbling with the doorbell.

"I think it's broken; I'm not hearing anything. Are you?" Julia proceeded to open the storm door to knock on the interior door. When she did so, the wooden door slowly creaked open.

"Oh nooo." Rain lifted a hand to her cheek. "Now we've done it." She added in a whisper through gritted teeth, "She's gonna think we purposely opened the door!" Rain bit down on her curled finger, waiting for the scolding to come.

Except no one came to the door.

"Tina?" Rain finally called out with trepidation.

"Tina, are you in there?" Julia hollered.

Still no answer.

Julia used this as an excuse to knock the snow off her boots and then step over the threshold.

"What are you doing?" Rain hissed.

"I'm going inside."

"You can't do that! What if she comes home and finds us in her house?" Rain said as she reached to grab Julia by the arm, to stop her. But it was too late. Julia had already stepped inside and rounded the corner behind the door.

"Then I guess we'll deal with that when the time comes," Julia answered, removing her boots and leaving them to drain on the inside mat. "Besides, the snow just stopped. So, wherever she is, she's probably hunkered down for at least a few more minutes. Look, there are no lights on in here. She's not here, Rain. And Wallace won't be comin' back either," she added gravely. "Just remember, that's why we're here."

Rain was horrified. And terrified. And ashamed that they were standing inside Tina's house without permission.

And yet, just like when they were youngsters, Julia could get her to do just about anything. Even if it got the two of them in trouble. Curiosity finally got the best of Rain, and she found herself following suit and removing her boots. "Well, at least we're conscientious burglars. Since we're not leaving a mess, maybe the police will give us time served for good behavior when we go to jail over this." Rain elbowed Julia, and then pointed to their boots lined up like soldiers and let out a nervous giggle. "I can't believe we're actually doing this."

"It's not like we're here to steal anything. We're here to help. Let's focus on that and keep *that* our end game mindset."

"I recall a time that you convinced me to steal the neighbor's canoe and do a lap around Pine Lake on a dare. Do you remember that?" Rain asked. "I got in so much trouble."

"We didn't steal it—we *borrowed* it," Julia reminded her. "And look, you did the dare, so . . ."

"Or the time we broke into that cottage. The one with the red roof? Remember that? That was totally your idea too." Rain frowned. "Luckily, on that one we never got caught."

"Rain," Julia huffed, "we didn't break in. If you recall, the door was broken off, and the fire department was doing a controlled burn on the place the very next week. We were just checking it out to see if anything of any value had been left inside by Old Man McCall after he died."

"Whatever." Rain rolled her eyes. "That's not the point. The point is, we shouldn't be doing this, Jules."

Julia clutched the sleeve of Rain's jacket and gave a hard tug. "Come on, we're wasting precious time. The sooner we do this, the sooner we leave. Let's stop the chitchat and hurry. Boots are off."

Rain looked down at her feet and curled her toes. She couldn't believe she was allowing Julia to talk her into this.

The two tiptoed into a front room where a large screen TV hung above the fireplace. To the side of it, a school of fish, painted a rainbow of colors, swam across the muraled wall. The two reclining chairs that were planted in front of the television were well worn, yet the couch that was against the wall was covered in muted pillows that seemed to be only for decoration. Clay figurines of large and small fish peppered the space, from the base of the fireplace to the walls. It seemed fish were everywhere.

"You think Tina made those?" Rain asked, pointing to one. "Didn't she say she was an artist or something?"

"I dunno about you, but I feel like I'm in an aquarium. It's definitely original," Julia answered out of the side of her mouth.

"I don't think we're gonna find anything of value in here. Let's keep moving," Rain said, scanning the room, giving it one last look before leading them to the adjacent one.

A home office was set up in the small space, with just enough room for a large desk and a rocking chair. Boxes and sheets of paper made it look as if a hoarder lived in the room or the space was being used as a closet. Except the office space wasn't closed off to the rest of the house. A bookshelf was tucked along the wall, with books haphazardly stacked on its shelves and tossed atop it. The librarian in her made Rain want to go and organize it by genre, or re-shelve the books according to size or color—anything to create order. She found herself literally taking a step backward in an attempt to hold herself back.

"This place is a freakin' mess," Julia said. "There's papers everywhere! We're never gonna even make a dent in these piles."

"I know. I feel claustrophobic in here. I'm guessing Seth isn't gonna have to worry about a lien being filed. I doubt you could find anything in this room," Rain said, lifting a sheet of paper off the desk. She looked at the paper in her hand and then set it aside. "An electric bill from last month. This place needs an overhaul!"

"We could be here all day and still not get through all this paperwork," Julia said as she flipped through a stack that had been piled high on the desk. "This looks like invoices for plaster and paint. I'm assuming they must be receipts for Tina's tax write-offs or something. Does she sell the stuff? Or is it just a hobby, you think?"

The furnace kicked on, and the rumble of it was startling. Rain's ears suddenly heightened to overdrive. A noise beyond the room caused her spine to go rigid. "Did you hear that?"

"Sounded like a car door slamming."

Rain pounced to the window and took a quick glance beyond the curtain. She noticed a familiar blue truck with lettering on the side that she assumed said "Wright Installation." A familiar figure soon entered the house across the street.

"It's Ryan," she whispered. "He must be doing a quote or an install across the street."

"Or he's following you." Julia's brow rose teasingly.

"Yeah, that's it." Rain answered sarcastically. "Just keep looking, will ya."

Rain pulled out the middle drawer beneath the desk and a legal document stared back at her. "Wait. This could be a lien—it looks formal," she said excitedly. "Julia, I think I've got something!" When her eyes scanned the top line, she realized otherwise. "No, it's not a lien—it's divorce papers. Wallace was filing for divorce!"

"Let me see that!"

Julia's eyes darted over the paperwork, and she flipped through the stack of papers until she reached the end. "Rain, these aren't signed yet. Tina might not even know about it." She handed the documents back to Rain.

"How could she *not* know about it? I found 'em right there in the desk. And come to think of it, even her neighbors thought they were on the outs, because Cassie's grandmother told me Tina and Wallace might have been on the brink of divorce when I met her over at the library."

"Well, out of the two of them, it looks like Wallace was the organized one, because all the papers I've sifted through so far seem to be hers. And that pile, my friend, is a disastrous mess."

"So that's what the note was about," Rain said under her breath.

"Note?"

"Yeah, didn't I tell you? Wallace left me a handwritten note inside one of the cookbooks he had borrowed and alluded to the fact that he knew now what he had to do. I bet he was talking about signing those papers!" Rain said, reaching out again to reread them.

"Could be," Julia agreed with a nod. "Could it be we also uncovered a new motive for murder?"

"I haven't a clue . . . It's hard to be sure. Like you said, did Tina even open those drawers? It looks to me that her stuff was a heap of a mess." Rain dropped the papers to her side. "But one thing I remember after reading all those mystery novels off the library shelves is that love can prove a far more dangerous motive than hate. We might be onto something."

Chapter
Thirty-One

"Let's put these papers back exactly where we found them." Rain tucked the legal document back in the top drawer where she'd found it and closed the drawer tight. Her mind flashed back to when she'd first met Wallace, how he'd cowered from her touch. A meekness about the man had subtlety shown itself. Marge had been right; she was extremely sensitive and sympathetic to others. Even if she never experienced spousal abuse herself, she felt the signs were there. Wallace had been abused.

"That's definitely interesting information," Julia said, interrupting Rain's reverie as her friend flipped through more papers that filled the desk in a heap. "I'm just not sure it's enough. We have potential motive, but at this point, all we really have is speculation."

"We need more," Rain agreed.

"I haven't seen a lien on Seth and Kim's property either. Instead, this seems to be years' worth of bills and invoices," Julia said with a hint of frustration. "I'm not sure how anyone would find anything in this pile."

257

"I wonder if it's an organized mess to the owner, like, if Tina wanted to, she could put her finger on exactly what she was looking for. Let's just hope for Seth's sake the lien paperwork is long gone, if it ever existed in the first place."

"I'm not finding any other legal docs either—I mean, nothing else that might flag us to think Wallace had an issue with anyone else. I don't even know what to look for at this point," Julia said, hunching her shoulders in defeat. "This is overwhelming."

"Hey, you were the one that wanted to dig into Wallace's paperwork."

"Yeah, I just didn't think the stack of papers would be the size of Eagle Peak!" Julia exclaimed. "Did you look inside those drawers?"

Rain noticed the two drawers that flanked the middle one, and pulled one open. "Yeah, maybe he's the only one to file paperwork in this household," she said as she flipped through the file folders.

"Anything?"

Rain pulled a few folders, scanned the information, and then put them back exactly how she'd found them.

"It looks like the paperwork from the handyman stuff that he'd been hired out to do is in order. I'm not seeing Seth's lien, though, or anything that proves he even did work over there. Looks like the clients are alphabetized, and I don't see Seth's name as a customer. Maybe he had the file somewhere else if he was working on it." Her eyes darted to the piles around the room, looking for a folder that might be the same color, but she came up empty. It was like looking for a needle in a haystack.

"Well? The other option is we can always ask our new friend Tina about it next time we see her," Julia offered, grinning.

Rain mirrored her smiled and then let it fade, "Speaking of Tina, maybe we better just get outta here before she comes back."

"Okay," Julia said, resignedly. "But first, one quick sweep of the house. Maybe we'll find another clue that will trigger something else."

"Like what? The murder weapon?" Rain teased. "Tina certainly has motive. The guy was leaving her!"

"True. It sure would be nice to find something and button this up tight. But I'm assuming if she was the killer, she'd be smart enough to get rid of any evidence. Wouldn't she? I'm guessing, like Jace said, the weapon was probably tossed down the hole in the ice, never to be found again."

Julia shrugged before pulling Rain along by the arm. "Come on."

After a quick poke through the house, coming up empty of further clues, they stumbled on a room that was closed off from the rest of the house. The space seemed to be an addition that had once connected a detached garage to the main house, as you needed to take a step down to enter it. When Rain opened the door, they were greeted by what was obviously an art studio. Plaster casts of fish and amphibians waited for paint on multiple shelving units while others, scattered across a table, looked back at them with beady eyes.

Julia gently rubbed her hand along the top of one of the plaster casts and said with a hint of admiration in her tone, "Wow. Quite the artist we have here. These are definitely an improvement over the ones in the living room. I wonder if she sells these. I bet she makes a pretty penny, though I haven't ever seen anything like it at a local shop."

"Yeah, they're actually growing on me too. Some are kinda neat. Definitely original."

A rumbling sound shook the walls and then abruptly stopped. Rain and Julia froze in position and looked at each other in horror.

Julia's eyes doubled in size as she put a hand to her mouth. When she dropped her hand she said, "Please tell me that wasn't what I think it was? I think I just wet my pants!"

"Yeah, we're screwed." Rain winced. "I think the garage door just opened up."

"Julia puckered her lips and tried to hide a sheepish grin. "Sugar snaps, we're in deep. I'm so sorry, Rain—don't hold this against me for the rest of our lives. Promise me?"

Rain kept her mouth silent, and mouthed, "Now what do we do?" She pointed to the door where they had entered and shook her head, downcast. "If we go out that way, we're doomed. We'll be caught for sure. There's gotta be another way outta here. Maybe the studio has an exterior door." She held her hands up defenselessly as she desperately searched for a way out.

Julia's eyes then followed suit, darting about the space. Her glance finally landing at their stocking feet. "Guess what, Sherlock? Even if we did find a back-door exit, we don't have our dilly-dang boots!" she hissed. "So much for cleanliness! If we'd kept our boots on, we wouldn't be in this mess now, would we!"

"Don't give me another reason to hate winter. Ugh!" Rain replied.

"There's no way we can go outside without boots. It's not even an option. We'll be frozen before we hit the truck, never mind the evidence of footwear we're leaving behind."

"Seriously, Jules, what are we gonna do to get outta this mess?" Rain's hands shook nervously by her sides. All she could think of was how Jace was going to react. How would he feel when his sister was charged with breaking and entering? After his brother-in-law was already on shaky ground with the police. Jace might never forgive them. Any hint of a romantic relationship or possibility with the man would fly swiftly out the door. She couldn't believe at a time like this that Jace was what she was worried about.

Julia moved behind one of the art shelves filled with plaster pieces and scrunched down on one knee and Rain followed. "So, this is your idea? We just hide in here? *Are you kidding me?* It's not like she's not gonna find us, Jules! Nick's plow truck is in the driveway, and our boots are by the front door. I say we just man up and get it over with." Rain attempted to stand, and Julia pulled her back down.

"Not yet. We need to think," Julia whispered, kneading her forehead with her fingers until an imprint remained. "Just give me a sec."

Rain acquiesced, sat on the floor, and folded her legs beneath her. The two sat quietly, holding their breath as Rain gave Julia a moment to gather her thoughts. She noticed a dark canvas bag tucked deep beneath the shelf, with "WB" embroidered on the side. Rain tilted her head to get a better view. The bag looked as if it didn't belong there, and the initials seemed to indicate that it belonged to Wallace. And yet none of his other belongings seemed part of this art studio. Curiosity prompted her to see what was inside. She dug her hand deep beneath the shelf until she could reach it and grunted after missing a few times. After finally pulling the bag free, and opening it, she blinked several times, because her eyes couldn't believe what she'd found—Wallace's glove. The one that had been missing from his other hand, the day of the murder. And it was caked in dried blood.

Chapter Thirty-Two

Rain gasped, and then let out a squeal like a puppy whose tale had been accidently stepped on. "Julia! Oh my god, Julia!"

Julia covered Rain's mouth with her hand. "Shh. You're gonna get us caught!" she mouthed. "And we're quickly running outta options here."

Rain lowered her voice, "Juliaaaa! Do you know what this is?" The canvas fishing bag sat open in her lap, and the evidence stared back at her like an accusing witness.

"Clearly. It's a bloody glove," Julia answered gravely after taking a peek.

"Yes! It's not just a bloody glove. It's *the* bloody glove! The one that was missing from Wallace's hand. Don't you remember he only had one hand that was covered that day? I can't believe it—this is the other one!"

Julia leaned in closer, "Yeah, but something isn't adding up. Wallace's hand wasn't covered in blood the day of the murder. Not a drop of it, from what I can recall. I only remember it was blue from . . . well . . . you know."

"Oh. That's true." Rain sat back on her heels. "So how did the blood get there?"

Julia shrugged. "I dunno. Haven't a clue. I'm still trying to figure out how I'm gonna get us outta here!" Her whisper came out as a hiss.

Rain plucked a Kleenex from her jacket pocket and fished around inside the canvas bag.

"What are you looking for, Nancy Drew?" Julia asked.

"The murder weapon."

Julia did a double take. "What makes you think the murder weapon is in that bag too? There's no way—"

"I'm not saying it is. I'm saying I hope it is."

"I'm doubting the entire state of Wisconsin we could be that lucky," Julia taunted.

"I'm guessing the killer used the glove to hide the knife—*that's* why it's bloody." Rain dangled the glove in her hand, for Julia to view, using the Kleenex, so as not to contaminate the evidence. "Look, the blood is on the *inside* and soaked through to the outside. Not the other way around."

Julia sat in stunned silence.

"Do you know what this means?"

"It means, that Tina knows something about her husband's murder. Maybe she hired someone to do it after he slapped her with divorce papers," Julia answered. "Or she did the deed herself."

Rain clutched her heart. "It also means we're locked inside the house of a potential murderer."

"Yeah. That's not cool. We're in a bit of a pickle here, huh?"

"Wait. You think Tina is really the killer?" Rain asked before she was interrupted by a sound off in the distance.

"Hellooo! I know someone's in here. Come out, come out, wherever you are!"

Julia slid a hand over each of their mouths, to quiet them, and they shared a horrified glance.

"You want to play hide and seek? Don't worry—I'm good at this game," Tina added in a creepy singsong voice, clearly moving farther away from them instead of closer, buying them time. But time was not on their side.

"She sure sounds like a murderer! Did you hear that? What a freak!" Julia whispered, "She's acting like this is some weird game!"

"I know, it's spooky, right?"

"Damn straight!" Julia grimaced.

"What do we do now?"

Julia used her own winter glove to search the canvas bag. "I don't think the murder weapon is in here. The only evidence we have is that stupid bloody glove. Rain, we need more. They won't convict her on that. We need to link her directly to this crime!"

"How?"

"First of all, I'm texting Jace to send the police over. Let them do a complete search over here, just like they did my house. Maybe she hid the murder weapon somewhere else in this room." Julia plucked her phone from her pocket.

"Or the chloroform. I can only guess that she needed it to knock Wallace out. I mean, he was a big guy, and I can't imagine that she could overtake him otherwise."

Meanwhile, Tina's voice continued to ring out, sounding closer: *"I'm gonna find you—it's only a matter of time . . . You may as well come out!"*

"Oh nooo." Julia sounded deflated and then held up the phone over her head. "I can't get a dang signal in here! Remind me, if we ever get outta this, to buy a new phone."

"I can't believe this. My phone is in your truck." Rain exhaled a long breath. "This really sucks pond water."

"Hurry—shove that bag back under there exactly where you found it." Julia said, her voice starting to rise in panic. She lifted it from Rain's lap, utilizing her winter gloves and folded the flap of the bag over to close it.

Using her feet, Rain shoved the bag back beneath the shelf as deep as she could. She scrambled to her feet. "We need to get away from that, so when she finds us, we won't be anywhere *near* that evidence."

"Good thinking." Julia nodded, then scampered behind another shelf. She banged her arm on it, and when she did so, plaster art crashed to the ground, like tumbling rocks in an avalanche.

The noise from the broken plaster was undeniably loud. Julia looked at Rain in stunned horror.

"Yep. Now, we're in trouble," Rain said, sighing resignedly. "We need to come up with a reason for why we're in here, and we need to do it fast!" she said, pounding her fists on her thighs but not feeling even the slightest pain.

Meanwhile, Julia looked at the plaster fish that had fallen to the ground and tried to piece them back together.

Rain looked at her incredulously. "As if that's gonna make it all okay? I think it's a little late for that, Jules!"

Julia ignored her and kept at it until she held two pieces together and looked at Rain and said, "I think I just found something."

"What?"

Julia held the two pieces of plaster together, and although there were missing clumps because bits of plaster had broken off, it was clear that the form she held together in her hand was a plaster cast that had produced a knife.

Rain's jaw dropped. "You mean, she *made* the murder weapon with plaster?"

Just as the words came out of her mouth, the door to the studio swung open.

"I know you're in here."

Rain heard Tina's boots clicking against the hard floor and coming closer. "Come out from behind there," she demanded. And when they did so, they were greeted by Tina pointing a hunting rifle in their direction.

"What are you doing in my house?" Tina said, her voice steady.

"We wanted to check on you," Julia rushed. "My husband was released from jail because the police know he didn't do it."

"Yeah," Rain interrupted, "and we wanted to come over here to help you. We think we can help you find Wallace's killer."

A flicker of fear crossed Tina's face. "I don't believe you," she said finally.

"She's right," Julia said, her voice quivering. "After we plowed your driveway, we came to the door, and it was unlocked . . . and we weren't sure if the killer was coming after you too. We just wanted to make sure you're okay. We were so relieved to find you weren't home, right, Rainy?" Julia nudged her. "You should thank your lucky stars it's just us!"

"Can you put that thing down?" Rain asked, pointing to the gun.

"Put your hands above your heads." Tina demanded. "Do it!"

"What? Why?" Julia asked, bravely walking slowly toward her.

"Yeah, we're here to help," Rain suggested again, but then was interrupted when Tina looked at their feet to where the broken plaster, and the piece that resembled the mold for a knife, stared critically back at them.

"Don't take a step closer," Tina said, holding the gun steady on them. "Where did you find that?"

Rain gulped.

"It kinda found us," Julia admitted. "It must've been at the top of the shelf, 'cause when I accidently banged into it, all those pieces fell."

"What is it?" Rain asked as innocently as she could.

Tina let out a throaty laugh, filling the room with an eerie sound. "You know exactly what it is. It's a trophy," she added proudly.

That comment made the bile rise in Rain's throat, because in that moment she was confident they were standing face to face with Wallace's killer.

"Where is it?" Julia asked. "I mean, if you're gonna kill us, I may as well know how you planted the knife in my husband's fishing gear and used the plaster one to kill Wallace. I wanna know. How'd you pull it off?" Julia's tone was one of curiosity, not one of disdain. Rain thought her friend might be playing into the sickness of Tina's mind.

"You'll never find it," Tina said defiantly.

"Try me," Julia pushed.

"It melted, you idiot!" Tina spat and then shock swept across her face, as if she realized she'd said too much.

"Melted," Rain repeated under her breath, and then clicked her fingers together. "You used the mold to make an ice knife! And now it's gone."

"Rather brilliant, actually," Julia said, seemingly still trying to appeal to the woman's depraved mind. "Then you planted the *real* knife, the one you used to *make* the mold, into my husband's bag to frame him and throw off the police's investigation."

And Julia's comment worked too, because a sick smile formed on Tina's lips before it faded. "Put your hands up!"

"Why would you do that to her husband? A man you don't even know! And lucky for you, Nick cut himself with it, implicating himself further and ending up in jail. That was your plan all along wasn't it? Only Julia's brother was smarter than that and told the police to run prints and swipe DNA samples off the knife. You're really not as smart as you think," Rain said with all the emotional strength she could muster.

Tina responded with a sneer, swinging the gun between them as if she didn't know which one of them would be more fun to knock off first.

"You realize killing us is a very bad idea," Julia said. "You'll get away with your husband's murder, since the murder weapon melted. But you can't melt bullets," she added, flipping a hand toward the weapon.

"I don't need to; I'm defending my property," Tina said proudly. "And you two came in here and attacked me. That's what I'll tell the police anyway." Her eyes flickered approval at her own brilliance.

"That won't work," Rain said. "The police would never believe that, especially now that Nick has been released from jail. There'd be no motive. You might want to think this through a little bit longer," Rain encouraged her, softening her tone.

Tina swung the rifle in the direction of Rain's head and took a step closer. "You! Open that box," she said, pointing the gun for a mere second in the direction of the corner where a Rubbermaid container sat in the corner. Rain did what she was asked, and then Tina added, "Tie up your friend here with that jute."

Rain returned with a roll of natural twine that she'd found inside the container and stood defensively.

"Go on." Tina nudged Rain on the arm with the barrel of the weapon. "Tie her hands behind her back. Do it!" she spat.

Julia thrust her hands behind her back and waited for Rain to do what was asked. Rain didn't pull very tight on the string, but left it loose, and hoped that, in a pinch, Julia might even be able to break free. But then Tina checked her work and shook her head disapprovingly. "Tighter!"

Rain acquiesced but still tried not to pull too tight. Julia winced, and Rain thought she was acting like it was tighter than it was, to appease the woman. She thought Julia should get an Academy Award. If they ever made it out of here, she'd provide her with one.

"Sit down!" Tina demanded, and Julia complied. "Tie her feet too!"

Julia watched as Rain tied her feet together and mouthed the words, "I'm sorry."

"Why'd ya do it, huh?" Julia spat. "Why'd ya kill your husband anyway?"

"Oh, we have a mouthy one here, do we?" Tina mocked. "My *husband* thumbed his nose at me just like you are doing right now! He insulted my art. Said I'd never make a living with it. Well, I showed him! I just sold a piece for a good penny. And now I'm not sharing one dime of it with that loser. He thought he was gonna divorce *me* and have *me* share my money as marital assets? Not a chance! Especially after he quit his high-paying job. I killed him with the art he said would never amount to anything. Ha!" An evil, throaty laugh echoed in the room.

"Wow. That's rich." Julia shook her head in disgust.

"Enough of your mouth!" Tina removed a winter scarf from around her neck and said, "Cover her mouth with this."

When Julia was totally defenseless, Tina nudged Rain again with the barrel of the gun and said, "You. You're coming with me."

The last thing she saw was Julia's eyes closing in defeat as she turned on her heel and was led out of the art studio.

Chapter
Thirty-Three

"You realize you'll never get away with this," Rain said, as Tina pushed her along with the barrel of the gun, poking it into her back. She nudged her to the front room, where the stupid fish on the wall now made her dizzy.

"May I remind you, it was you two women who broke into *my* house. I'm sure the cops will understand. They'll see it my way."

"Julia's brother is a police officer, and I promise you, he'll hound you for the rest of your life until he proves otherwise. Trust me when I say you're making a very big mistake."

"I doubt that very much," Tina said icily. Her tone was colder than a Northwoods winter.

"You didn't stop by the library to apologize, did you? Instead, you came to tamper with my windshield wipers! What did I ever do to you?" Rain asked. "I mean, I think I have the right to know. I'm surprised you didn't finish the job when you had the chance."

"I did apologize! And besides, it was too busy that day to do anything to your car."

"You just solidified the fact that it was you!" Rain spat.

"Look, I was trying to warn you to back off. But clearly you didn't heed the warning. See? It's your own fault you're in this position," Tina said, jabbing her in the shoulder, with the barrel of the rifle.

"And Seth too? Did he ask you too many questions when he was here? Is that why you tried to have him die a slow death inside his ice shanty?"

Tina let out a throaty laugh. "I knew they would release that Nick guy once they discovered Wallace's DNA wasn't on the knife. I needed more time . . . I needed a new form of misdirection. Seth was just another way to thwart the investigators. I think I did a great job covering my tracks. With two men attacked inside their shanties, the police would never believe a woman was capable. They would think it was some lunatic out attacking local fisherman. Men can be so stupid!"

"What are you gonna do with us now? You should just let us go, Tina, before this gets even more outta hand," Rain pushed. "I mean, seriously. Aren't you in enough hot water?"

"What? And let you both run to the police and tell them I killed my husband? I don't think so!" she shrilled.

"Instead, you're just gonna shoot us? Is that it? Is that really your best option?" Rain took a brave step toward Tina, but the woman raised the gun to her shoulder and then held it steady, pointing toward Rain's head.

"Stop it! Stop it!" Tina said through gritted teeth.

Rain continued, "First Wallace, then Seth, now us. How many people are you gonna leave in your wake? The murder list is getting a bit long, don't ya think? You keep this up, and you'll be on death row."

"Just shut up. Shut up! I don't know what I'm going to do! But I will remain in control!" Her eyes blazed, and she poked Rain on the arm again with the gun.

Rain took a steady breath. Trying to reason with a psychopathic woman who might or might not be hormonal wasn't helping. She closed her lips and gazed toward the window. But the window was too far away to get a good look out. She wondered if Ryan was still at the neighbor's house. He'd find out someday what had happened not far from where he had been. And Rain wasn't okay with that. Not one bit.

Rain looked down at the bracelet on her wrist given to her by Max on their last Christmas together, and wondered if they'd soon meet again. He had given it to her with a promise. A promise they would try in vitro fertilization again. This wasn't exactly the way she thought she'd reacquaint with him or meet her maker. The bracelet shimmered a reflection off the window, giving her an idea. If she could blind Tina, even for just a moment, she might have a chance to break free. But if she broke free, Tina might hurt Julia. She needed to get control of the gun. There was no other choice.

"I have to go to the bathroom," Rain uttered finally. She hoped her bluff could provide a way to disarm her.

"Nonsense," Tina hissed.

"Seriously! I'm gonna make a mess on the floor if you don't let me go, right now."

Tina pushed her to move with the barrel of the gun. "Go if you must, but I'm coming with you, and you're keeping the door open. No funny business," she added as she led Rain down a short hallway to a bathroom. The gun nudged uncomfortably at her back the entire time.

When Rain entered the bathroom, she turned to Tina and asked as meekly as she could muster, "Please, one last private moment before you kill me. Please let me shut the door." She willed a tear to form in her eyes but quickly realized the woman lacked empathy, and she was barking up the wrong tree.

"No! Just do your business. And hurry it up!" Tina shrilled, pointing the gun momentarily in the direction of the toilet before returning it to aim at Rain's head.

Rain acquiesced but then turned and pleaded one last time. "I need to turn the water on, you're stressing me out, and I need . . . the help."

"I thought you said you needed to go? If you really had to go that badly, you wouldn't need help."

Rain begged the woman with her eyes before Tina finally acquiesced. "Oh, go ahead and turn the water on." Tina let the gun settle to her side, giving Rain a momentary reprieve from a gun pointed at her head.

Rain moved toward the sink, her heart beating hard in her chest. After flicking the hot water on, she waited for steam to come. She lathered her hands thickly with soap.

"What are you doing? The water's on—you don't need soap. Do your business! Now! Before I change my mind!" Tina screeched.

Rain put her hands under the hot water until she had a cupful and then attempted to splash Tina in the eyes with the soapy water. She hoped this would cause Tina to blink and render her defenseless. Instead, she merely splashed the wall, angering Tina further.

A shot rang out in the air, and for a moment Rain stopped breathing before she patted her body down, feeling for an entry wound. Thankfully, none was found.

A bloodcurdling screech escaped from Rain's lips after she noticed a hole in the bathroom wall. She felt her legs grow weak as she breathed in the scent of gunpowder. Tina had narrowly missed her. "You are crazy!"

Tina smacked Rain in the side of the head with the hot barrel of the gun, causing her to feel woozy for a second.

"Don't you try that again!" Tina hissed. "Now, move it! Your chance to use the bathroom is over!"

Rain put her hands above her head in an act of defenselessness. Her body trembled as she was led, with the gun nudging her shoulder with each step, back toward the front of the house. As they passed the window, she darted a quick glance out and noticed Ryan running across the street in the direction of Tina's house. She held her breath. He was on his way over, and she feared for his safety, but there was no way to warn him.

Before long, the sound of the doorbell and a hard knock at the door could be heard.

Tina's eyes flashed and then she lowered her voice. "Go look out the peephole and find out who's here," she directed with a hiss. "Do it!"

Rain already knew who it was, even before she heard Ryan's voice ringing out on the other side of the door.

"Hey! Anyone in there? I heard a gunshot!"

Rain turned to Tina and whispered, "It's a friend of mine who's been working across the street, and I'm sure he's already called the police," she bluffed. "Didn't you just hear what he said? He heard gunfire."

Tina's eyes ricocheted around the room, and she lowered the gun away from Rain for a second. Rain wondered if she could overpower the woman and take it from her, but it was too dangerous a move. If she missed, it could have dire consequences for not only her and Julia but now for Ryan too.

The sound of hard banging continued on the wooden door. "Hey, if you don't open up the door, I'm gonna call the police! My friend's plow is in the driveway! I know she's in there!"

Rain waited for Tina's direction. Her shoulders fell, and she eyed the woman carefully.

"What do you want me to do?" Rain asked finally. "If you don't hurry up, he'll call the police, just like he said."

Tina seemed to weigh her options as her gaze momentarily darted back to the floor.

"You better make a decision pretty quick here," Rain pushed. "You're running out of options."

"Open the door and make him go away. If you don't, I'll kill both of you," Tina said finally as she eased behind the door, hiding away from sight. "Don't think I won't," she sneered.

Rain slowly opened the door, and when she did so, Ryan immediately reached out a hand to her.

"Rain! What the heck is going on over here? I saw your friend's truck in the driveway and heard gunshots and screaming—am I losing my mind?" His eyes were eager and expectant.

"Good to see you too, Ryan Wright," Rain answered with a feigned smile as she purposely begged him with her eyes to understand. She hoped that by saying his last name, he'd picked up on her clue. She hoped he'd understand that everything he'd said was RIGHT. *Call the police!* she begged with her eyes.

"Where's your friend? Is she here with you? Is she hurt? Rain, please tell me someone wasn't shot!"

"No." Rain shook her head violently. "You need to go," she added and slowly backed away from him, hoping she could just slam the door and he'd run for help, but he didn't. Instead, he pushed his way inside.

Rain's shoulders slumped, and she blew out a breath of frustration when Tina kicked the door closed behind Ryan and held up the gun, swinging it between them. "Welcome to the party," Tina said, her words dripping in sarcasm. "Don't people know how to mind their own business in this silly little town!"

A look of complete shock swept over Ryan's face as he said, "Whoa! Easy now! What's going on here? How 'bout you put down that gun."

"You just walked into a hornet's nest." Rain gestured a hand toward the crazed woman. "Ryan, meet Tina Benson. This happens to be Wallace's wife . . . well they were married before she killed him," Rain said to him quietly, biting her lip. She then turned her attention back to Tina and said, "Now what are you going to do? Shoot all of us—including Ryan here? You still think you can claim we all broke in here to do you harm? I don't think so!"

"Yeah, that wouldn't be wise. I've already called the police. They're en route as we speak," Ryan said calmly.

"Liar!" Tina screamed.

"'Fraid not." Ryan said firmly. "I was bluffing earlier. You really think I would come over here without calling them on my way?"

"What did you tell them?" Rain asked.

"The truth. I told them I heard gun shots. And to send a squad out pronto."

"Shut up! Shut up! Shut up!"

Tina was apparently at her breaking point, and Rain knew, deep within her heart, if she didn't act soon, they were all done for. Waiting for the police might put them in a hostage situation. Especially with Julia not at her side, there was no way to protect her best friend. She darted a quick glance at Ryan and then back at one of Tina's plaster fish leaning against the wall on a side table, not far from them, but far enough away that she couldn't easily reach it. She eased her body slowly toward it when Tina took her eyes off her for just a second, and looked to Ryan for approval. Rain hoped he understood her cue, and he took a daring step toward Tina.

"Put the gun down," he said calmly. "Just put it down."

"What are you doing! I'm warning you: Don't take another step! Back up! Back up!" Tina's nostrils flared, and her eyes blazed like fire.

Rain noticed Tina had swung the gun like a pendulum in Ryan's direction, and she availed herself of the only opportunity she thought she'd get, snatching the fish from its stand. She swung as hard as she could at Tina's head, but missed, hitting her in the shoulder instead and causing the gun to fly from her hands.

The three stood with mouths agape when the tables turned, as they all seemed to watch in slow motion as the gun bounced to the floor with a crash.

Ryan was the first to wake from the haze and shoved the crazed woman backward, causing Tina to teeter, lose her balance, and fall.

Rain snatched the weapon from the floor, shock vibrating through her entire body as she pointed the gun back at Tina. "Don't move a muscle."

Ryan put his hands together in prayer, closed his eyes, and sighed heavily, "Thank you, Jesus. I wasn't quite ready to meet you today," he uttered under his breath.

"I think we're done here," Rain said defiantly as she watched Tina rub at her eyes and then blink back at her with a stunned expression.

Chapter
Thirty-Four

"Any chance you can hold this for a moment?" Rain handed the gun to Ryan as they waited for the police to arrive. "Keep it steady on her, will you?"

She turned on her heel, but before she darted from the room, Ryan asked, "Where are you going?"

"There's something I gotta do!" Rain hollered over her shoulder; pure adrenaline pumped through her veins, as she ran to set Julia free. When she threw open the door, Julia lifted her head from her knees, her eyes wide.

Rain removed the scarf from Julia's mouth first.

Julia gasped through sobs, "Oh, Rainy! Rainy! I thought Tina shot you!" Julia cried out, rocking back and forth, her head slamming against her knees. "I've never been so glad to see you!"

Rain then rushed to untie Julia and the two embraced like long lost friends.

"I'm so sorry," Julia sobbed. "I never should've convinced you to . . ."

"It's okay," Rain said soothingly, brushing back strands of Julia's hair, wet by her tears, from her friend's face. "We're all okay now . . . Everything is going to be okay."

Rain held her friend, and the two rocked back and forth until Julia held her at arm's length. "How? Where—are the police . . . is Jace?"

"It's okay, Jules, I'll tell you everything. I just want to make sure you're okay. Are you woozy? You okay to stand?"

Then the women heard the most beautiful sound—sirens—causing the two to share a relieved smile.

* * *

Rain and Julia watched as Jace led Tina away to a squad car. The whole cavalry of police and ambulance had come, blocking the road. Rain wondered why half of Wisconsin's police force came out from adjoining communities. But then she recalled the size of police force they had in Lofty Pines, and the potential that Julia and she could be held hostage, locked inside with a lunatic, and she guessed the overkill was worth it. The most important thing was that they were safe now.

While Ryan was giving his statement to an officer, Rain noticed Nick dodging the vehicles between them as he ran in their direction. Julia met him halfway, in a bear hug, and the two clung to each other in a long embrace. Rain followed, to talk with them.

"I'm so glad you guys are okay. You are okay, right?" Nick finally released his wife and reached out a hand to Rain, giving hers a quick squeeze.

"Yeah, we're fine." Rain smiled weakly. The adrenaline was waning, and she could feel her legs growing a bit wobbly, but she held back from sharing.

"Nothing a stiff drink won't cure," Julia added with a grin. "And I, for one, am ready," she added, jutting a thumb to her chest. "Pour one to the top! Maybe two!"

"I have a bottle of wine waiting at home with your name on it, honey. But first, let me look at you. What happened here?" Nick lifted his wife's arms and eyed her wrists, "Let's go over to the EMTs. I want to see if they have anything to put on that."

Julia had worked on freeing herself from the twine, to the point of ripping skin and leaving rings of dried blood around her wrists. "I don't think it's necessary." She shrugged. "Seriously, I'm fine. I just wanna go home."

"It's either that or I take you to the hospital myself," he said adamantly. "Is that what you want?" Nick sent a conspiratorial glance to Rain, and they both grinned, knowing how much Julia hated hospitals.

"Fine," Julia huffed. "How about you, Rain. You comin'?"

"No, I'm good. But I might have to join you for that drink," Rain said lightly. "A little alcohol might do the trick."

She shoved her trembling hands into her pockets to hide them. Someday, she'd share with Julia how close to death she had come, but not today. Today, they were gonna celebrate life and clearing Nick's name once and for all.

Nick tossed a set of car keys in her direction. "Rain, would you mind taking Julia's car home? And we'll take the truck. Come on over when you get there. I'll play bartender." He grinned, throwing an arm over his wife's shoulder and pulling her close protectively.

"Yeah, sure. You two go on ahead. I'll meet you back at home."

Before they left, Julia reached for Rain one last time and hugged her tightly. "We did it again, friend. We did it again!" she said proudly while they rocked back and forth before Julia let go and held her at arm's length. "Maybe the Lofty Pines Police Department can get us like a badge or something?" she teased. "Or maybe ya know, at the very least, a brick with our names on it down at the station? Or maybe just a big write-up in the local paper?" Julia held her hands up in demonstration: "Two local gumshoes solve the murder investigation of Wallace Benson." she grinned.

It was good to see Julia back to her old self. Rain couldn't fathom what had run through Julia's mind when she heard the gun shot. Obviously, her friend had thought the worst. If their roles had been reversed, she'd have thought the same.

"I don't want to hear another word." Nick momentarily cupped his hands over his ears. "Enough of that nonsense. You guys are off the case for a bit. No more sleuthing!" Nick added with a warning finger, and then he tugged at his wife's arm and encouraged her in the direction of the ambulance. "Come on now. The sooner we get you taken care of, the sooner you can get home to that drink."

Rain watched as the police cruiser with Tina and Jace inside pulled away from the curb. Ryan finished giving his statement to an officer and headed in her direction. He summoned her with his hand on his way over, and she went to greet him.

"You holdin' up all right there, Sunshine?"

"Yeah, yeah, I'm fine." Rain hid her trembling hands in her pockets.

"You know, you're pretty tough," he said, studying her. It was as if he could see right through her, as if he was trying to reach deep within her soul and figure her out. Little did he know how shaken she was.

"Yeah, maybe," she said shyly, looking at the ground.

"How did you even get involved in all this?" Ryan asked with a shake of his head.

Rain chuckled. "How much time do you have?" she asked with a raised brow.

"All the time in the world . . . if it's with you?" he answered cautiously.

Rain felt a hot rush to her cheeks but cooled it quickly by saying, "By the way, thanks again for coming to our rescue. I don't know what would've happened if you hadn't recognized Nick's plow truck in the driveway and come over. Had you not given Julia that lesson with the plow, you would've never known . . . funny how life works sometimes."

"Yeah, I probably wouldn't've gone to the door at all and would have just waited for the police to come."

"Why did you?"

"A hunch," he admitted with a shrug. "I was worried about you. I thought there was a chance you might be with Julia . . ." He clearly held back more words that were ready to fall from his tongue by clamping his lips tight.

"Well, I appreciate you following your gut." Rain leaned in closer. "I'm just glad it all worked out, but you didn't catch my clue, huh? Ryan Wright?" she said with a smile, folding her arms across her chest. "I was trying to tell you—you were *right*!"

"Hey, I had a feeling you were under duress; I mean, your expressions were priceless! What I didn't know was that she was on the other side of the door with the gun to your head!" he added with a frustrated chuckle. "And anyway, I would've taken a bullet to the chest for you. If it kept you safe."

"Well, thank heavens it didn't come to that, and it all worked out. I'm just glad we *all* made it outta there in one piece." A rekindled shiver of fear ran though her before his winning smile and comment made her laugh.

"Hey, you can't go wrong with Mister Right on your side."

"Yeah, I'm learning that to be true." she folded her arms across her chest and noticed her hands were still shaking.

Ryan must've noticed too because he reached to take hold of them and gave them a comforting brush with his thumb. "I hope I'm not out of line with my timing, but do you think maybe when things calm down . . . I can maybe take you to dinner? Or a drink perhaps?"

Rain smiled. "I'd like that."

Chapter
Thirty-Five

The library was cozy and warm, heat emanated from the crackling stove, and the scent of hot cocoa filled the air. Children were gathered around Marge's feet, along with Rex, who lay obediently curled by her leg. The children sat wide-eyed for story time; ears perked to Marge's every word. Her eyes were animated, and her enunciations right on cue, causing Julia to laugh aloud at her antics. Rain was convinced the older woman was in her happy place. And so was she as she hung a loose arm around Julia's shoulder.

"You know, if it wasn't for you, we wouldn't be here right now," Julia whispered in her ear.

"Where on earth would we be but our favorite place on the planet? No place I'd rather be than here with you guys." Rain looked around at the leather spines that surrounded them and felt the books' comfort like that of a long-lost friend. Any chance to escape in an author's words, for just a moment, was pure joy.

Julia looked over both shoulders, lowered her tone further, and said, "Jail."

Rain led Julia away from the children, a few aisles away, where no patrons were perusing shelves.

"What are you talking about—jail?" Rain asked finally when she was sure they were alone.

"For breaking and entering!" Julia teased with a bump to the shoulder. "Although I did some breaking, I don't think that was the charge that would've stuck," she added with a chuckle. "Especially since it led to the murder weapon. Boy, what a cluster, eh? I still can't believe we solved another crime in Lofty Pines."

"Oh that." Rain waved a hand of dismissal. "Who are the police gonna believe? A cold-hearted killer? Or two witnesses who distinctly remember Tina inviting them inside?" Rain grinned. "I suppose the thorough search they did at Tina's, uncovering the history on her computer and finding the chloroform, helped. And of course Ryan coming to our rescue. His statement alone probably saved us."

"When do you think Tina planted that knife in Nick's gear? That's the one thing that's really been bothering me. The not knowing."

"Oh, Jace told me. When they questioned her down at the station, she finally came clean. When she saw Nick enter Wallace's ice shanty and heard them arguing, she slipped into Nick's, dropped the weapon in the gear, and voilà! She created what she thought was an instant alibi. She had it planned all along to choose a victim for her scheme. She just didn't know Nick would be the one until she heard them arguing."

"When did you talk to Jace? He hasn't called me?"

"Oh, he called first thing this morning and wanted to know if he could bring anything to the bonfire tonight. I'm so glad we're all getting together. It's important for Seth and Kim to be there too. Hopefully, he and Nick will be able to mend fences so to speak. It's time, now that the murderer has been caught. We need to put this all behind us once and for all."

"Figures, Jace'll talk to you about it," Julia said with an eyeroll. "Lucky for you, because my brother is still on my case about it. Say's we need to stick with what we know here at the library and leave the policing to him," she added with a sly smile. "If you can imagine."

"Yeah, I suppose he's right," Rain said wearily. "I've certainly had enough adrenaline rushes for a while; a little peace would be nice for a change. Curled up by the fire, reading a good book, with a hot drink, sounds about perfect to me."

"Oh," Julia said deflated.

"Why? Doesn't that sound good to you?" Rain leaned against the shelf and folded her arms across her chest.

"Yeah, but I do like a puzzle . . . maybe we should start a book club? For mystery books only?" Julia's eyes danced with merriment.

"What? And stay away from historical romance? I'm shocked," Rain mocked.

"I'll stay away from romance books for a while. I have enough of that back at home now that Nick and I've been making up for lost time, if you know what I mean." Her eyebrows bounced, and she shot Rain a wink.

Rain laughed aloud. ""Get a room! Will ya?"

"Oh, you don't know how thankful I am that we have one! Luckily we don't have to depend on conjugal visits. Can you imagine what could have been?" Julia said wide-eyed. "Yes, it could've been awful. But I'd much rather talk about something else."

Surprisingly, Julia dropped the subject.

"I think it's a brilliant idea, by the way," Rain said.

"What's that?"

"A book club. I'll print up some fliers to stick inside the books so when patrons check out, they can learn about it. And I'll post a few fliers throughout the library too. That way, we can see how much interest we can attract. I think a book club would be a fun way to get through the long winters up here. And the library *has* been bustling. I say we do it! What have we got to lose?"

"Marge will love it too," Julia said as they stepped back into the aisle, and the two turned to look at the older woman's animated storytelling continuing to unfold. Marge must've noticed them looking her way, as her eyes sparkled, and then the three shared a knowing smile.

The sound of the bell alerted Rain to glance toward the door. She walked deeper into the center aisle, where she saw a man standing in the doorway with a large bouquet of flowers covering his face. Julia followed.

"Lookie there. Speaking of romance . . . Looks like lover boy is here to see you," Julia teased, poking her head over her shoulder.

Rain couldn't determine who it was, and neither could she decide if she'd rather the man holding the flowers be Jace or Ryan. She looked to the floor, noticed the familiar boots, and smiled.

Recipes

Comfort food to share with friends (Nick's favorite!)
Rain's original recipe for Enchilada Lasagna Bake

Ingredients List

1 lb lean ground beef (you can substitute with either ground turkey or chicken if that's your preferred meat or you'd like to go leaner)

½ sweet onion (such as Vidalia), finely chopped

RP's fresh lasagna noodles (these come in gluten-free too!). They're found in the refrigerated section at your local grocery store, or substitute with another fresh lasagna noodle

Two 1.5 oz packets of powdered McCormick enchilada sauce seasoning mix

Tomato sauce per directions on McCormick enchilada sauce (one 8 oz can of tomato sauce for each packet; you will have a bit of extra sauce, but one packet is not enough)

Frozen corn (preferably from a Wisconsin garden, picked in August, blanched, and then frozen in Ziploc bags for the long winter, as it's the sweetest corn you'll ever find)

1 small can green chilis (7 oz can, or bigger if you prefer spicy heat!)

One 14.5 oz can chopped tomato with jalapeño (you can omit the jalapeños and go with straight tomatoes if you don't like too much spice)

Shredded cheddar cheese or jack cheese (Again, if it comes from Wisconsin, it's the best. Order online!)

Optional additions for topping: sour cream, sliced avocado, diced green onions, olives—the additions are endless and to preferred taste

Directions

Preheat the oven to 350 degrees.

In a large skillet, brown the beef, and then add onion and cook until translucent.

Add frozen corn (right from the bag), green chilis, and tomatoes with jalapeños to the pan with the beef mixture.

In a separate saucepan, cook the enchilada sauce with water and tomato sauce until thickened, and according to McCormick's package instructions. Set aside any additional sauce for leftovers or freeze.

Using a 9 × 13 baking dish, layer the enchilada sauce, noodles, meat mixture, and then cheese, and repeat layers just like you do when you're making traditional Italian lasagna. *Or* roll up each individual noodle with meat mixture and cheese to make roll-ups.

Bake, covered with foil, for 45 min.

Remove foil and add a top layer of cheese to melt, then bake an additional 5–10 min.

Let the pan sit for a few minutes before slicing.

Add a dollop of sour cream, avocado, or any of the additional topping options, or, better yet, choose your own. Have fun with the options, and be sure and enjoy with friends.

This freezes well, but you may need to add additional enchilada sauce to reheat as it freezes drier than traditional lasagna.

Acknowledgments

Thank you again, Faith! You continue to amaze me with each additional manuscript. Sandy, cheers on another one! Melissa, Madeline, Rebecca, and the entire CLB Team, I owe you *big* time. Jesse Reisch, two thumbs up!

Thank you, Heather, for listening to all my ramblings, making things cozy for me in GB, and bouncing between us cozy ideas; and to Conor for your invaluable insight on this one. Dan and Sammy, thanks for the ice-fishing and shanty info; and Mark, too, for the ice-fishing equipment (augers, etc.). I am continually learning about all things fishing. But most of all, thanks to Mark for your love and continued support. Without it, these books just wouldn't happen—that's the truth. And finally, dear readers, it's always my goal to provide an escape for you from whatever life stresses come your way. Did I succeed? Reach out and tell me. I'd love to hear from you. Until then, happy reading!